To Eleanor
Hope you enjoy the book!!
All
Gene Pisasale

ABANDONED ADDRESS

THE SECRET OF FRICK'S LOCK

GENE PISASALE

Outskirts Press, Inc.
Denver, Colorado

Other Books by Gene Pisasale

Vineyard Days

Lafayette's Gold- The Lost Brandywine Treasure

DEDICATION

To Phyllis - my love, my light and inspiration... to Paulette - for your kindness and insights... and to all the gifted minds in every field of human endeavor who receive the Divine spark that enriches mankind...

"In trying to perfect a thing, I sometimes run straight up against a granite wall a hundred feet high. If, after trying and trying and trying again, I can't get over it, I turn to something else. Then, someday, it may be months or it may be years later, something is discovered either by myself or someone else, or something happens in some part of the world, which I recognize may help me to scale at least part of that wall.

I never allow myself to become discouraged under any circumstances. I recall that after we had conducted thousands of experiments on a certain project without solving the problem, one of my associates, after we had conducted the crowning experiment and it had proved a failure, expressed discouragement and disgust over our having failed 'to find out anything'. I cheerily assured him that we had learned something. For we had learned for a certainty that the thing couldn't be done that way, and that we would have to try some other way. We sometimes learn a lot from our failures if we have put into the effort the best thought and work we are capable of..."

-Thomas A. Edison 1921

Chapter 1

"Nothing in life is to be feared, it is only to be understood..."
--Marie Curie

"I did it!!" The door slammed hard behind him as he strolled in the side entrance to their home, knocking the carved wooden angel they'd gotten at San Miguel Mission in Santa Fe slightly ajar as it hung on the wall, its beautiful tan wings outstretched behind the angel's welcoming arms. "Sorry about that." He straightened the umber trunk to vertical, the body carved from a solid piece of scrub oak growing near one of the many ancient Indian ruins they'd seen the year before on their trip to Sedona. He thought about that relaxing journey, leaving him refreshed and rejuvenated after an extended stint without a vacation working in the investment industry. This moment felt the same.

"Did what?" Natalie entered the kitchen from her home office next to the Conservatory. She studied his face to see any signs- positive or negative- to interpret.

"I'm retired. After 24 years of conference calls, managing portfolios and analyzing companies, I'm ready for a change.

As much as I enjoyed it, I'm done." He grinned, wrapping his arms around her waist, the touch of her smooth peach-colored top a welcome delight from the feel of the steering wheel on the tense drive home.

"Yes!! Was this your last day there?"

"Not quite. Gary's been a superb branch manager and a gentleman. I gave him two weeks notice."

"So, that's when you'll finally be out of your office?"

"Maybe much sooner. Just need to clean up my work area. He was gracious- said I can leave any time I'm ready. It'll be in the next week or so. I'll fill up some boxes and get completely out of there. Had another run-in with Sean, though." Resting the cell phone on the counter, he loosened the bold maroon and navy blue silk Enzo Fellini tie, one of his many prize possessions from his days working as an investment executive at Paine Webber in the mid-1980s.

"I hope no one got out of control."

"I didn't. He *always* does."

"What was it this time?" She watched as he shook his head and laid the tie on the black granite island in the center of the kitchen.

"With him, there doesn't need to be a reason. If you say one thing that differs slightly from his thinking- World War III. I'd walked out of my office to check the thermostat- it was getting warm- then went over to the empty conference room to turn off the lights. No one was using it that I could tell. He marched up to me, stood within a foot of my face and yelled 'Don't turn off the lights in there. I want them on!!' He glared at me for 30 seconds until I finally walked away."

"Did he tell you why?"

"No, but I took the right course. Didn't want a repeat of last year."

"Oh, my God. No way!"

"Don't worry. I avoided a melee. No donnybrook, but it could have been, shall we say, a bit rough." He pondered over the last time he fell into Sean's trap, getting pulled into a ridiculous argument over – nothing. The day had been beautiful. Returning from a great lunch at Elizabeth's with Natalie, he could still taste the garlic croutons and the peppery tomato soup as he entered the back door of their red brick building, heading to his office. Sean was there, standing in the hall by Jim's door, talking with a sales rep they both knew. The rep looked directly at Jim. Not wanting to want to make it appear like he was avoiding him, Jim said hello and chatted for a few seconds. Sean was incensed and stormed away into his office. A bit bewildered, Jim gazed at the rep as they both tried to discern what caused the bizarre incident. After Jim thanked him for his time and walked back into his office, he was surprised to see Sean strut right up to Jim's desk, watching in amazement as he berated him, beet red for almost five minutes, not allowing Jim a moment to explain.

"How DARE you interrupt me when I'm talking with someone! You are the lowest form of life! You are a non-person to me!!! Don't *EVER* speak to me again!" He marched back to his office and slammed the door, without giving Jim a chance to respond.

Jim studied the grain in the gleaming oak floor, his biceps stiffening as Sean's voice echoed, re-living the physical altercation that could have occurred so many times. "How could I have avoided that? Avoided him? He's always right there, in your face." The troubled smirk hung menacingly in front of him. "I should have let him have it at least once…" Stepping back from the edge, his eyes wandered up to the painting on the wall by Cezanne of Mount St. Victoire, bucolic, serene, a temporary respite from the drama. He re-lived the arguments over and over in his mind, the aggravating e-mails. "What rational person would ever say those things? He's *not* rational. He's a wounded animal that just reacts, jumping out at you and …" His neck ached, then Natalie's hand on his shoulder shifted his gaze to the engagement ring he'd given her on the 5th anniversary of the day they'd first met, proposing at sunrise on the balcony overlooking Horseshoe Bay in Bermuda. The tension left him as her turquoise eyes locked with his, their hint of grey shining above her freckled smile.

"You're back in it again, aren't you?"

"No. A special day won't be ruined. It's ours to celebrate. I'm past it."

"Sure you didn't say or do anything that'll start the bombs flying again?"

His head shook as he managed a small grin. "If there's a war being fought for no reason– don't pick up a gun to fight." The scars remained. Blood pulsing through his fists diminished to a relaxed pace, her delicate touch on his wrists a brief, but welcome massage after the encounter.

"Good."

"Let's have a toast." He took her hand and brought her close to him, kissing her. His eyes opened to see her smiling.

"We have a bottle of White Star on ice. I took out the two beautiful filet mignon you got yesterday at the Country

Butcher, plus the Portobello mushrooms and some wild rice. Were you secretly planning behind my back, with all this great food?"

"Boy Scouts. Be prepared."

She brushed the near-black hair from his temple and exclaimed "Let's get the party started. You pour the champagne while I put on something you like." Bringing her lips to his again, she then crossed the kitchen to the staircase. "By the time I come back, I want to see a glass of champagne waiting."

"Your request is my pleasure, madam." He ambled over to the stainless steel refrigerator, opened the double door and grabbed the bottle. "Have to enjoy life's special moments. They're so few." Removing the colored gold foil wrapping, he pressed up on the cork. POP!! "Love that sound."

Approaching the terrace, the ice-cold bottle numbing his fingers, he slid the door open and stepped onto the slate-colored flagstones. River birches and tulip poplars stood along the forest edge as he contemplated his mother's words many years before. Her face was younger as she sat below the pictures of her favorite cat Max on the wall, smiling across the small white kitchen table.

"Always treat others with respect- even if they're not doing the same."

"Sometimes that's hard to do, mom."

"Life is hard. Live it in a way that'll make you proud when you look back someday..."

Reaching forward to hug her, he realized with sadness she was far away. "You're right. Thank you for showing me how to be a better man." The sun slipped below the tree-line as he proceeded back inside.

"You have a bottle. Let's put it to good use."

The deep V-neck of her fur-lined bathrobe captivated him. "Very... nice."

"Glad you like it." She glided across the room, her white thigh highs and high heels gleaming as she took the two platinum-rimmed champagne glasses from the counter. "What are you waiting for?"

"This is certainly overdue." He poured the amber liquid into each glass, bubbles frothing up to the edge, popping at the surface.

Meandering into the family room, she settled onto the rust-colored couch, her right leg outstretched, the four-inch heeled shoe dangling on the tip of her toe. "I'm ready to relax."

"Here's to a new start. We found gold coins from the Battle of the Brandywine- a miracle. That'll cover us for many years. This is the official beginning of our next endeavor- the treasure hunting company we've talked about for so long. This area is filled with buried artifacts from the Revolutionary and Civil Wars, just waiting to be found."

"That's the best idea you've proposed in quite some time. Here's to upcoming adventures." The crystal glasses clinked together and the ring echoed off the stone fireplace.

"Let's get started. You can be my first mate."

"What about Captain? I've become an expert at canoeing down the Brandywine. There's no pile of mud or dark cellar I can't handle."

"Captain it is." The glass went to his lips as she did the same. The corner of his eye revealed her one hand on the cord to her robe.

"Well, we can do the planning in the morning. Tonight, it's

pure fun." The cord loosened and fell to the floor. "Never mix work and pleasure…"

———— ∘《●》∘ ————

The digital radio alarm on Natalie's night table showed 6:00 a.m., the song "Summer Breeze" whispering into the room as her finger hit the 'STOP' button. "Time for us to get up."

"Have to open our eyes first. That'll take twenty minutes."

"No. We're not going to let another beautiful morning slip away. If you get us some coffee, we can have it here in bed and plan the day."

He pushed the bedspread away and slid out, half-asleep as he ambled slowly to his brown leather slippers. "If you hear a loud noise going down the stairs, call an ambulance." The bust of Shakespeare came into view on the landing and he examined it briefly before turning toward the double windows. "William, hope you remembered to set the timer last night."

"Beep… beep… beep." The final note signaled the coffee was brewed. "I love the scent of dark roasted Sumatran in the morning. Smells like… victory." The steaming liquid poured into the colorful French Market ceramic mugs, their coffee bean grove emblem surrounded by 'Will Tickle Your Palate' and 'Pure Coffee' shining as he returned the pot to the warmer.

Entering the master bedroom, he noted she was sitting up, reading a large book. "Anything of interest?" He set the cup of coffee on the table next to her, then lumbered over to his side, stepping out of the slippers and dropping his robe on the bench. "Stories of priceless artifacts unearthed near tranquil home sites?" He climbed in next to her.

— 7 —

"Close. Sue and I were talking about the abandoned towns and hauntings highlighted on that show 'Ghost Hunters'. This book 'Weird Pennsylvania" mentions a ghost town not far from Phoenixville. Looks fascinating."

Raising the mug to his lips for a moment, his attention shifted to her side of the bed. "Here, I can take the book while you drink your coffee." Jim sat up and started reading the opened pages. "Saw a lot of ghost towns out West in Arizona and New Mexico. Didn't think there were any nearby."

"It's called Frick's Lock. Oldest house dates back to the 1700's. The land was bought up by PECO Energy before the1980's when they built the Limerick Nuclear Plant. Guess they didn't want another Three Mile Island scaring the hell out of the local residents."

"I remember the movie 'China Syndrome' had people terrified of a meltdown. Can't blame them."

"Let's check it out!! Never know what we'll find. We can drive up and then have lunch at a cozy, back-country inn on the way home."

He finished his coffee as she started to get dressed. "I'll meet you downstairs. Need to feed the fish and put out the cats before we go."

"I want to do a quick web search first." Sitting in her office, Natalie opened Internet Explorer and Googled 'Fricks Lock'. Fifteen entries popped up and she clicked through the first few. "Hey, this is interesting. Tells about the formation of the Schuylkill Canal. The Lock was part of the system which was built in the 1820's on farmland acquired from local farmer John Frick. Locks 54 and 55 on the system were part of the inland waterway in the area, which allowed easier transport of goods, kind of an early turnpike system." She read the next three articles, her grip on the mouse tightening with each story. One blog appeared, its headline claiming there was an unreported incident of forced evacuation, residents given only hours to vacate their homes, leaving behind most of their possessions and uneaten dinners. She pondered the words, then looked at the title of the blog- 'Wild Tales'. "Probably hype by some local restaurant owners to bring in more business. Should've been titled 'Wild Tales from Sam's Deli'." Turning off the computer, Natalie announced "I'm ready to do some exploring. When do we set sail?"

"After you, Captain."

She beamed. "Do you have the collecting bag?"

"Sure do. One canvas sack filled with 2 flashlights, gloves, gallon plastic baggies, rock pick, trowel and paper towels." He twisted the top of the sack into a loose knot.

"What about the four sticks of dynamite?"

"Leave it here this time. They don't need a new extension off the Blue Route yet."

"Thanks for remembering the paper towels. Last time I had to wipe the mud onto my pants."

"I liked the look. Tiger stripes. Very retro."

"Let's go."

"Phoenixville is almost an hour. You're our navigator. Just let me know where to go after we hit town." His hands gripped the steering wheel firmly as the car turned out of their complex.

"Should be an easy drive. Take Route 724 north, then go right onto Frick's Lock Road after a few miles."

The pale mist of early morning was breaking up into patches of azure on the first Saturday in June. Along the horizon, milky clouds were forming, ready for their Eastern trek across the sky. Jim could feel the heat. "Should be a gorgeous day- but it's getting warm already."

"It'll be perfect!" Natalie relaxed, the greenery blanketing the hillsides interrupted only by her glance at the LCD navigation screen on the dashboard. "Bear left ahead onto Route 23, then Route 724. I'll watch for the turnoff."

"I love a woman who's in command. There's a few other commands I can think of for later tonight."

"Don't blow a gasket." After another 10 minutes, Natalie indicated "Here it comes- turn left just ahead. Hey, look!! The Colonial Theatre has a sign for 'Blobfest'!!"

"What in the world is that?"

"Phoenixville has a special place in sci-fi motion picture history. Part of the movie 'The Blob' was filmed here at the theatre back in 1957. It was one of Steve McQueen's first roles. They celebrate the event every year now. It's a big deal."

"Scintillating."

"Phoenixville was also a major steelmaking town back in the 1800's all the way up to the 1970's. They made joists and pre-fab structures for hundreds of bridges, railways and viaducts around the nation. The Historical Society of Phoenixville has a large collection of memorabilia documenting the history of the industrial town, said to be the 'Gateway to Valley Forge'."

"Now that part sounds interesting. Millions of railroad cars and automobiles must have rolled over those bridges..."

The SUV slowed as it arced onto Frick's Lock Road, gravel and jagged rocks flying up from around the tires, pinging loudly against the undercarriage as the car bounced past the potholes. A few one-story businesses poked their aging roofs skyward, remnants of a 1960's industrial park. A gravel lot spread out before a yellow iron gate blocking the road ahead. The scene was deserted except for two men in their late forties working on the engine of a 1980's vintage tractor trailer, their heads buried under the hood. Jim studied the sign across the gate. "Should have checked first. See that? 'No admittance – Violators Prosecuted'."

"Come on!! We can at least look around." The car door slammed as her hands gripped the camera. Advancing toward the anchored yellow poles which prevented cars from proceeding down the narrow lane, a curving line of broken blacktop, partially overgrown with grass and weeds came into view. Three-foot wide breaks in the nearby brush indicated nothing impeded foot traffic despite another sign in bold lettering reading 'Under 24 hour surveillance.' "It is warm today- feels like it's already 80 degrees."

Jim took his keys and pushed the door hard behind him. "This is as far as we go." He nodded toward the white and black "NO TRESPASSING" sign on the telephone pole, then scanned the parking area. His gaze wandered along past the gate about 50 yards away where several antiquated brick homes stood behind pine trees which had witnessed a long line of Presidents. Facades behind their boughs exposed windows and doors boarded with plywood. "Don't see any cameras around, but it's not worth taking any chances." He frowned as Natalie continued ahead.

"Don't worry, nobody's here. Besides, in this economy- who's going to spend the money to monitor a bunch of abandoned buildings? I say they're relying on the fear factor – and I'm fearless. I'm going in."

"NO!!"

"Hey, what happened to your motto? 'If it says 'No Admittance', that's where you want to go'."

"That applies when there isn't a sign indicating you'll be having dinner in jail. Just take a few quick photos from here and we'll head home."

"We drove all the way here- to do nothing? I'm going in and checking out some of those buildings." She studied the sign again and glanced back at him. "OK, we won't go in *right here*. Maybe there are some cameras hidden nearby, but I seriously doubt it." She surveyed the tall overgrown shrubs and trees fringing the edge of the property. "Let's go investigate those woods over there and see if we can find a back way in." Her mauve blouse contrasted with the olive foliage as she pushed through the dense brush and trees.

His eyes targeted the telephone poles and adjacent trees for cameras. "Wait!!" She was almost 75 feet away, heading quickly into the thicket without looking back. Pulse racing, he bounded after her, slipping on some loose, grey-green serpentine pebbles. After stepping carefully around dozens of hanging vines and getting caught three times in sticker bushes, he stopped. She was still more than 20 yards ahead, disappearing into the thick scrubland. "I'm going back!!" he yelled, his voice dampened by the hanging moss around the trees and wet leaves all around his feet. Curses pierced the silence as he turned away, catching his collar on an overhanging prickly vine. "Damn it!" Probing his way back through the thicket of intertwined vegetation and wild rose bushes, lush in their early Summer pose, his eyes pleaded to see a clearing.

"Looks like poison ivy. I can see an opening over there"

she remarked, bending the leafy branches away, then gawking at the 18th century brick building whose crooked, dilapidated chimney poked through the treetops. Wandering through the underbrush, sensing the ground becoming uneven, her feet couldn't avoid slipping on some loose stones. "Owww!!" Sliding several feet downwards, her rear end fell directly onto a muddy, jagged rock at the edge of a ravine overgrown with ferns. A sharp pain throbbed as her view descended to inspect her right ankle, bleeding slightly onto the edge of her Topsider. Pulling burrs slowly from her shorts, her thumb was pricked on the last one. "Ouch!! Might have to backtrack. Looks like a dead end- or a good way to become chopped meat." Crawling back up the edge of the embankment, swatting gnats from her face, she steadied herself below the canopy of towering trees. "Got to be a way in somewhere."

Escaping through the copse of trees, he brushed a spider web from his forehead as he spotted the SUV. "Finally." Scanning the parking area, he noted the two men putting tools onto the heated blacktop. Their attention focused directly at him as he trekked toward his car, its black exterior shining in the mid-morning sun.

At the edge of the forest, a small break in the undergrowth appeared as she plodded slowly in the direction of what looked to be a deer path. Maneuvering past a dense patch of sticker-bushes, she veered left up the small hill and saw it. "Awesome! Looks like- an old chicken coop?" The small wooden building was partially covered in a shroud of wire mesh, rusted and broken, hanging like a weeping willow over the open window- the little wooden cubby-holes still covered in straw for chicks to rest. "Any 30-year old eggs left behind? Suitable for tee-shots."

Several feet away, the scattered remains of a burned out building stood hulking in the Summer sun. Rotted, moldy wooden boards collapsed around its edges, commingling in a pile of debris 10 feet deep. Stepping inside the roofless structure, her gaze rose briefly up to the cloudless sky as her feet carefully tiptoed around, avoiding rusted nails protruding from piles of beams, worn tires and decaying metal objects completing the scene. "Must have been an old garage or storage place that caught on fire- or maybe was set on fire?" She leaned onto a broken beam, feeling it giving way- then backed off. "Nothing useful here- unless you work for Sanford and Son."

Navigating around the shabby pile of wreckage and peering at the next building about 20 feet away, she continued, trudging through three-foot tall weeds. "Someone's home once. Not pretty by our standards- but 100 years ago, maybe a respectable residence." As she stepped onto the back stoop, the pale-green porch came into view exposing gaping holes through broken linoleum and a dark, murky basement below. In the middle of the floor an old white porcelain washbasin lay on its side, rusted and chipped. Entering the narrow doorway, she noticed plastic plates strewn about the floor, wallpaper peeling in giant folds from every corner. "Martha Stewart would *not* be pleased." She could barely make out the unlit spaces and waited several seconds for her eyes to adjust. Surrounding the dingy rubble, a few rays of sunlight danced into the room, highlighting walls painted a blindingly bright sunflower yellow, edged by iridescent green trim. "Lord, who was their decorator- Peter Max?"

Collapsed doors, broken wooden chairs and kitchen utensils haphazardly completed the scene of destruction. "Where is my bag?" Touching her left shoulder, her fingers searched for the strap which was not there. The canvas bag she'd hoped to feel lay back in the car. "With no flashlight, this would be way too dangerous." Natalie squinted and strained to see down a gloomy, wooden staircase toward what appeared to be a blackened basement. "I can't see anything!" She blindly pointed the camera down the steps, hoping the flash would outline the scene, then played back the photo on the LED screen. "Hmmm- looks moldy and wet, with stone walls and what might be a dirt floor. Probably hundreds of spiders... If I had a shovel, I might get something worth taking home, but not on this trip."

Leaving the house, she hiked over to another aging structure, the outside a drab cream stucco, cracks indicating where fragments were about to break off. Finding an entrance in the back, a shattered wall announced the work from years of random assaults. "Another victim of vandals." No roof or second floor- only the dilapidated remnants of a former building lay strewn in a hazardous pile before her. "This is one of the older dwellings- 200 years, easy." The walls showed a patchwork of irregular stones, over 18 inches thick. Touching one, she saw it start to move, the crude mortar crumbling to dust. Above a debris-filled fireplace rested a thick wooden beam, heavily charred- an 18th century mantle below which a family once cooked their meals. Several rusted iron rods protruded from inside its scorched walls, decades ago holding cooking pots. Glancing up, the outline of what was for later generations a bathroom stood amidst the wreckage, white tiled walls rimmed in black.

Roaming behind the structure, a line of wide, massive stones poked above the earth. Stepping along the path, traces of the top of a wall stood intact, encased in dirt, now home to wild grasses and tiny blue flowers. At the end of the path lay a partially excavated turn-wheel, three feet in diameter, its stone teeth the notches of a giant gear. "This is it!! This was Frick's Lock! Hundreds of boats used to go by here- highway of a bygone era. Very cool!" The ground around her feet with generations of memories provided her foundation. "Looks like someone was trying to dig this thing out– must weigh several hundred pounds." The edges of the structure rested firmly in the earth, motionless as her view moved to each undulation of the ground where it once directed human activity. "How many merchants worked their hands raw, bringing their daily work to earn a living here? What a different life."

Her gaze shifted to the expansive ravine and the rise above the Schuylkill where they stood, looming over the town- two giant, chalky grey cooling towers, steam billowing from their crests. The Limerick Nuclear Power Plant dominated the horizon. "That's eerie. A sign of progress to some- doom to others, including this town…"

⸺⫷◉⫸⸻

"ABC News. This is Mark Jenners. Thank you for joining us tonight. Breaking news from Pennsylvania. There has been a leak from the Three Mile Island nuclear plant. Emergency personnel are on the scene and reporters have been prevented from getting within one mile of the plant, not far from Harrisburg, Pennsylvania." The camera flashed across the scene, darkness punctuated by floodlights from dozens of crews covering the story from around the world, from London to Sydney, Rio de

Janeiro to Mexico City- all huddled around the entrance to the facility, their reporters standing in the eerie twilight, hoping to get inside the plant for a look at what happened.

"Sir, hello!! Are you a local resident?"

"Uh, yes- I live about five miles from here."

"So, what's your view on what happened here tonight? Are you concerned?"

"Well, I'm always concerned about safety. I don't know what happened here. I heard somethin' on the radio as I was comin' home from my shift and I wanted to see what was goin' on. Some guys back at the hardware store said there was some kind of an incident- radiation got out."

The cameraman scanned the countryside, dozens of cars and trucks parked all around the edge of the facility, people standing near their vehicles, hoping to get a view of the scene.

"Well, there you have it- comments from a local concerned citizen- someone whose life could be in danger. We have reports that there was a leak. How serious, we just don't know. There isn't a way to understand exactly what happened without more information from the authorities, the people in charge here, but they're not speaking to the press as of right now. Meanwhile, look at the protesters, folks. They're everywhere…"

"NO NUKES!! NO NUKES!! NUCLEAR POWER, NO WAY!! NUCLEAR POWER, GO AWAY!!" The chants grew to a deafening roar as the cameraman pulled away from the scene.

"It's an interesting atmosphere here reporting from the Three Mile Island nuclear power plant near Harrisburg, Pennsylvania. It's a scene of both concern and excitement, as we ask ourselves- "What is the future of nuclear power in this country? Are we really safe? Will this event turn out to be nothing- or will it change the way we look at the production of energy in this country? That, we just don't know… Signing off, Mark Jenners, ABC News, March 28th, 1979…"

———— ⋙«(●)»⋘ ————

The towers refused to release her gaze for a few more moments as they stood defiantly across from the edge of the Lock buried in its grave, the victim in repose across from the modern grey edifices which made that way of life obsolete. A screeching cry jolted her to attention. Turning toward the noise, she beheld the grizzly feast. A dozen large black vultures slowly raised their heads from a bloody carcass, unrelenting in their glare, beaks trailing shreds of meat. Natalie flinched as her eyes met their resolute stare. "How appropriate. Better back away, or I might be dessert." Their deadpan eyes followed her every move, turning to the right as she retreated. "Should get some distance from those guys."

Heading towards the narrow blacktop road which snaked through the small town, the long winding surface revealed their car was out of sight. Straight ahead stood a plantation-style home, statuesque windows lining the first and second floors, their glass panes boarded with weathered plywood. A third row of undersized windows sat above them, blocked by rotting, mustard-colored shutters. The entrance was preceded by a once elegant porch, the roof bowing from the weight of neglect. Vines grew up one side of the house, its white paint chipped and blistering away, the scene a eulogy to the families who lived there, children growing up in sight of the Lock which gave sustenance from commerce flowing East and West to Philadelphia- and all the memories that were now gone, buildings abandoned, crumbling relics of an era no longer relevant.

Standing on the porch, the cooling towers caught her attention again, not wanting to release their magnetic grip. Peering down at the flowers, as if planted on a grave- she viewed a monument to the past, testimony to technology now gone, yet somehow still wanting to be alive beneath her feet. Natalie's mind worked to find a way into the structure around her. The doors and windows stood blocked by fallen timbers and heavy wooden boards. Rounding the last wall, a grin emerged as she viewed a well preserved bird feeder perched on a pole. "How many starving finches found a snack inside there?" Then she saw it- an open window. Rotting plywood lay crumpled nearby. "I'm entering, but at least I'm not breaking anything."

Crawling through the window, her blue eyes canvassed the deserted room- met by grimy grey carpets, vacant cabinets and rusty radiators barely visible through the shadows. "Only forsaken memories here." Light from the upper level marked a potential path as she worked her way towards the staircase leading to the second floor. "Looks clear– a bit brighter, too." Proceeding carefully up to the top of the loosely carpeted stairs, a hallway of debris from yesteryear lay before her. "Good Lord!!" she shrieked, ducking down instinctively after viewing the ceiling. Above her, hundreds of albino bats hung upside down as they watched unwincingly, ready to attack. "Wait, get a grip!!" She refocused, then chuckled, shaking her head. "It's just paint peeling off the ceiling." Proceeding down the hall, she inspected a 1950's vintage bathroom, pale-grey paneling resting proudly above cracked Formica counters, fringing an open window just inches from the toilet.

On the floor lay a deeply yellowed, torn newspaper. Natalie bent down and gingerly turned the pages, barely touching the edges while examining the worn newsprint. "Hmmm... never heard of this one. 'The Mercury', dated 1980- pretty weathered, but otherwise intact. Might make some interesting reading when we get home." Taking the paper, she thought about the construction of the nearby plant and the lives that were forever changed.

Crudely made bookshelves lined the walls of the next room, the rough wood bare except for a thick layer of grime and dead flies. More 'bat wings' hung from the ceiling. Eerie lime-colored light emanated from a shattered window. Natalie stopped abruptly in front of a ghoulish skull gazing at her through the jagged shards of glass. Shoulders repulsed, she stood before it enraptured in the strange scene. "*Very creepy!!*" Stepping closer, she touched the peeling two-dimensional skull, its void eye sockets grotesque above a narrow smirk. It was just a sticker, about eight inches high- that had been placed on one of the panes, behind which someone had painted the storm window green. Turning back toward the room, her eyes met something more bizarre. An old, rusting metal chair sat alone in the middle of the floor below a three-foot wide hole in the ceiling above it. She stepped forward, steadying herself on the chair as she peered up into the darkness. "Damn it!! How could I have left my flashlight in the car? I can't see anything up there." Remembering the camera, she held it up, shooting several flash photos into the opening- and played them back. The images revealed an attic with a roof and walls of rough, hand-cut wooden timbers. The underlying area in the photos appeared vacant- until something square-shaped loomed in a back corner.

The attic was stiflingly hot as she climbed up and wiped the sweat from her brow, the moisture mixing with the dust and dirt on her face. She pulled herself up toward the rafters, clicking another flash shot to light the way. Crawling along the floor, she continued, using the flash to guide her. "Screeeeeeeeeech!!" A fur lined body brushed by her cheek. "What the hell was that?!" she exclaimed as she felt something swat at her right leg. Her eyes now used to the darkness, the space near her feet came into view- and she saw it. "It's so CUTE!! A baby raccoon!!" His eyes met hers as he jabbed his paw against her left foot, examining the intruder. "These guys are relatively harmless- but they can *carry rabies*- so keep your distance, Natalie." Moving slowly toward the back corner of the room, the darkness and heat enveloped her. Her right index finger pressed for another shot, the flash a strobe-light spectacle of momentary clarity. "Looks like a large cardboard box- covered in cobwebs and dust." She peered inside during another camera flash and several indistinct objects came into view- crude tools and weathered pieces of paper, coated with mildew and mouse droppings. A large dead black spider, its legs curled in a death grip, was visible in the pile. "Don't touch anything" she thought. As she gripped and lifted the edges of the box, she set it down quickly. "Way too heavy. I'll just slide it across the floor. Hopefully we can check out the contents at home with gloves on- and a lot of bug spray."

Blindly making her way back toward the opening, glowing yellow eyes emerged from across the room. As she crawled, they also approached, pacing her to the hole. Her heart raced as she pushed the box faster. Wiping sweat from her eyes, she swung her feet over the edge and dropped down. She grabbed the box above her head and nudged it quickly toward the opening, dropping it onto the chair, the echo of the impact ringing out. Above, she could hear the chilling scrape of claws approach the hole. "Must have been its mother. Don't want to come between a mom and her cub." Putting her arms around the perimeter of the box, she knew it would take a strong effort to return it to the car. "Time to head back." She stepped carefully around the broken beams lying behind the decaying frame, putting one leg out the window onto the cracked flagstone, then gaining her balance as she set her left foot down securely. A sharp breeze blew her hair into her face. "Where did that come from? Strange… smells like mint." Shutters around the upper windows slammed against the side of the house, startling her. Grabbing the box, she moved quickly through the backyards toward the car.

"Where the hell is she?" he thought, sitting in the front seat, the air conditioning on full-blast. Jim glanced at both side mirrors, then shook his head. The trunk door opened and he turned around in his seat.

"See what I got? A whole box full of stuff!!" She pushed it into the trunk and put the newspaper on top.

"Of JUNK, most likely. OK- let's get out of here."

"Not just yet. I have a couple more houses to check. They're nearby. It shouldn't take long. You'll be able to see me from the car."

"NO WAY!! Look, those guys we passed gave me a strange look- and it wasn't Happy Birthday. We're outta' here- now!!"

"Calm down. No one's watching. This place is deserted."

"Stop! If anyone IS watching, we could be in serious trouble. Now you're putting us *both* at risk. This is unacceptable!! Get in *immediately!*"

She slammed the trunk door and started toward the buildings. "Don't be such a chicken, which reminds me, I found a chicken coop back there!! Hey, what's an adventure without a little risk?"

Pressing the button near his seat, the window rolled down as he started to yell. "You are acting like a 12-year old!! Get in the car- we are LEAVING!!" Enraged, he threw the door open and ran to catch up.

"Look, I'll be gone just a couple of minutes. You can watch me from here. I'll be in those two brick buildings right over there."

"You're NOT going back there!!"

"Yes I am." She headed toward the overgrown yards rimming the houses, trying to avoid walking directly past the No Trespassing sign.

His cell phone hit the ground as he marched back to the car, pausing to open the door to get in. Looking down, he stopped. "Hope I didn't break it." He bent down, grabbing the phone, then got back into the SUV, the door handle already hot from the sun. "I don't believe this." He flipped it open and the green signal indicator was shining brightly. "At least I have communication if something bad happens." Turning toward the driver-side window, he saw the two men glaring at him intensely. "Those guys don't look like they appreciate guests." Fifty yards behind them, dust was rising from the road, shrouding something large and he saw it – the black and white car, slowly approaching. The vehicle cruised to a stop and the two men walked up, the driver rolling down his window. "That's a cop!" His chest tightened and his heart started to race. Spasms of pain pulsed through his neck as he grabbed the phone and dialed Natalie's cell number. He heard the familiar ring- coming from the passenger side floor of the car. Gazing down, he saw Natalie's purse, the phone ringing inside. "Damn it!!"

One of the men pointed toward his car and Jim looked down at his shoes pressed against the tan floor mat. His heart was pounding harder, sweat beading all along his forehead. "This feels like that night…"

―――――⋙((◉))⋘―――――

Danny was driving, four 17-year olds bunched into his new 1974 Celica GT. They pulled up to the stoplight, which had turned red. Jim was in the backseat and had just taken a sip out of the large bottle. Chas in the front was laughing as he crushed the beer can beneath his right foot, next to the unopened cans still in their plastic housing.

"Number five- and we haven't even gotten to Dave's party!!" Chuck in the other back seat laughed as he took the last gulp of Schlitz.

Danny chuckled and turned around to look at him. "Who's in a rush? We got a party right here." He put his foot on the accelerator, then stopped as he saw the light was still red and pushed hard on the brake pedal. "Oh, shit!!" The car screeched to a halt a few feet past the light, the cross-traffic swerving slightly at the intersection. Within thirty seconds, flashing red and blue lights shone through their rear window.

"FUCK!! It's a cop!!" yelled Chas as he pushed the Budweiser cans under the seat.

Jim stiffened up and started to panic as he shoved the bottle beneath his knees. "What can I do with this??!! I'm sittin' on a fifth of Jim Beam!!" He felt the bottle cut into his legs as his eyes widened, mouth hanging open.

"Hide it!!" Danny yelled as he tried to gain some semblance of composure seeing the police car stop right behind them, the door opening slowly.

"Where??!! There's no place to put it in here!!" His mind raced as he wrapped his legs around the container, forcing both knees together firmly to cover it.

The police officer tapped on Danny's window as he started to roll it down. "Do you know what you did wrong?"

"Yes, officer. I ran a red light." Danny's voice was weak as he barely got out the words, his gaze fixed blankly on the traffic swirling around him.

"No, you didn't. You entered the intersection on a red light. That is against the traffic laws. Can I see your license, please?"

Danny fumbled in his jacket and pulled it out, handing the card to the officer as his left arm trembled. Jim looked down at his own feet, his knees shaking as the red and blue lights flashed again and again on the rear of the small seat in front of him.

The officer scanned his flashlight on the license, reading it carefully, then handed it back to Danny, inspecting each of the boys in the car for over a minute. He focused his gaze directly on Danny, then leaned onto the edge of the car and took a second long look at Jim. He stood back away from the vehicle, erect, the flashing lights glistening on his badge for an eternity. "Well, you look like good boys. I'm gonna' let you go with a warning this time, but don't let me catch you 'round here again."

"Yes, officer!! I'm sorry about that." Danny briefly made eye contact, then tried three times to put the license back in his wallet. "I won't let it happen again."

"You take care out there, tonight. There's a lot of bad drivers. Go on home now, boys. Good night." Tipping his hat, he strutted back to the police car, getting in. Within a few seconds, the flashers stopped, the darkness a welcome change to the scene.

"I almost had a *hernia!!*" Jim yelled as he felt the rim of the bottle biting into the bottom of his legs.

"You?!! *I* would have gotten the ticket!!" Danny shouted, then started laughing.

"Bud – we would've *ALL* been in jail – or perhaps you forgot our cargo."

"Oh– right!!" The light turned green for the third time and Danny floored it. Chas burped. Jim's knees were still shaking as they sped away, the police car's tail lights shining in the distance…

———◈———

The red and blue lights flashed on the sides of Jim's SUV as the patrol car moved slowly forward. One of the men continued to point toward his car as the police cruiser turned. The vehicle approached the edge of the lot, stopping in front of the "NO TRESPASSING" sign.

Jim froze in his seat as he watched the officer get out and walk past the gate toward the abandoned buildings. "Natalie, where the HELL are you??!!" he shouted, the windows completely up so no one could hear. Jumping out, he moved quickly toward the entrance area where the rutted road led into the abandoned town. Then he stopped. Natalie was standing behind one of the buildings, staring up at the boarded windows and doors, her back to him and the approaching officer.

The policeman proceeded directly toward her. His voice boomed over the abandoned lot in front of him. "Ma'am, you are trespassing on private land." Natalie flinched and spun around as he continued, his monotone speech a dire indication of her being out of bounds. "This area is well marked. You must have seen the signs back there."

Natalie stood silently as she saw the blue-uniformed male behind her- and noticed the cruiser parked 40 feet beyond him. "Um, well…"

"There's a reason why people are not supposed to come in here. These buildings are over 200 years old and falling apart. One kid got in last Summer and cut himself up pretty bad- had to go to the hospital. We can't let that happen. What is your name?"

"Oh, officer- I am so sorry!! I'm Natalie Peterson. I won't do this again."

"Can I see some identification, ma'am?"

"Oh, yes!! Well, actually, it's in the car."

"That's fine- you can show it to me at the station. You're coming with me. You're under arrest for trespassing. You have the right to remain silent and the right to an attorney." The officer stood directly in front of her as he quickly put the handcuffs on both wrists, completing the Miranda statement as her eyes began to tear. She looked away.

Jim proceeded quickly to within ten feet of the patrolman's back. "Officer, do you really have to do that? I'm her husband, Jim Peterson. She didn't hurt anyone."

"That has nothing to do with it, sir. She's broken the law-trespassing on clearly marked property is forbidden. Stop right there or you'll be under arrest." He pulled Natalie back with him as he strode toward the cruiser, the lights flashing across her face. Then he glanced at Jim. "You can follow us to the station. It's just down the road, off Route 724." He pulled the back passenger door open, nudging Natalie's head down as he pushed her in.

Jim was seething as he saw the images in slow motion, the cruiser pulling away, Natalie turning to see him, tears streaming down her cheeks. He ran back to the car, jumped in and sped out of the lot, noticing the two men grinning in front of the tractor trailer, a full ratchet set spilled in the sunlight on the ground in front of them. He heard a noise as he neared the highway, a large rock bouncing up, hitting the rear window.

⬥ ⦿ ⬥

She sat fully erect in the olive green, drab chair as she listened to the officer finish reading the charges. Natalie was still crying as the words entered her ears. Her mind was racing, considering what her family would say if they found out.

"Did you remove or damage any property from the location today?"

"No."

His veins caught on fire as he heard her voice. "My God!! What are you doing??!!" he thought, his hands wrapped anxiously around the sides of his chair ten feet away. His stomach was in agony, spasms wrenching his insides as he fixed on her eyes, her tears still flowing. Her eyes met his for a moment, then she looked away. His chest was convulsing, his breathing faster and faster as he thought about what she said- and about the box she put in their car. Turning bright red as he considered the possibility they would question him and search their SUV, he labored with each breath as he analyzed questions they could ask *him*. "Knowingly giving false information to a police officer in the commission of a crime is a felony." He coughed loudly and focused on the thick layer of dirt covering her shoes. His body was starting to shake, the night with Danny washing all around him.

"Do you have anything to say, Mr. Peterson?" The officer finished filling out the form, pushing it in front of her on the metal desk and watching as Natalie signed the bottom.

"Yes. When can we go?" Jim gawked at his weather-beaten face, wrinkles around his eyes the roadmap of many years on the force.

The officer ignored his question. "Mrs. Peterson, you'll be receiving notice in the mail of these charges and a court date." Then he peered over at Jim. "You can *both go*. You're done here."

Standing up slowly, she tried not to look at Jim or the officer. Her gaze turned to the "WANTED" posters on the corkboard across the room and the filings of arrest reports stacked on the long table next to his desk. She felt Jim's hand and stepped lightly toward the exit.

Silence engulfed them for the first ten minutes of the drive home. The two-lane highway loomed ahead in the mid-afternoon sunlight as the car's speed reached 55, then he turned up the air conditioner to the maximum setting, the noise a dull roar around them.

"OK!! OK!! You were right!! I feel... so horrible. I can't believe I did this." The trees flashed by at the side of the road, the rose and white petals of the dogwoods unable to bring the smile they normally did. "It was so humiliating, riding in that car, people at intersections glaring at us, mothers with children pointing at me, shaking their heads. I couldn't look at anything except the mud on my shoes. That's something I NEVER want to experience again."

"What, getting mud on your shoes?"

"No, you bonehead!!" She shook her head as she pushed his right shoulder. "Being handcuffed in a police cruiser." She gazed out her side window and tried to smile, the sun shining brightly through the trees warming her.

"Let's make damn sure it never happens again." He brought her hand up to his lips as he accelerated back onto the interstate.

Frick's Lock entrance

Frick's Lock Plantation House

Frick's Lock – Room with ceiling hole

Chapter 2

"What we do during our working hours determines what we have;
what we do during our leisure hours determines what we are..."
                                                    --George Eastman

"She got what was comin' to her." Floyd put the ratchet wrench down on the blacktop.

"I just want our hundred bucks!!" Dexter laughed. "Hand me that 3/8ᵗʰ socket, will ya'?" The early morning sun was on his forehead, small beads of perspiration already breaking through. "Gonna' be a hot one today and it's only the first week of June."

"I hope *she* feels some heat when she goes to court and pays a big fine. Those rich city folks, think they can do anything- trespass on other people's property, say the hell with the rules- just to get what they want." A sparrow landed on the asphalt in the shade of the truck. Its speckled brown chest bobbed up and down as it hopped toward him, hoping for some food. "You're a cute little guy, but sorry- no food 'round here. Might try over there near that oak tree." As he finished speaking, the bird chirped and flew off toward the edge of the forest in the bright sunlight.

"How long you figure it'll take us to get this one fixed?"

"Oh, a good part of the mornin'. We have to take apart most of the transmission and it needs a full lube." His shoulders ached, reminding him of all the hours he'd spent working on trucks since his father lost his job years ago, all the days he wished he was out having fun with his buddies… then his expression turned dour. "You and me, we gotta' work for a livin'. Them, they got all the money they want, drive around like her in their fancy Mercedes, think they own the place!!" He stood up for a break and focused on the 200-year old red brick building at the end of the nearby property, its back walls crumbling into a pile of debris, left untouched by caretakers for so many years. "Look at that- my great grandfather used to live here- it was his home. Now it's fallin' apart!!" His shoulders drooped as he frowned, limestone pebbles scattered all around his feet on the gravelly edge of the lot. "They took dad's caretaker job away- without any notice!! Some dude drives up here- it was a Friday, as I recall- and goes up to dad. They talk for a few minutes, then I heard dad cursin' somethin' fierce. He started to take a swing at the guy, but his buddy stopped him. Then the dude yells somethin' and drives away. Car's worth more than our house!! That was the day dad came home really drunk, more than usual- and lays into me. 'You gotta' get a job NOW!! You hear??!!'" He searched the lot and nearby oak tree for the sparrow, but it was gone.

"Hey, Floyd, let it go, alright? That was what- 30 years ago? Come on."

"I won't let it go!! Look at what's happened. This place was sacred- somethin' special to me. Those houses were part of a town way back when. Frick's Lock used to MEAN somethin'. Not the way it is now. This place did a lot of business, with the canal and all. Even when the town kinda' closed down, my dad had his job here with PECO, takin' care of all the houses. With Three Mile Island, everybody started worryin' about some meltdown, like we were all goin' to get cooked by some nuclear reactor!! After a while, Power company didn't want the risk- so my dad lost his job. It's been downhill from there."

"Floyd, look. That was then, this is now, man."

"NO!! I HATE people who come up here in their expensive cars, snoopin' around. I had to quit school, get a job as a clerk at the Post Office- remember that- AND start learnin' how to be a mechanic at Smitty's Garage on the weekends just to put food on the table. Nobody handed *me* nuthin'!! Once went three days without any food in the house until mom brought home some bread she stole." His nose was deep red, his bloodshot eyes the signposts of an early morning drinker. "One thing I haven't done since that day."

"What's that?"

"Never worked on a god-damn Mercedes- and never will!!"

Dexter laughed so hard, tears started streaming from his eyes. "Floyd- don't sugar coat it- give it to me straight!!"

Floyd managed a smile and got back down to work on the truck. "Least you 'n me- we make an honest livin'." His fingers grasped the wrench in his right hand. "My grandfather was a crackerjack mechanic. Hard workin' man. Used to fix the old Model T's. Said he went to some fancy trade show back in the 1930's and saw Henry Ford himself!! Those first cars- people were so nuts about 'em- they'd travel twenty miles by horse just to see one!! Used to show 'em off in road races, too." Floyd felt the wrap of his grandfather's strong arms, picking him up in the air. He was talking slowly, gently about what it was like working on the first cars, how everything was new back then, moving away from the horse and buggy era. "Pops told me once 'No more horse and buggies…' I didn't know what he meant because we didn't have a horse and buggy. I think what he was tryin' to say was… technology was changin' the world and we gotta' change with it." Floyd held the ratchet in his right hand and studied the wall of bolts, hinges and gaskets all around him. "Just hope this technology binge doesn't take *our* jobs away."

"It won't, Floyd. They'll always need guys like us to fix these things."

"Yeah, guess so… Just wish they'd pay us decent." His fingers wrapped around the metal instrument as he tightened the two large bolts. "One time old pops told me he was in a road race himself- on Old Route 66!! Wasn't even fully paved back then."

"Must've been in the '40's."

"This is *way* back- around 1927, bud. They used to drive out into the desert- nuthin' around but tumbleweeds and rat-tlesnakes!! Whoever got there first won a prize- probably a tank of gas to get to the next pit stop." Floyd imagined the old roads before superhighways came in. The four-stool diners serving chicken-fried steak and mashed potatoes in the middle of no-where. Lonely signs, frosted by the desert windstorms. 'Next gas- 87 miles'. His eyes closed and he saw his grandfather again, his big smile and hands around Floyd's shoulders, his firm hug welcome despite the scrape of the two-day beard.

"I think Joey Falcone's dad had a Model A. He was a car

nut. All Joey's brothers used to steal parts from it and bring 'em to school." His attention turned from the set of wrenches on the ground to Floyd. "You miss him, don't ya'?"

"I do." A smile formed slowly, then the pain of that day returned. He was in sixth grade, came home from school and sat down at the kitchen table when his mother told him his grandfather had died. "He was my real dad- when dad was out drunk somewhere. Which was most of the time." The edge of the hip flask jutted into his side from the hidden pocket as he grabbed the two bolts off the ground. "Ya' know, I drove part of Route 66."

"Yeah, when?"

"Remember that Summer back in '79 when I disappeared for a few weeks? Me an' Mike Jackson hopped in his dad's old Studebaker- he gave it to him because it always broke down- and we started headin' West. I said 'Let's drive as far as we can before this thing explodes!' Made it out to Oklahoma... Saw those plates 'Oklahoma is OK'. Then on to Arizona before the car started shakin' every few miles. Decided to turn around before somethin' bad happened. Got back in one piece- and saw some pretty nice country. Petrified Forest- got some rocks from there sittin' in the garage. A lotta' prairie dogs and jackrabbits. Great trip."

"Think we'll ever be doin' anything better than workin' on these rigs? I'm kinda sick of it." Dexter shook his head as he held the screwdriver and loosened the four screws in the under-carriage, straining to get the last one out.

"Look, it's all I know. Besides, it pays the bills- and with three kids and a wife that can pass everything on the road except a "SALE" sign, I'll be at it for a while." He thought about the night they first met at the high school dance… He strutted up to her, admiring her nice butt in those tight jeans- then she turned around just as he reached out to touch her shoulder. "Did you want to ask me to dance?" She smiled, her generous coating of pink lipstick exciting him as he answered "Uh, yeah!!" He asked her out three more times and then knew they'd 'go steady'. He didn't see any other girl throughout the rest of his Senior year- and it was a sunny day the next April when they walked down the aisle in the old Nottingham Church. They both had a few miles on them since then, their life a tour through tough times and raising kids. Yet they'd made it this far. He tried to keep his eyes on the road ahead- not the scenery.

"When do ya' think the cops'll get us our money?" Dexter was thinking about lunch at the diner and his first beer of the day. His stomach growled, the dull ache of too many drinks the night before, along with three-alarm Mexican food.

"Ya' mean the hundred bucks for turnin' that lady in for trespassin'? Captain Ferguson says he always pays within a week- so by next Monday, I guess."

"Another hundred for us!!" Dexter leaned over and gave him a high-five, straining as he laid nearly on his side.

"Yeah, that deal with the cops has gotten us over a thousand bucks so far this year! An easy hundred each time we see someone goin' into Frick's Lock. I'm sure they make enough in fines- we deserve a cut."

"Hundred bucks buys a lotta' brews!!" He could feel the ice cold beer in his hand at the bar, ready to take another long drink- until he remembered the wrenching grip on his shoulder shaking him on the night Ferguson arrested them both.

The Super Bowl crowd at Sally's Bar had gotten a bit wild, people throwing food around, yellin' and pushin'. "Remember that night- when Ferguson took us in?"

"Yeah, like a toothache…

———————

The bar was packed three-deep, mostly with men in biker T-shirts angling to get closer to the bartender. "Hey- Joey!! Two more Buds over here!!" Floyd slapped the ten dollar bill down, feeling beer soak through as he watched him nod back, the suds flowing smoothly from the tap at the center of the room. Just then a hot dog landed in front of him. Floyd's gaze shot over to the other side, bringing two guys into view, both in their early 20's, smirking as they held paper plates with remnants of a snack.

"Hey, knock it off!! I'm tryin' to have a drink here." He glared at them both, then turned around to get his change. Floyd focused his attention across to the far end of the bar where two girls in mini-skirts were swaying to the loud music coming from the jukebox in the corner. "Now that looks pretty good to me… Wonder if they're… available." He winked at the buxom blonde and she winked back, then got up on a table, jumping up and down to the beat. Swaying her hips wildly to the music blaring in the corner, she laughed, taking a bottle from her girlfriend, chugging a very long gulp before giving it back.

"Woo-hooo!! Yeah, baby YEAH!!" She started to fall off, but was caught by two very willing bikers in full black leather gear, chains dangling from their waists.

"This place is gettin' a bit wild. Wonder what's next?" Floyd thought as he searched around the room for Dexter. A bottle hit him at his waist and he turned around quickly after he put the two beers back down on the bar. "What the…?"

"Hey, down in front!! We can't see the game, *bozo*!!"

"What the *hell* are you doin'?!!" His eyes burned with rage, but Dexter's arm caught him before he could approach the offending parties.

"Back off, Floyd!! Those guys are Warlocks!! Check out the skull-and-crossbones tattoos. They *kill* people. I know- saw a story in the paper a few months ago. Don't mess with 'em." He kept his grip on Floyd's shoulder, holding him back.

"Jerks!! I oughtta'…"

"Cool it!! Wanna' get your head kicked in? They don't fool around… Let's go down to the other end. It's not as rowdy over there."

He handed Dexter his beer and they slowly made their way to the end of the bar. Floyd marveled at three shapely, full-figured girls strutting around, each one in skin-tight, hip-hugger jeans and low-cut, V-neck tops, pushing their chests into the faces of willing onlookers. The redhead at the front of their group grabbed one patron, her arms wrapped around his head, pulling his face into her ample cleavage. He smiled as she held him down for several seconds, then yelled "Marry me- now!!"

"Dexter, this is the craziest I've ever seen this joint. All we need is for some of those chicks to strip naked and put on a little entertainment for the troops!!"

"Wouldn't rule it out. Take a look over there…"

Floyd nudged Dexter's knee with the ratchet. "He didn't have to do it- the whole place was outta' control, not just us!! Marty was stone drunk, fallin' off his stool at the bar. Then those guys at the other end hollerin' 'BOO!' every time the Eagles scored. It was startin' to get to me. Look, the crowd was rowdy- so shakin' up that Bud and sprayin' it at them was nuthin' compared to what was goin' on in the back. That one chick was dancin' on the bar, startin' to take her top off. Too bad we couldn't see the end of *that* show! Jimmy took that waitress into the Men's Room. When she came out, her dress was hangin' pretty crooked." Floyd pondered if he'd ever have gotten a date with her.

"I remember that! Hot babe, as I recall."

"For sure, but I think she was the one who called the cops!! I made a crack about her bra bein' down around her waist, showin' off her assets- and she stormed out. Never saw her after that. Next thing, the cops barge in and grab me an' you since we was closest to the door!!"

"Couldn't believe he arrested us. Glad he was open to bargainin' when we brought up that we worked next to Frick's Lock. Said the place was strictly 'OFF LIMITS', orders of the Fire Marshall and the power company. He knew we were mechanics. Just makin' a phone call every time someone goes beyond the 'TRESPASSING' sign was the best deal I heard all night. Least we got off without a record." Dexter wiped a drop of motor oil from his forehead as he tightened the two bolts on the undercarriage. "Think we should say anything about the box that lady took?"

"NO!!"

"Why not?"

"Cuz' I wanna' know what's in it- maybe worth some money. Remember that one guy who came up here last month? You were workin' on the other truck. I went up to him, holdin' a big wrench and got him to drop what he had and run. Slipped and skinned his leg, he was so scared!! Well, I got a decent watch, a nice clock and a radio out of it. Sold them at the auction for over five hundred bucks! One guy told me he thought the clock was some kinda' Art Deco antique, or somethin'. Good way to earn some money. That's why." Floyd stared at him until Dexter turned away. The sparrow was gone.

"Did you get that lady's license plate?"

"Sure did. Wrote it in the dust on the windshield. I'm callin' Joey over at the DMV later today. He's gotten me a lotta' info over the years and he owes me a favor. Have to find out where she lives."

"Let me know when. I'm up for a road trip..."

Chapter 3

"Every right implies a responsibility; every opportunity,
an obligation; every possession, a duty..."
--John D. Rockefeller

Jolting pain from the incident at the Lock the day before
pierced her abdomen as she sipped the mug of cinnamon
tea, her stomach churning as she tried to assimilate what happened. "How could I be so careless and stupid??!! Just to see a
few old deserted houses and get a box of junk." She ruminated
on all the 'bad kids' in high school- the ones who were con-
stantly in trouble, some who actually did go to jail. The steam
billowed from the cup and she was back in Home Room... The
problem kids were the last ones strolling in to get to their seats,
being scolded as the strong odor of cigarettes emanated from
their clothes toward Mrs. Hotchner at the front of the room.
Natalie considered herself more responsible than them- studying and always in class on time, respecting authority. "What's
with those guys? Don't they realize they're only hurting themselves?" Natalie watched as the final few- the real troublemak-
ers- got to their desks, flaunting the teacher with smirks as she

started to write at the blackboard… She considered her situation, observing the petunias and snapdragons bowing slightly in the early morning breeze. "I'm going to have a criminal record!! I can't believe this!!" She set the cup down gently, knowing it would take Jim months to completely forgive her. Picking up the phone, she clicked through the pre-programmed numbers, stopping on 'Sue Home'. Natalie heard the first ring, waiting for the one person who could lift her spirits.

"Hello?" came the hurried and somewhat agitated voice on the other end.

"Hey Sue! How are you doing?"

"I'm fine, hold on a minute. I'm watching 'Supernatural' and it's right at the interesting part." The phone was lowered to her waist as the images flashed on the TV.

"No problem." Natalie sat back, hearing the faint sounds coming through the receiver. She pondered the troubles in her sister's life- much tougher than Natalie's, raising three kids alone after a divorce and no child support. A string of unusual jobs at low pay, sometimes working 12 hour days, seven days a week for months at a time – anything to make ends meet. It was fodder for family jokes, like her job in Minnesota with Campbell Soup, removing the eggs from dead chickens all day long. "Sometimes you have to be thankful for the things you DON'T have in your life…"

Some of the tension left her chest as she recalled Sue's jobs improving over the years from rigorous factory work including one plant where she operated a 50-foot long 'Thermatrol' machine to stamp out trays for TV dinners, then on to office assistant answering phones and working on computers. Without any formal technical training, Sue showed herself to be a natural in the area and was usually the first in their family to get the latest tech wonder- digital cameras, multi-option cell phones for texting. Sue's little house on the edge of Downingtown came into view, its cramped rooms filled with cat toys, gardening magazines, scrapbooking supplies, DVDs and an adjacent room with two computers- one Sue's and the other for her current employer. Working from home entering chemical formulas for patent applications, the job paid all the bills. Sue's life had appeared hectic- a series of ongoing mini-dramas, but she seemed truly happy now, with seven grandchildren to fawn over and a higher paycheck to allow her to spend money and time on her favorite hobbies. Natalie contemplated their more comfortable life, with few major challenges- until yesterday.

"Sue, are you still there?" The drone of the TV in the background was suddenly interrupted by the chatter of birds squawking and flapping against the cage.

"Damn it Stella, cut it out!" Sue swatted at the tabby cat, forcing it to jump away from the intended target.

Natalie grinned, picturing feathers and seeds flying all over, coating the nearby furniture and floor. The cat and the birds were a gift from Jim and Natalie a few years back, helping Sue get through yet another tough situation- a break-up with a boyfriend of over 11 years who showed little interest in 'committing'. The birds were still squawking when Sue's soft, uplifting voice came through on the line. "Stupid cat, couldn't even watch the end of the show. She always wants to be petted right as the good part comes on!! So, what's up?"

Natalie hesitated for a few seconds, dwelling on how best to phrase her run-in with the police. "Well... I just wanted to talk."

"I'm listening."

The pressure returned again in her chest. "Something bad happened." Her eyes shifted to the fuzzy pink slippers beneath the breakfast table, giving her a moment of joy. "Remember I told you about that book 'Weird Pennsylvania'?"

"Sure, what about it?" She swatted again at Stella, keeping her away from Bonnie and Cassidy, the two parakeets inside the cage. "Stop! You two are flying around like you *want* her to have you for lunch!!"

"We drove up to a place called Frick's Lock yesterday. It's an abandoned town from the late 1700's up near Phoenixville- it's mentioned in the book. Really neat boarded up houses, some falling apart, quite eerie. Well, I did some exploring, even though the place is cordoned off with 'NO TRESPASSING' signs and a warning that the premises are under surveillance."

"Yes... and...?"

"Jim didn't want to go in- said it was too risky- and stayed back at the car most of the time. I got into one house and it was amazing- even a bit scary!! There were things hanging from the ceiling, broken timbers everywhere. I found a big box of items almost too heavy to carry, but I got it back to the car. I told Jim I wanted to go back in and he was furious. Got into a brief shouting match, but I went anyway and roamed around the other abandoned houses- until the cops came."

"Don't tell me…"

Natalie frowned, barely able to look outside again as the sun shone on the black wrought iron railing at the edge of the terrace. "Sue, I got arrested for trespassing."

"Oh, God!! That must have been horrible. Now what?"

"I don't know!! They said I'll get something in the mail

with the official charges- and a court date sometime soon. I'm nervous about what could happen… and ashamed of myself. I've never done anything like this in my entire life. I was always the 'good girl'… followed the rules… now I'm a criminal."

"I love that show 'America's Most Wanted'. Maybe you could be on there."

"Sue- stop!! This is serious. What should I do?"

"I think they pay pretty good, like a thousand bucks if they take you on the show."

"You bird brain! This isn't about money, it's about keeping me out of jail!!"

"Still think the thousand bucks might be worth a try. Sounds like you have a good story."

"Sue!"

"Just joking!" She pondered the question, trying to think of something useful to solve Natalie's predicament. "Hey, didn't you meet some cute FBI guy a while back in that investigation of the antique dealers? Maybe he has some connections and could help."

Natalie's mind raced as she recalled how he sat with her in their parlor, discussing the case- and his offer to help her anytime. "Yes!! That's a great idea." She deliberated for several seconds before a possible solution started to emerge. "He was good looking- even flirted with me a bit. When he gave me his card, I suspected he was looking for something more than just lunch."

"Who cares? You don't have to date him!! He might be able to help. Give him a call!! If he wants a date, give him my number. Hope he likes pets…"

"You're right- he could have some connections. If you're in

the FBI, you don't stay there for long without getting to know a lot of law enforcement people. I just have to find his card."

"Do it today!! Look, what's the worst that could happen? He says 'No' and that's it. You've got to at least try." The cat jumped on her shoulders, causing her to drop the phone. "Stella, you nitwit!!" She tossed the pillow at the cat, chasing her away. "There, now let me talk for a few seconds!!" She picked up the phone. "Sorry, kitty needs hormone replacement therapy. She's going bonkers. Just call that guy now!!"

"It's Sunday. I'll call him tomorrow. Thank you so much. I think you might have helped me out of this mess. If this turns out well, I'll buy you dinner at your favorite place."

"Just ask if he has a cute friend. That way I won't have to fly solo. The way you described him, he was ridiculously good looking. Hey, I have to run a whole bunch of errands. Call me soon and let me know what happened!! This is exciting- better than the last episode I saw of CSI!"

Her laugh filled the room. "I will. I'll call you when I find out something. I owe you one!!" She hung up the phone and watched as two squirrels feasted on a small pile of nuts they'd managed to pull out of the bird feeder, the smaller one with the larger pile, contentedly nibbling as the larger one looked back up at the feeder, sensing another climb ahead. She strolled back to her office and sat down at the desk. "I know I kept it. Got to be in here somewhere." She took out the writing pad from the Hotel du Pont, a keepsake from her birthday dinner with Jim- and saw it, his card sitting on top of other assorted business cards she'd received over the last year.

"Hey, you took a lot of photos there, might as well see what you got" Jim commented, entering Natalie's office.

Startled, she closed her desk drawer. "Oh, you mean of Frick's Lock?"

"No, Hoover Dam. Of course. You risked your freedom to get them. Let's have a look."

"Alright. They're already downloaded onto my computer. Should only take a second to pull them up." She tapped the key, opening the file. The screen showed numerous thumbnail images.

"Can you enlarge each one? I'd like to see them up close, check out the details."

"Sure." She clicked again and the first image filled the screen.

"A scene of destruction… Hiroshima after the bomb." He leaned closer.

"Not quite, but everything appeared in ruins. I'm sure vandals played a large role."

"Weather, vandals, just normal deterioration. The place is a mess."

"You haven't seen anything yet." She advanced to the next photo.

"Wow. Tons of debris. Was it a home? I can see the semblance of walls amidst the squalor. How did you ever walk through all that junk?"

"Wasn't as bad as it looks. Actually, it was really interesting. Now this one's kind of eerie." A tap on the keyboard moved the view to the next shot, showing the nuclear plant.

"Cooling towers. That's the Limerick Nuclear Plant. What a backdrop for an abandoned town. You know, after Three Mile Island happened, there was such an outcry against nuclear power that all nuclear plant development was halted. In 1979,

Comanche Peak in Texas was the last plant commissioned. That was 31 years ago. Hard to believe."

"So the outcry from environmentalists killed nuclear power?"

"Pretty much. It's ironic. Even though nuclear power when used appropriately is among the safest and lowest cost of all methods of electricity generation, it was given the axe. It was just hard to argue that you should build a new plant after Three Mile Island scared the hell out of a lot of people. Then, in 1986 Chernobyl put the nail in the coffin. That was it." He glanced at the Daily Local sitting on the edge of her desk, the headline 'Limerick Plant May Be in Jeopardy Due to Japan Safety Concerns'. "What just happened in Japan is a tragedy. I mean, they know they're in a major earthquake zone, so those plants should all have been constructed to withstand at least a 9.5 temblor- and had ready access to several alternate supplies of energy to back them up. The news reports on T.V. were showing some horrible scenes of destruction. Those poor people- they're all paying the price... My heart goes out to them..."

"It's a dilemma with far ranging implications."

"Maybe. Unfortunately, as with Three Mile Island and Chernobyl, the real tragedy could be that we don't build and retrofit our utility *and* chemical plants more safely to protect against things like this. The more we delay, the worse off we'll all be. It's interesting to note that the French, who are pretty liberal as a people, get 78% of their electricity from nuclear power- almost four times the percentage we get. Now, if a liberal country like France can construct these things and feels nuclear power is safe, why can't we use it more extensively in the U.S.- and around the world?"

"Good question." She clicked to the next shot.

"Tragedies are God's way of teaching us to do things differently. Think about it. If we'd spent the last 30 years designing a variety of more safe and efficient sources of power, we'd be far down the road toward energy independence."

"The BP blowout in the Gulf of Mexico didn't help any. Now there's millions of people protesting against any drilling in the U.S., further setting us back, causing more oil to be imported from countries in the Middle East, which don't have a particularly high concern for our well-being."

Jim shook his head, then looked directly at Natalie. "I've always argued that we should develop *all forms* of energy which can be utilized efficiently and safely. If we did- we wouldn't be in this situation."

"Agree completely." The next few pictures came into view, showing the antebellum houses in their disarray, walls collapsed amidst huge piles of debris.

"Well, I think I get it. A once thriving town, built to take advantage of new technology is abandoned and left to rot in the shadows of… yet another new form of technology. Joseph Schumpeter was right. He used the term 'creative destruction' to describe what happens as humans find and develop new scientific advancements and leave behind the old ones. Perhaps it'll all come full circle someday."

———— ((●)) ————

Monday started out sunny, the circular outdoor thermometer showing 74 degrees at 9:10 a.m. "Jim's at work, so I can do this now. Should call from my cell phone just to be safe." She proceeded through the kitchen and stood outside the back door as the phone rang on the other end.

"Special Agent Clark here."

She studied the name on the card. "Hello, Jack?"

His ear pressed firmly against the receiver, sensing a familiar voice. "Yes, this is Jack."

"Jack, this is Natalie Peterson. Do you remember me?"

"Of course, hello Natalie!! How are you?" He noticed the open door to his office and he shuffled toward it, nudging it closed.

"Oh, I'm… fine, I guess. How have you been? Solved any more interesting cases?"

"We're always busy. The Mob never sleeps. What's new there with you?"

Breathing in deeply, the Russian sage came into view surrounding the driveway, a calming feeling settling in. "Well, I was just wondering. Is your lunch invitation still good?"

"Of course it is." He stood up straighter near the desk and grabbed his pen, noting her number from the caller I.D. screen, ready to write the time and place of their rendezvous.

"That's great!! Maybe we could check out Catherine's in Unionville sometime. You know where that is?"

"Great place- ate there once." Sitting up in the large black leather chair, he opened his Franklin Day Planner. "I'm actually free on Thursday. How about 11:30 a.m. before the lunch crowd comes in?"

"Sounds wonderful! I'll meet you there." Standing in the sunlight, the phone pointing upwards for several seconds, she pondered a plan to get away. Puffy grey-white clouds moved slowly by, breaking the sunlight into patches across the lawn.

The phone came to rest back in the charging station and he felt a lift as he stepped back toward the office door to open it. "Sounds like a deal to me. She's older- but definitely attractive." He dwelled on the memory of their last meeting- her clingy, low-cut top, the tight jeans, touching her face gently just before he left. "It almost happened... now it will." All the attractive women over the years he'd met in his job, the images drifted into view- some came close, stopping in for a brief 'visit'- others were just trains rolling away in the distance. "This one's married, buddy boy. Could be problems. Better be very, very careful." Then one of the 'encounters' came back to him...

Watching the tan octagonal clock at the edge of his cubicle strike 5 p.m., he closed his notebook, putting his pen into his jacket. Strutting out the door, he rounded the corner at 15th Street and saw her- one of his fellow FBI trainees sitting inside as he approached the entrance of the Capital Grille. "Wow- she looks even better than at lunchtime" he thought. "Must have put on more make-up... but she doesn't need it." Scanning the area as they were taught for stakeouts, he noticed none of the other agents were there. "Hi there. Mind if I join you?"

"Oh, hi!! Take a seat next to me here. I'm ready for a Manhattan!!"

He nodded to the bartender, a handsome man in his late twenties, with strong biceps bulging through his partially rolled up blue shirt. "A Manhattan for the lady. Chivas on ice for me." The bartender nodded back and turned to get their drinks.

She straightened her shoulders, raising her head as he nudged his chair toward hers, the high-backed dark walnut stool a perfect accent to her stunning figure. "So, what do *you* think of all this training?"

He loved the way her lips curled slightly every time she spoke. "Actually, I find it fascinating. A lot to know, but we're getting the best education in the world." The bartender put both drinks on the bar and they each took a long sip.

"I like it, but it gets a bit too much at times. Wish I had my girlfriends from Georgetown here to party with." Her eyes showed long dark lashes fringed with grey-blue mascara.

"You have to distance yourself, or it takes control of you." He shook the ice cubes in the tumbler and drained it to below half full. Looking back over at the bartender, he nodded for another one, pointing to his glass. "Another for you?"

"Oh, yes!!" She finished her drink, then giggled. "I'm such a quick drunk. Two and I'm done for the night." She admired his handsome square-cut chin as the bartender brought the drinks.

"So, what do you do for fun around here? Any good clubs, restaurants you like?" The scotch was starting its buzz down his throat, into his chest.

"On what they pay us as rookies, I've turned into a pretty good cook- even though there's a nice little Italian place about four blocks away which I love."

"I'm 50% Italian- and I *love* to cook."

"You do? That's *great*. So do I!!" Her left leg brushed up against the edge of his pants. "We should exchange recipes sometime. Maybe you could come over and show me some of your favorite dishes."

"Would love to." The hemline of her skirt had risen two inches higher on her thighs as she leaned in closer to his chair, exposing the tops of her sheer nylons.

"I'm getting… a bit… tipsy. This is my last one… but if

you want to stop over for coffee afterwards, I can show you my place." She leaned within a few inches of his chair- and put her hand on his shoulder, painted crimson nails tracing the edge of his suit.

"Check, please." He made sure the bartender heard him before putting the twenty on the bar. "Sounds good to me. I could use some coffee before I head home." He glanced at the bill. "We're done here. Ready to go?"

"I am!!" She followed him out to the street. "My apartment's only two blocks away."

"That must be so convenient every morning. I loved living downtown when I was in San Diego. I thought of all the people fighting the traffic driving down Interstate 5 as I strolled past the fountains."

"Here we are." She pushed the button for the 8th floor and started to move closer to him as the doors shut.

The lighted numbers flashed slowly in the small square above the door line... four... five... six. Trying to focus on anything but her, he held the door open as they both went into the hallway. She stopped in front of a beautifully carved, heavy oak door. "This is the place. Make yourself at home." She went directly to the kitchen to start the coffee.

"You have a nice place. What a great view!!" He wandered over to the couch and sat down, waiting to see if she would join him.

"Do you like it? I rent mostly for the convenience, but it's comfortable." Pressing the button to get the coffee brewing, she gained her balance and smiled before taking the seat right next to him, her gaze rising to meet his. "Your eyes are my favorite color!!" She moved within inches of him and closed her eyes, then pressed her lips against his.

"Mmmm… that felt… nice." They kissed again, his arms wrapped around her waist, briefly touching her rather ample chest covered by the cream-colored silk blouse. The wire-rim of her bra gave him a twinge, the excitement causing him to straighten up.

"Well… it's getting a bit warm in here… Why don't we… get more comfortable?" She undid the first few buttons of her blouse, then stopped. "I am…a bit drunk… and so sorry!! I know you're Jack, but I've totally forgotten your last name."

"Clark. I have the same confession. You're Judy…??"

"Cunningham." She undid the middle button and opened her shirt just enough to show the top of some magnificent cleavage, smiling as she noticed him admiring her chest. "Do you like that?" She licked her pink lips as she watched his reaction, resting her hand on his shoulder.

"Very… much." He sat up and tried to swallow through the dryness in his throat. "You're not related to *Field Director* Cunningham, are you?" The stern warnings from their first three instructors NOT to become involved in any intra-office relationships rang loudly in his ears. The Director highly frowned upon it.

"He's my uncle."

"Your *uncle*??"

"Yes, why?" She undid the last few buttons and opened up her blouse, exposing a full view of her breasts as they jiggled in a very low-cut, padded push-up bra. "How do you like the view from here?"

"Oh, umm… I didn't know you were related to… the Director." His eyes were locked for several seconds on her tantalizing cleavage, her breasts swaying each time she moved closer. He felt his left hand being placed firmly on her knee. "I really... need to be going." His pulse was racing as he got up quickly and went toward the door.

"Why? What's wrong?" The smile ran away from her face as she stood up.

"Nothing... just not *quite* what I thought. It was very nice meeting you. I'm sure we'll see each other in the next few training sessions." He glanced back once more at her chest, avoiding her eyes, then closed the door behind him, hurrying to the elevator... promising himself he'd never do that again. "Six... five... four..." flashed on the screen as the heavenly sight remained before him... "That was a close one... so tempting..."

The inviting sound of Natalie's voice that day in her parlor, the curve of her chest which first caught his attention and her tight jeans around the very curvaceous waist brought him back with a jolt of excitement. "For an older woman, she is definitely hot. How many have I dated over the years? There was that 48-year old divorcee in Downingtown. God!! She couldn't keep her hands off of me... Then there was the receptionist- 50 going on 20- who worked at that engineering firm we investigated. She didn't mind showing off her curves in those shiny satin tops. Can't believe I actually dated a woman who was 15 years older than I am... but they're so... giving. Got to start finding women who are closer to my age!! Only problem is, they all want to get married right away and have kids. Not my cup of tea..." he thought as he planned the lunch meeting with Natalie. He viewed the schedule for the week ahead. "Let's see today- pretty open. Tomorrow- need to finish the report on that drug gang in Norristown to complete the file. He flipped forward to Thursday and wrote in large bold letters 'LUNCH APPOINTMENT'. "I'll wear my Austin Reed dark blue pin-stripe suit- always gets good comments. That red and silver tie is perfect for it." Then he thought of her again. "Mmm... Natalie, I am definitely looking forward to this..."

———⊙———

As Natalie ruminated on the last few hectic days- stopping by to bring her mother toiletries, driving the next day up to Bryn Mawr to visit Connie who she hadn't seen in over six months and then going over to John's house to drop off items he need-ed for his computer, she realized the week was more than half over, then remembered the last words Jack said before hearing the dial tone in her ear. "Catherine's- 11:30. Wait- that's today!! Where has the time gone? I never get a chance to just sit down and relax..." Ruby and lavender petals poked skyward, the pansies, dianthus and hydrangeas in the garden below calming her, but she knew the lunch meeting could be... intense. Her stomach growled, a tinge of pain piercing her ribs. Turning from the glass doors, she noticed Jim standing at the island in the kitchen.

"This morning is flying by. Errands to run- need to get a few things at Lowe's and I also want to go to Michael's to get some frames- they're having a sale. I'll be stopping in at work first to say goodbye and pick up the last few boxes. Probably won't be back until mid-afternoon. OK?" He put his arms around her shoulders.

As she tried to smile up at him, she thought about how

Jack could help her, make some connections- get the situation resolved- and the irritation was mostly gone from her stomach. "Not a problem. I have some things to take care of myself. I'll see you back here later on." She put her chin up to kiss him gingerly as he advanced toward the garage. Hearing his car leaving and the middle door closing, she picked up her keys.

She rounded the turn past the hand-written wooden sign into the cramped rear parking lot. 'Serving Breakfast and Lunch Now, Too!' Natalie debated how best to get the first words out. "How am I going to say it?" She proceeded through the back doorway and recalled something her mother had told her when she was just 16 years old, about to take her Driver's Test. "Honey, if you want something from a man, wear a short skirt and show a little cleavage." Her left hand adjusted the neckline of her top slightly lower to show a bit more skin as she stepped toward the table. "Hello!! How ARE you?"

"Doing great. I hope you're well." He pulled out the chair behind her before taking his place at the small round table with white linen and silverware.

"I'm fine. Things are going well... Actually, I wanted to share something with you... and maybe you could help."

"Sure, I'd be glad to." He recalled the 15 minutes together with her last year. She was wearing the same suggestive top that first captured his attention.

"I'm not sure if you know where Frick's Lock is- up around Phoenixville?"

"I do. We completed a case near there maybe six months ago with the sheriff. There was a tie-in between some local gangs and drug trafficking through several states coming into that area, so it was a Fed issue. Our team helped them out quite a bit and secured several arrests. Why, what about Frick's Lock? I believe that's an abandoned town."

"I… I did something stupid. Drove up there with Jim and we did some exploring. I ignored the trespassing signs. It was wrong. Who pulls up- a local cop- and he promptly arrested me. I'm a bit scared… and don't know what to do." She rubbed her temple, then scanned the floor and noticed two small cracks in the pine near the edge of the wall before gazing back into his teal-colored eyes.

"Oh, I'm so sorry to hear that!" He put his right hand towards hers below the wine glass. "Trespassing is actually a fairly minor offense- unless you committed another crime like burglary, so you should be OK." Noticing her lips pointed downward, he awaited the next words, hoping she would share more.

She pictured the box still sitting in the trunk of her car and the pain ripped through her abdomen again. "What do you know about the laws on trespassing? Is there any way to… maybe get the charges dropped? I've never done anything like this before in my life." Small flecks of emerald in his eyes gave her the same tinge of excitement as the first time she saw his ruggedly handsome face.

"Well, it's rare that any jurisdiction will press formal charges while insisting on a maximum penalty. Usually a plea bargain is agreed upon, the defendant swearing not to engage in any illegal behavior, never setting foot on that site again and the plaintiff allowing a de minimis charge- something really minor." The lines on her brow showed worry, but he let his gaze drop briefly to the narrow opening in her blouse. "Nice- but relax, Jack" he thought as his view turned back to her eyes.

"So, I'm still going to have a criminal record?"

He pondered for a few seconds before speaking to sense if she comprehended the seriousness of the matter. "Look, you did break the law, so it's now on the books. You can't change that. Yet, you were important in helping to solve that case for us last year with the mob and the stolen antiquities ring. Without your help, we may never have gotten Caniletto and his group of thugs. Partly because of you, they're off the streets." He considered what he'd have to do and who to discuss a strategy with. "Actually, there is a chance- a small chance- I might be able to get this, shall we say… fixed. I know the local sheriff and his team pretty well after our investigation and in a way, he owes me one." He leaned closer to her, almost knocking over the crystal wine glass as the waiter came up with their menus. "I can try to pull… a few strings. No promises."

"Oh, that would be GREAT!! Here's my cell phone number." She took a black pen from her purse and wrote it on his napkin, pushing it toward him. "Please call me if you find out anything!!" Her left arm extended out across the white tablecloth and she rested her hand gently onto his, showing her platinum wedding ring and one-carat diamond. Leaning in closer, she ignored the waiter standing within inches of the table.

He glanced at the ring and felt a tinge of guilt, but the excitement of her touch quickly chased it away. Recalling the near misadventure with the rookie agent a few years back, he straightened up in his seat. "It looks like she wants you, boy- but lay low on this one for the moment. Could happen… don't push it" he thought. "I'll see what I can do. Now, this menu looks pretty appetizing." He caught her admiring him as he read the first few entrees for the 'Specials of the Day'.

"Yes, it does…" Two levels of excitement lifted her- the

charges being dropped and watching his strong arms holding the menu, but then she stopped. "Wait, Natalie!! You're happily married. That's where this ends. If you were single, maybe- but not now." She perused the menu, then glanced briefly up again. "Everything looks good." Smiling, the anxiety vanished completely as his eyes met hers. "It's still legal to look... and the scenery is pretty nice from here" she thought as she made her selection.

———)((◍))———

"You know where they live?" Dexter leaned against the warehouse door.

"Yeah, some fancy neighborhood in Kennett Square. Joey at DMV was pretty helpful. Not far from those mushroom farms, where people earn a real living, with their hands- not connections with high-priced lawyers and corporate types in monkey suits. The kind you never see at Wal-Mart."

"So, what are you gonna' do, Floyd?" Dexter watched as he raised the vice-grip.

"I want that box. Maybe some good stuff in it. I could use a few extra bucks- kids need sneakers for the Summer. How come *we* never got new sneakers every Summer?"

"The only thing I got every Summer was a tan. I remember my dad finding an old baseball in the garage, grabbing the broom, breakin' off the bottom and saying 'Look- here's a bat and a ball- go over to that field and knock yourselves out.' That was about it. Kids these days- they're spoiled. They want everything- NOW... and it all costs a fortune." Dexter raised the wrench up to the large bolt, giving it a quick twist.

"You're tellin' me- like a hundred bucks for a pair of those stupid air-soled tennis shoes. Add in a wife who can't say "No" to a dress that's on sale- and its credit card bills out the yin-yang... forever." The gear found a resting place on the ground as Floyd felt the oil oozing onto the edge of his Phillies T-shirt, making a brown patch around his shoulder. "Shit!! Another shirt gone."

"My wife only knows two words." Dexter locked the wrench around the large bolt and gave it a quick twist. "Ugh!!"

"What's that?"

"Charge it."

"My wife only knows how to make one thing for dinner."

"Spaghetti?"

"Reservations."

"We gotta' find a way to earn more money, Floyd."

"Tried the lottery, but the most I ever won was ten bucks. Rather invest in a six-pack."

"What six-packs cost ten bucks?"

"I'm a refined gentleman. *I insist* on only the best- Heineken. A Grey Poupon kinda' guy."

"Hand me that Phillips screwdriver, will ya'?"

Chapter 4

"I dream of painting, then I paint my dream."
--Vincent Van Gogh

Ignoring her usual caution, she pushed the accelerator and watched as the speedometer shot past the 40 mile an hour speed limit on the drive back along Route 82 from lunch, grinning as she thought about the charges being dropped. The early afternoon sun cheered her as the sunroof opened. "What a lovely day!!" The call numbers for her favorite station gleamed into view on the satellite radio, 'The Bridge' flickering along the digital screen in front of her. "Mellow is perfect right now... Mmm... nice." Patches of sunlight flashed onto her neck and shoulders as the car wound its way through the oak and maple-lined streets approaching the Borough of Kennett Square, the 'National Historic District' sign a welcome home banner. Noticing small clumps of dried mud clinging to the garden tools hanging on the garage wall, her plan for the afternoon evolved. "Perfect day to get some weeding done, then maybe plant more begonias."

"You're in an exceptionally good mood. Win the lottery?"

Jim glanced over at her from the counter where he was reading through the latest issue of 'Islands Magazine'. "Now here's a place I could relax- St. Kitts in the Caribbean. Look at those beaches!!"

"Got my chores done. A sunny day puts me in a great mood. Makes me want to get back in the garden."

The words interrupted his attention on the article. "That's a turn around. A few hours ago you were worried about having your profile on the wall of the Post Office. Now you're thinking about mulch. Something must have put you in a good mood." Every movement of her lips gave him clues, showing from years of conversations whether she was sincere or hiding something.

"Just love a nice day. We don't get that many and I never get enough time to garden. Seems like there's always something left undone." She glanced only briefly at him, then opened the refrigerator and grabbed the pitcher of iced tea. "Want some?"

"Ohhh… kay."

"Where did we put that box from Frick's Lock? Is it in the garage? I didn't see it."

"It's still in the trunk under the cargo guard where the cops couldn't see it. I can get it." He put the magazine on the counter and walked back toward the garage, scrutinizing her closer as he passed. "Sure there's nothing you want to talk about? You seem… in a … different mood."

"Just happy to be with you, on a sunny day and do some exploring- in that box!! We never got to examine the contents." The creak of the trunk opening entered the room, followed by a slight groan before the door slammed shut.

"Here it is. How the hell did *you* carry this out of that house? It's got to weigh over 25 pounds."

"I've been doing my bench presses- up to 150 pounds now. In a week, I'll challenge you to an arm wrestling contest."

"Give me at least six months, Mrs. Schwarzenegger. I'll have to work up to your level." He shuffled up to the granite island in the center of the kitchen and dropped the box. "Ugh!! I can't believe you got this down from that attic. Where was the forklift?"

"It wasn't easy. I actually had to drop it from about five feet up. Hope nothing broke in the fall. Let's see what's inside." She pulled back the water-stained flaps, corners ripped and moth-bitten.

"Here's an old newspaper. You can have that."

"Oh, yeah. I remember picking it up from the floor of the bathroom." Pulling the torn pages slowly apart, the soiled, oat-meal-colored sheets stuck together at the corners, not wanting to reveal the next story. "This paper is from October 1980. Weren't the Phillies on their way to a championship that year?"

"That they were. I remember the playoffs against the Astros- sending them to the World Series. I'll never forget walking down Sixth Street in Austin, Texas with Lee, yelling 'Go Phillies!!' as all the guys coming out of Maggie Mae's looked at us like we were traitors. They had a superb team that year- Joe Morgan, Pete Rose, Tug McGraw- Tugger!! What a character."

"Not much time for us to watch baseball these days." She examined each page, opening them gingerly, hoping not to tear the fragile paper.

"I always liked the World Series. I remember that year, when Tugger was hot on the mound- all the reporters were interviewing him, asking about whether he expected to get to the Series. One reporter said 'Well, Tug, what are you going to do with all the money you'll be making?' He said 'Well, the first 90% I'm gonna' spend on fast cars, loose women and good whiskey. The rest I'm just gonna' blow.'"

"Hah!!"

"Another reporter asked which he liked better, grass or Astroturf. He said 'I don't know. I've never smoked Astroturf.'"

"That was a great year for them. Didn't they go to the World Series a few years later, too?"

"Yes, in 1983... but they weren't as sharp as they were in 1980. The Orioles were young and aggressive and kicked their butts. Joe Morgan, 'The Teacher' who rarely made any mistakes- made plenty of errors in that Series."

"Talks here about the local Johnston Gang. I remember hearing about this on the news- their trial on a variety of charges, including murder. It was all over the papers."

"I was out West in Denver. Don't think it made the national news." Jim continued to view the items in the box.

She flipped slowly to the next page. "Now this was worldwide news- Three Mile Island. Mentions PECO purchasing the land around Frick's Lock and the opening of the Limerick Plant, which is right across the river. I could see the cooling towers from the edge of that abandoned town. Great picture of the towers here, too."

"Toured Limerick several years back when I was covering the power industry as an analyst at Wilmington Trust. Had a guy from Janney Montgomery Scott, who'd previously worked at PECO for many years, give us the tour. It was fascinating. After 9/11, we were all expecting the place to be rimmed by dozens of security guards toting M-16's, but there weren't any. In fact, I don't recall seeing *anyone* with a rifle. Made me and a few of the others wonder- what if a group of terrorists drove up, broke through the gate and threw some grenades into the reactor room?"

"Did you ask them about the security?"

"I did and all they said was 'We monitor this place very closely'. That was it."

"Glad to see that 50 megatons of explosive potential are being closely guarded. What *did* they carry for protection- water balloons?"

"Yes… but they were VERY BIG balloons. Actually, only thing obvious was that you had to go through the plant in 'stages'. You couldn't leave one area without an escort to the next 'zone'. One guy joked that he wanted to yell "Ahhh!!!" to see what the guards would do."

"Did he?"

"I recommended strongly against it."

"Paper says that by the 1980's the town was abandoned." She squinted to see the words on the weathered page. "I can't blame PECO. With all the talk about meltdowns, people were scared. The last thing they wanted was a town with dozens- maybe hundreds of people- affected by some kind of a leak from the plant nearby."

"Actually, PECO bought the property to protect the plant *from the* people – a 'no man's land' perimeter. This looks… odd." He pulled out a thin pewter-colored, stained metallic sheet from the box. "It's covered with tiny indentations."

Natalie rubbed her fingers across the surface. "What is it?"

"No idea. Never seen anything like it. Maybe… a piece of material from a metal press?" His view roamed from the top slowly to the bottom of the sheet, noting the heavy brown stains all along its length. "Whatever it is, pretty strange looking. There's three more in here just like this one." He put them aside and pulled out several items at once, laying them on the counter, the surface getting coated with dust.

"Watch out for dead bugs!"

"Well, I hope we have plenty of Fantastik to clean up this mess. Whoever invented that is probably a millionaire. Here's… what looks like… an old scrapbook?" He opened the pages slowly and saw relics of another era. "Natalie, check this out."

She leaned toward him and held it in her hands. "Oh, it's a scrapbook of old Valentine cards from… what looks like the turn of the century!! I see some dates… 1906… here's one- 1909."

Jim pulled out a scrap of paper less than five inches wide, torn on three edges. "Says, I can barely read it- 'Wishing you all the best in your many endeavors. –TAE'. Appears to be the very bottom of a letter to someone." Eyeing the lower corner of the box, he saw the rusted tins, labels brown and scratched. "Here's something you don't see too much these days- cans of chewing tobacco from the turn of the century." He took all four out and placed them on the counter.

"That's disgusting. I knew a guy in high school who used to spit brown gunk everywhere. Felt he was cool. All the girls thought he was *gross*."

"Way back when, it was actually popular to chew tobac- co." He opened the first can. "Whew!! What a smell… it's decomposed… almost like manure. Ugghhh!" He twisted the circular top off the second can with some effort. "This one's almost rusted completely shut… same gooey junk inside." Picking up the next tin, he noted the printing, colors still vi- brant. "Spearmint Chew- The Best There Is!" He grabbed the bottom and tried to twist the top. "Owww!! This one's not

GENE PISASALE

budging without a vice-grip."

"Don't bother. Probably just more stinky chewing tobacco. The kitchen already smells like a Wild West saloon." Natalie dug into the box and pulled out a rusted piece of iron. "What's this- some kind of a cylinder?" She held it up under the lamp.

"Looks like something from a machine shop- maybe part of a lathe. What else is in here?" His right hand probed down toward the corner and he felt something vaguely familiar. "Now, this appears to be a very primitive light bulb- although the filament is gone, maybe disintegrated. The same thing that lights up over your head when I say 'Where can we go for dinner?'"

"Let me see. Yes, it does look like a light bulb- small, but with the same basic shape." She reached toward the bottom of the box, pulling out a cluster of papers and some metallic instruments along with debris. "There's so much in here. It'll take a month of Sundays to go through. Everything's covered in cobwebs and disgusting mouse droppings."

"Sounds inviting. Shall we close our eyes and dig in with both hands?"

"Hold your horses, cowboy. This stuff is really old- and fragile. Its fascinating finding things like this. It would be even more interesting to know who the owner was."

"You think we'll discern anything meaningful in all this gunk? The papers here are barely legible. To decipher any of this, we should do some checking at the local historical society, maybe even visit the Court House where they should have the homeowner and tax records."

"Tomorrow let's call the Chester County Historical Society. They may know more about the town. The Court House has got to be in the phone book and probably listed on-line. I'll check while you get us a glass of cabernet."

"Still lingering on the Winter varieties? It's Summertime- what about a nice, chilled glass of chardonnay?"

"You choose. I'm going to the computer. Have a glass- red or white- waiting when I get back."

"Done. I have a bottle of Titus 2009 Chardonnay Los Carneros on ice. Ready for a bit of golden nectar?"

"Indubitably. Let's call it a day after I get done on the computer. We can discuss all these treasures relaxing in the Conservatory."

"If you call mouse droppings 'treasures', I'll bid eight cents for the whole box. Okay, I'll go as high as ten."

"Just go pour the wine- and stop whining!!"

He opened the bottle and paused to smell the cork. "No leaks, that's good. Color- very nice." His nose reached the rim of the pale green bottle. "Full, rich- exactly what I needed on a Summer- or almost Summer day." Passing her office into the Conservatory he announced "I'm in here hon, whenever you're ready."

"Be out in a minute." She printed the addresses and phone numbers, then carried the sheets to the olive colored couch. "Here's everything we need. How about a toast to an exciting day?"

"To our discovery- of historic mouse droppings."

"You goofball!! Could be something important in there- maybe even worth some money. You never know."

"Bat guano goes for about ten dollars a ton. Rodent drop-pings *might* be close."

"Stop!!"

⇒«(◦)»⇐

The drive up to West Chester along Route 52 brought back memories of her childhood, riding on her bike past Lenape Park, then down the back roads and onto the main thoroughfare into Chadds Ford. The trees overhanging the roadway were a welcome umbrella on the hottest days, keeping her out of the bold rays which could scorch you on a ride of 40 minutes or more. The patches of gold flashed into the SUV as he navigated the sharp turns, arriving at the Historical Society in less than the usual 25 minutes. "Everyone must be on the golf course or at the beach. That was quick."

"Perfect day for anything outside." She un-latched her seat belt. "Let's see what we can find inside. No more than one hour, OK?"

"I was hoping for less." He followed her onto the sidewalk. "With any luck it's all computerized, so we don't have to deal with boxes of files or microfiche."

"They haven't used microfiche in years. You're back in the Stone Age."

"I liked the Stone Age. In fact, way back when- I used to like the Stones. The tour in 1981 was their last good one."

"You've been to way too many rock concerts."

"Nope. Went to my last concert in 1997. Jimmy Buffett. Now that was a *fun show*!! Pacific Amphitheater out near Irvine, California. The people in the parking lot were as much fun as the concert! A guy built an entire volcano next to his car- lava and everything. One dude brought an enormous pile of sand and had girls in hula skirts dancing all around. It was hilarious. 'Wastin' away again in Margaritaville…'"

"Why was it your last concert? Didn't you have fun?"

"A *great* time, but something happened which told me

'This is the last one.'"

"What was that?"

"The crowd was wild. Everyone was drunk and jumping up and down. A girl in back of me was so delirious, she put her cigarette out- *on my shirt*. When I felt the burn, I turned around and said 'Excuse me!! You just burned a hole in my shirt!!' She tried to focus on the hole, then just giggled and said 'Oops!! I'm sorry!!' That was it- my last rock concert."

"Sounds like fun- NOT." Breezing past the counter, she saw the sign for 'Research- County Records and Historical Documents' and proceeded through the small entryway.

"Can I help you?" came the friendly voice from a young woman, early-twenties, plain-looking, but with a nice smile. "I'm Jennifer Logan, the assistant here for records. What were you trying to find out?"

Jim advanced to her desk and leaned forward. "We're doing some research on the abandoned town called Frick's Lock. It's near Phoenixville in northern Chester County."

"That'd be the black file cabinet over there near the far corner of the next room. We have historical and current maps, a few articles written about the area and some memorabilia. Please put anything you view on the large table in the middle of the room. No copying allowed without prior permission. Let me know if you need any help."

"Thank you."

Jennifer played the name 'Frick's Lock' over again in her head. "That takes me back…" She recalled her girlfriends during senior year at Phoenixville High School, wanting to meet boys and sometimes going places they weren't supposed to. "Those abandoned houses- I can't believe we used to party there!! Well, they were always deserted so nobody could see us. Except that one night…"

"Hey, Jenn- get in here!! This place is wayyy cool!! Look at all this stuff! People must have just left it behind." Caitlin's voice rang out over the debris as she panned the flashlight around the room and Jennifer stepped in amidst the wreckage.

"Not sure if I'd say way cool. Way weird, maybe!!" She hesitated before sitting down in the darkness, making sure there was a spot without too much grime.

"Jamie, bring those beers over here, dude!!" Rick yelled out as he glanced at Jennifer, noticing her very short skirt and inviting smile. "Jenn- you're lookin' very nice tonight!!" He took a long gulp of Rolling Rock, then put his thumb over the top of the bottle, shaking and spraying it all over the decaying walls of the house. "Woo-hoo!! Parrrrty!!"

"Rick, you're toasted already!!" Jamie crawled over the fallen boards to sit next to Jennifer and chugged most of a Genesee Cream Ale as the suds escaped from the edge of the bottle and streamed down the side of his neck. "YEAH!!" He grabbed a jagged piece of broken metal and threw it into the air directly above the group of four.

"Hey dude!! What the…?? You tryin' to kill us??!!" Rick yelled at the top of his lungs and grabbed another beer from the twelve-pack that lay on the broken rafters.

"Relax, guy. Just havin' some fun… Hey!! Let's start a fire so we can see. I got some matches. There's plenty of stuff to burn."

Jennifer sat up. "Wait!! That might not be such a good idea. It's hard to see what's around us and who knows? It could all go up in flames. I don't want to burn the place down. Don't, Jamie- please."

"Oh, cool it Jenn!! You're such a party pooper!! Sit back and relax." He took the matchbook out of his pocket as he kicked two cardboard boxes toward the old fireplace. "These should be just fine." He lit the larger box and pushed it up against the other one.

Jennifer lowered her voice. "Caitlin, I need to use a rest room. I'm going upstairs."

"Jenn, this place has been deserted for years. Even if you find a bathroom, it probably won't work. Just wait until we get back. We'll probably leave soon."

"I need to go NOW. I'll just be glad when we get out of here. This place seems dangerous enough without Jamie starting a fire, too. I'm going up. I won't be long. Hand me your flashlight."

"Watch out for spiders…"

Jennifer stepped gingerly around the rubble near the stairs, then slowly reached the second floor, shining the light down the hall. "I can barely see. Where… is the bathroom?" Tiptoeing, she felt her way along the wall, lightly touching the peeling paint in the darkness. She paused as she felt a cold breeze blow past her. "There must be a window open up here… but it wasn't windy when we came in." The breeze brushed her hair back again. "What was that?" She felt something rush past her side, then saw it- a six-foot tall shadow moving down the hall, illuminated by the weak beam of her flashlight. She turned around, but the others were still downstairs. "What is going on?!! I'm gettin' the hell outta' here." She spun back around and saw him, her jaw dropping open- an old man, dressed in a long, flowing nightgown, walking... hunched over with a light shining in front of him. "Holy shit!!" She slipped as she tried to run and got up quickly, bracing her hand on the wall for balance. The man approached within two feet, enveloping her in a frigid mist, even though the temperature was near 70 degrees. "Oh God, get away from me!!" She stumbled down the stairs, skipping the last three to jump back into the room where Caitlin sat, sipping her beer.

"Find a bathroom?"

"What?! No!! No, I didn't. Caitlin. I... I saw something up there!! I don't know what it was."

"What, a rat?" She giggled and finished the last two gulps before putting the bottle down at her feet.

"No. I'm serious. I saw... I can't say for sure. I... think it was a ghost!!"

"How many beers did you have?"

"I'm NOT drunk!! Barely had *one beer*. I'm telling you, there was this weird man in a long gown walking through the hallway- and he went right by me!! I am serious!!"

"Really?! So, what happened?"

"Well, nothing. I mean, he didn't touch me or anything. He was in this long shawl... maybe a nightgown... looked like someone from, like a hundred years ago... and he was holding, I know this sounds strange- he was holding what looked like a small glass ball or bulb. It was glowing. Almost looked like an old light bulb, but it couldn't have been... I mean- it was just in his hands, but it was glowing. This place is way too freaky for me!! I wanna' get outta' here!!"

"Well, you're gonna' have to persuade Jamie. He drove us. Too bad he wants to stay here all night and build a bonfire…"

"NO!! I want outta' here- NOW!!" She ran over to Jamie as he stood in the orange glow of the blazing boxes and grabbed his arm. He drained another bottle and started to put his hand around her.

"Hey, babe!! I knew you'd come 'round. Like your perfume… smells kinda'… minty. Wanna' go upstairs and…"

"No Jamie. I want to go home."

"What?? The fire's just gettin' nice. Isn't it romantic- that's what you ladies like- right?" he grinned, sliding his hand down her behind.

"Stop it, Jamie! We need to get outta' here… There's something wrong- strange- going on in this house. I wanna' go- NOW!! I mean RIGHT NOW!!"

"You're freakin', babe. Calm down… we'll go in a little while…"

She glanced over at the stairs and saw the ghost slowly descend towards them. Terrified, she screamed at the top of her lungs, her voice echoing off the walls and the sides of the other houses. "RIGHT NOW!!!!!! Get me outta' here NOW!!!!"

"OK, chill out!!! We're goin'." He looked over at Rick and rolled his eyes as the firelight flashed across his face. "One more for the road first." He opened another ale and chugged half before starting to head back toward the path.

Caitlin and Rick got up and walked quickly ahead, trying to avoid the overturned bookcase, tripping on fallen rafters and piles of beer cans. Once they were within 50 feet of the car, Jennifer looked back, the fire still burning, flames dying down slowly, throwing yellowy-orange shadows around the broken windows. Her eyes rose toward the second story and the shadow appeared, watching her, the small light glowing faintly in the darkness...

———⟫⟪⟨◉⟩⟫⟪———

Jim began roaming around the several rows of cabinets. "That must be it up there." He approached the oversized metal enclosure and noticed the alphabetical labels on each drawer. "Here's the F's." Pulling the drawer open, a row of tabs appeared, his fingers flipping past most of them nearly to the back.

"What do you see?"

"An old map of the town- circa 1848. Interesting. Doesn't label homeowner's names, though. This is more significant- a 1970's county record of the layout of the town, including the Lock." Each page displayed a long list of local residents. "Way too many to check each one. We need specific tax records and deeds. Could either go to the Municipal Court House or just try a quick search on-line."

"It looks pretty comprehensive. We can check the name on the Court House website against the location. Why don't you just ask to copy that list?"

"That would be intelligent." He took the sheets back to the girl at the desk. "Can we copy these? We wanted a summary of previous homeowners in Frick's Lock."

"Sure. There's a copy machine over there. It only takes coins."

He glanced around and saw the old unit toward the other side of the room. "You don't have a more up-to-date one that takes debit cards?"

"Sorry, that's the only machine we have right now. I

know- it's a pain. I use my debit card for everything. Just let me see those before you make copies." She inspected each sheet. "That's fine. Just place everything back where you found it in the cabinet."

"Thanks." He approached Natalie announcing "We have to go over there. The copy machine is from the 1960's- only takes coins." She followed him into the next room. "Reminds me of the scene from 'Blazing Saddles', where they're riding horses out in the desert and suddenly stop at a turnstile, in the middle of nowhere."

"What'd they say?"

"'Somebody's gonna' have to go back and get a shitload of dimes...'"

She laughed, then opened her purse. "I actually have quite a bit of change. Need some quarters?"

"Give me all you have. Use the Canadian ones first." He took the coins and proceeded to copy each page. "I remember in Catholic school, they had the old mimeograph machines with the roller. Each sheet would come out blue-black and you'd get ink all over your thumbs taking them off. My buddy Bruce would sneak into the copy room after school to get the original from the trash for the test the next day..." Sister Mary Catherine appeared before him frowning, as he put in the last quarter. "Done. Let's go home. We can search from the comfort of your office chair." He opened the cabinet and placed the sheets back in the folder, closing the drawer.

Crossing the street, they dodged fast-moving cars in the late afternoon sunlight. "That guy was *trying* to run us over. Could've at least been subtle about it." He opened his car door and shrugged it off.

"I hate that! One tractor trailer can ruin your whole day."

"We're checking out the courthouse files on-line when we get home. You look them over and I'll make us a snack." The car pulled past the intersection at Bayard off of Route 1 and turned, going around the edge of the lot where Hill's Seafood advertised 'Fresh Pacific Salmon- $2.00 off/pound'. "How about fish for dinner? Omega-3's are good for you."

"I know, but we already have those center-cut pork chops thawing."

"Pity. Pork overrules salmon so rarely, but I can cope with it." He stopped the car just short of the stacks of shells, assorted beach chairs and buckets from their last Summer trip. "We need to get back to Bethany sometime. The Atlantic View Motel had the best spot, right on the beach."

"I'm game." She closed her car door and jogged to the house before him. "I'm on the computer. Bet it only takes me ten minutes to find out who lived in that house."

"Not without these, you won't."

"Come on, detective. I need the evidence to fully investigate the crime."

"I'm too easy." He handed her the pages. "Fifty bucks says it takes you at least twenty minutes."

"You're on." She grabbed the pages and raced to her office. Clicking the "Power" button, the monitor lit up. "OK, Chester County Court House Municipal Records". The screen flashed quickly and she selected the third tab at the top. "Homeowner and tax records." Clicking again, 'Survey maps - homes and businesses' came into view. Another click brought access to what she wanted- a layout of the abandoned town. "Yes!! Here are all the homes- I recognize them from the parking lot."

Scanning each one, she stopped and looked at her watch. "It's only been eight minutes... I know I can do this."

She studied the sheets and tried to match each name with the map of Frick's Lock on the screen. "Allen, Browning, Callaway, Driscoll, Edwards- three Edwards." Glancing at each home, then at the long list of names from the Historical Society, her eyes started to grow weary. "No match. Wait, I'm in the wrong area!! They're the houses in the front!!" She turned to view the other end of the map. "Here are the houses near the back, overlooking the cooling towers." Inspecting her watch, she saw time was short. "Eighteen minutes!! Two minutes left..." Each dot had an identification, the writing so small she had to squint with her reading glasses perched on her nose. Then it appeared- the location of the house where she got the box. "That's it!! Says... Larson. Daniel Larson." She studied the sheets Jim gave her. "Friedrick, Halsam, Kilkenny- the Irish came over here in droves in the late 1840's." Then she saw it. "Larson!! Daniel Larson!!" Hitting 'Print', she grabbed the copy and walked out of her office. "This is worth fifty bucks- and several nights of toe rubs."

"Time's up. I win." Jim stood near the granite island with a plate of garlic hummus and wasabi rice crackers.

"You counted your chickens way too early." Natalie handed him the sheets and the print-out of the map identifying the house. "Fifty bucks and unlimited toe rubs for the next year."

"Wait." He examined the sheets and saw the obvious link between the locations. "You win, but there's a time limit on toe rubs. It's cruel and unusual to be sentenced to a years' worth. I say dinner and three months. That's my best offer, Detective."

"Deal, but I get them every night- several times a night if I want!!"

"I need to start using those metal hand grips for strength. You win. Good job."

Her grin widened as she felt a sense of accomplishment. "I knew I would win."

He turned as the phone rang and reached over to pick up the receiver. "Hello?"

"Hi!! It's Jacalyn. How are you two doing tonight?"

"Well, we just discovered some interesting files, old homeowner records for houses dating back to the 18th century around Frick's Lock- and she just won a bet."

"Sounds exciting. Put Natalie on."

"It's Jackie. Tell her about how you won the bet." He handed her the phone as he scooped up some hummus with a cracker. "Mmm- I love these."

"Jackie, how are you?"

"Jim said you were at Frick's Lock. I actually grew up not far from there in Pottstown. Used to go to Frick's Lock when I was in my teens to paint. Started my artistic career there. Falling in love with great painters like John Singer Sargent, Winslow Homer, Eakins... Did quite a few oils and watercolors."

"I didn't know you were from that area! Did you paint any of the old houses? We found some interesting things in one of the abandoned homes. I'd love to see your work!"

"OK, but they're all stored in the basement somewhere. Haven't seen them in years... You know- it's hard to look at the things you did when you were just starting out. They seem so... crude... rudimentary."

"I want to see them!! Let's get together sometime soon..."

Chapter 5

"It is a terrible thing to see and have no vision."
--Helen Keller

The room exuded a brilliant glow, dappled sunlight warming the air. "I checked on-line at the East Coventry Township site. There's quite a bit of information available about the Lock area, but the website only shows titles, not detail. It does give the name of their local historian." Natalie glanced at the few sheets she'd printed as Jim finished doing the morning dishes.

"Who is it?"

"Name is Sherry Donahue. I guess she's the point person if you have questions. They list a phone number and an e-mail." He read the first few lines on the page, noting her name and went over to the phone. "Worth a try."

"Do you think it's a bit early to call?"

"It's 9:15. Someone should be there." A voice came through sharply on the other end.

"Hello, East Coventry Township, Records Division."

"My wife and I are doing some research on Frick's Lock and

structures in the area. Is there a chance we could talk with you or someone there, maybe even stop by to review your files?"

"Sure, I'm available from 9 to 5 today, Monday through Friday and by special appointment if needed." Her voice was firm, but pleasing- authoritative without sounding overbearing.

"Excellent! Could we stop over this morning?"

"You can do that. What is it specifically that you're researching?"

He hesitated, not wanting to even hint about the trespassing encounter. "Actually, we're trying to find some information about homeowners- who lived where, at what times, perhaps even some local color about a few of the interesting personalities."

"That's fine, we do have a fairly extensive database on property owners and related tax and civil records. Just let me know if you'll be coming around lunchtime so I can make alternate plans."

"I wouldn't think of interrupting your lunch." He smiled, wondering when he'd ever experienced a civil servant not only so pleasant, but accommodating with her schedule. "We live in Kennett Square, so it'll take us roughly an hour to get there. If we leave shortly, we should arrive around 10:30. How is that?"

"Sounds great. Come through the parking lot. The building is a tan, five story brick structure. Go to the elevators and press the fifth floor. I'm down the hall on the left about 50 feet."

"Wonderful! Thanks so much. We'll see you soon." He put the receiver down and could feel a good morning ahead. "Says we can stop by now. We're done breakfast- unless you wanted another cup of tea."

"I'm fine. Just give me five minutes to do my hair and we can go."

Moving toward the parakeets as they stood on perches near the window, the tidal basin came into view as he observed its fringe of white and pink wildflowers. At the end of the basin was the wash-pond where they'd caught a few tadpoles the Summer before, bringing them to their small garden fountain where Natalie had hoped to see them emerge into frogs. "Well Linus, you and Lucy stay alert for any critters eating flowers in our yard." The previous year, he'd built a simple shelter next to the house using leftover paving stones and put food inside for Frankie and Francis, plus the local feline visitors- Dadcat, Bear and Tiger Lily. One morning he'd found a large red fox- about 25 pounds, 36 inches from tail to nose- curled up and sleeping in the protected space, happy to snooze on the old towels and burlap that lined the small shelter's floor. "Time to re-build the motel" he'd decided, removing several of the stones to make it just large enough to accommodate a food bowl- not an overnight 'guest'. Lucy chirped and jumped over to stand next to Linus. "That's right, Lucy- you're on point. Eyes open."

"Ready?" she asked, approaching his side.

"Next stop, the Township Building- where many secrets lie…"

"We'll see. Was she helpful?"

"Much more- even offered to change her lunch schedule to meet with us."

"A saint. Hopefully she's a knowledgeable person."

"I think we're in luck. At the very least, she'll point us in the right direction." The bushes lining the highway swayed as they sped onto the intrastate. "Wild roses- nice."

"My father loved them. Planted several varieties around the house. He knew quite a bit about gardening."

"My mother always planted Lilies of the Valley. Had them growing near our back door when I was a kid. Used to see the tiny white flowers first thing when I went outside to get the ice cold bottles of milk in the morning."

"That goes way back. Remember having milk, butter and eggs delivered to the house? I was maybe six... seven years old and I used to greet our delivery guy every week."

"Once I said to my buddy next door- 'You don't look anything like your father. You look more like the milkman'."

"A bygone era. How have we functioned without getting fresh milk delivered to our doorsteps?"

"I loved picking up the glass bottles in the Winter. They'd be covered in snow and ice on some days. He'd leave milk in a metal crate with four slots to hold the bottles, tin foil crimped around their tops with the local dairy logo. I miss that." He focused on the short line of traffic ahead.

"I think you look like *OUR* milkman."

"Cute. There's the turn-off. We should be there in less than a minute." He steered into the lot and saw the building. "Safe arrival. Now we just need the most valuable commodity known to man."

"And that is...?"

"Information." The door closed and he stepped around to join her. "Shall we?"

She took his hand and they entered the building, proceeding the thirty feet over to the elevator. "Press five."

The gray metal doors came together and the elevator began a slow, steady ascent. "This is an old one- feels like it's moving at about 3 feet per minute. I could walk up faster."

"Relax. We're not in a rush."

The elevator continued its steady rise when the overhead light flickered and a deafening screech came from above them. "What in the …?!" Jim said as the elevator lurched and abruptly stopped… before starting a quick decent.

Natalie fell backwards, then hit her head on the railing as she dropped to the floor. "Ahhhhhhhh!!"

"We're in free-fall!!" Jim yelled, grabbing both edges of the railing as he tried to steady himself, the inertia forcing him up toward the ceiling. He fell onto the floor as the car came to a jolting halt, throwing Natalie flat on her back. "Are you OK?" He got up on one knee, putting his arms under her.

"Ohhhh!!… I hit my head on that thing. It really hurts… Am I bleeding?" she asked, lifting her hand to the spot.

He turned her head to the side. "No, but you've got a new landmark in the shape of an 'L' above your ear."

She stood slowly, shaking her head as he kept his arms around her waist.

"Sure you're OK? You look a bit dazed."

"Guess you're supposed to lay flat on the floor when an elevator falls, but I didn't have much time to plan. I just want to get out of here! There's the Emergency button. Press it."

He reached over to the red knob above the Certificate of Examination. 'This Otis elevator represents the best technology available today. We are proud of our long heritage, dating back to 1853. If you have any questions, please call our toll-free Comment Line at 1-800-OTISELV.' "Yeah- I have a question. If these elevators are so great, why did Otis accept a used cannon for payment on the first one?" He pushed the button… silence.

He pushed it again and again. Nothing. "The Emergency button's not functioning."

"Try the phone" Natalie said, pointing to the receiver.

"That was my second choice." He picked up the black handset from the receptacle and heard only static. "I don't believe this!! Now we're stuck between floors. Left my cell phone in the car, too. How about yours?"

Natalie pulled out the phone and flipped it open. "No good… can't get a signal. Metal walls must be interfering."

"*Now* what do we do?" He pounded both fists over and over against the metal plate surrounding the phone, the vibrations reverberating around the cabin, shaking the floor. "GOD DAMN IT!!" Pounding harder and harder with each blow, his wrists reddened with the impacts, the noise echoing throughout the chamber and into the space above. "Damn it!!" His right hand bled as he hit the edge of the phone receptacle. "Owww!!" Bringing both fists crashing onto the wall, he stood back, exhausted.

"So, what did that accomplish?" Natalie asked, her calmness in contrast.

"Other than an appointment for hand surgery?"

She took his wrist and examined it closely. "You'll live… for now… Gangrene takes at least 48 hours. Let's just find a way out of this thing."

He stepped back, then jumped up and brought his right shoe crashing up against the phone, the cabin shaking slightly with the impact.

"Feel better now?"

"Kind of. My grandmother used to say 'Anything mechanical- give it a good bash'.

"Bash... you probably broke it! Now we're talking damages to the county."

"Who cares? Get me the HELL OUTTA' HERE!!" he yelled, kicking the door.

"Done with your tantrum?"

"Who knows? Maybe somebody heard me."

She stepped closer to the receptacle. "Let me try." She picked up the phone and heard a ring. "Guess your grandmother was right. Didn't you say she knew Alexander Graham Bell?"

A voice answered on the other end. "Security. Can I help you?"

"YES!! We're stuck in this damn elevator somewhere between the first and fourth floors. Can you get us out?"

"Hold on, ma'am. I'll try resetting the power switch." The phone went silent for several moments, then the lights went out. Jim and Natalie froze, expecting the worst. After more than a minute in total darkness, the lights came back on. "Ma'am, try pushing the button for your floor again."

Natalie pressed the button and the car began to move slowly upward, coming to a stop, the light above the door showing '5'. "That worked, thank you." Natalie placed the phone back on the wall.

"YEAH!!!" He grabbed her hand as the doors opened, pulling her out of the car.

"That's one adventure I *didn't* need."

"My grandmother was a pretty smart lady. Think she worked on escalators, too."

They proceeded quickly to the first office and noticed a woman at a metal desk which was covered with several stacks of manila folders.

"Hello!! You must be the guy who just called." The woman walked around the desk right up to them.

His hand received a strong shake. "Yes! I'm Jim. You're Sherry?"

"Yes. How are you?"

"Well, we almost became two-dimensional with a free-fall in your elevator... but other than that- OK."

"Goodness, I'm so sorry. Those old elevators can be a bit quirky. I took the liberty of helping you a bit with your research by taking out some files for you to peruse." Turning her back to him, she leaned over and grabbed several folders from the desk.

Jim tried to focus on the materials she was taking off the table, but couldn't help noticing her rather curvaceous figure. "I'm guessing she's... about 45? Face and neck say that...but she has the figure of a 30 year old" he thought. Natalie's tightening grip around his fingers redirected his attention to the files and away from Sherry's curves. "That was extremely kind of you. Don't know much about this specific area, except that Frick's Lock was an important stop-over along the Schuylkill Canal way back when."

"That it was. Are you familiar with the history of canals and locks?" She smiled at him, then glanced at Natalie.

"Kind of doing a first run. We could use an overview" Natalie remarked.

"Perfect. There are two basic man-made channels for water- aqueducts and waterways. Aqueducts go back to Roman times and earlier, allowing conveyance of potable water for human consumption, municipal uses and irrigation. Waterways- often called canals- were a means of navigable transportation for both goods and people. They also date back thousands of years, but gained widespread usage during the blossoming of the Industrial Revolution in Europe and then here in America, as merchants strived for an easier way to carry heavy cargo over difficult terrain."

Jim enjoyed the firm, yet pleasant sound of her voice so much, he hesitated to ask a question. "I know there have been several famous canals built over the centuries."

"The most famous one here in the U.S. was the Erie Canal, first recommended by Robert Fulton, the steamboat inventor to President George Washington in 1797. The goal was to allow a route for commercial transportation from the Hudson River through to Lake Erie. Construction began on July 4, 1817 and the first passage from Lake Erie to New York City occurred on October 26, 1825." Sherry's expression revealed she truly enjoyed her work.

"How many years before it became a popular route?"

"Not long at all. Commerce rapidly expanded in the region all along the length of the canal, becoming a major boon to the economy. Merchants and entrepreneurs started building canals in many industrial areas to transport goods to places they'd never considered reaching before. These waterways were the first true industrial interstates, allowing important items like coal, iron ore, cotton, even fruits and vegetables to reach distant markets more easily and quickly. Because of the canals- prices for many goods dropped dramatically, so consumers enjoyed the benefits the new technology brought them. They were precursors to the development of the railroads, which revolutionized commerce even more a few decades later."

Sherry took two folders and placed them in front of Jim.

"These have a fair amount of information on canals in general and Frick's Lock. You can go through them on your own, but I'll summarize to make it easier." She stood right next to Jim. "Canals quickly competed with poorly built overland roads for commercial transport. Aside from the Erie Canal, which transformed America by allowing people to leave the farm and work in factories, other states developed vast systems for their own commerce. By 1840, over 3,000 miles of canals had been built in the U.S."

He sensed the depth of her knowledge, nodding as she shared it with them. "Didn't they also try to develop a national road system?"

"They did. Albert Gallatin, Thomas Jefferson's Secretary of the Treasury wrote a landmark document in 1808 titled 'Report on Roads, Canals, Harbors and Rivers'- which was gargantuan in scope. It was the first official survey of what we'd call infrastructure projects. The plan was to develop a vast array of routes from Maine to Georgia, explore better ways to navigate major rivers and give the country its first set of interconnected commerce pathways. Sadly, most of his ideas were never fully developed, except for one. His 'National Road' was begun in Maryland to connect Indiana with Washington, D.C. Also called the Cumberland Road, it was the precursor to the interstate highway system and later became U.S. Route 40, which now runs coast to coast."

"Fascinating." Focusing on her sensuous lips, he craved the thrill, but the old feeling he'd known for so many years was gone. Instead of attraction, a deep and growing respect built as she spoke, admiration for the intensity, the passion for what she knew. He felt transformed, his gaze remaining above the curves he'd seen first and now disregarded for the smooth, firm sound of her voice and friendly smile.

"I didn't know the highway system started way back then." Natalie examined the first folder.

"I drove on Route 40 and parts of old U.S. Route 66 when I moved back from San Diego to Philadelphia. Route 40 is pretty broken up in spots out in New Mexico. It was like driving on railroad tracks." He started to read the second folder just as she spoke.

"Funny you mention railroads. They eventually made most of the canals obsolete. By the 1860's, railroads were being built across many states. The Transcontinental Railroad was completed in 1869. Railroads became the 'new' technology, allowing even more efficient and cost-effective transportation."

"I know some of the larger canals like the Suez and Panama are important. Are any others still in use?" Natalie asked after reading the first page.

"Not far from here, the C&D Canal in northern Delaware is one of the most active canals in the world, allowing an easy connection from Philadelphia and ports to the North through to Chesapeake Bay. It's the only commercial waterway built in the U.S. in the 1800's still in active use. The 14 miles from Delaware to Maryland carry 40% of the ship traffic in and out of Baltimore, one of the busiest U.S. ports. It's a National Historic Civil Engineering Landmark and is on the National Registry of Historic Places."

"We love going down to Chesapeake City, having lunch at the Chesapeake Inn, right on the water."

"Yes, if he had his way, we'd be sailing all the time. We usually have lunch there, walk around the town, which is really quaint- then take a riverboat ride out toward the entrance to the Bay. It's great fun."

"Nice place. I've been there. You folks travel a lot?"

"Whenever we can get away. We take mini-vacations, three to four days- and visit our favorite spots." Paging through the next few sheets in the folder, he was engrossed in the history of the region. "So, in terms of Frick's Lock, what can you tell us?"

"Well, it was originally called Frick's Village before the extensive system of locks was built. In 1792, two companies were chartered by the state of Pennsylvania to build a navigable waterway between the Susquehanna and Schuylkill Rivers and a canal from the Delaware River to Norristown. Work began, but the companies had exhausted their funds by 1794 and the project stopped for many years. In 1815, the Pennsylvania Legislature voted in funds for a new firm- the Schuylkill Navigation Company- to complete the job."

"So the project nearly failed?"

"Almost. Luckily there were some business-savvy people in government who knew that letting the project die would not serve the citizens well. The Schuylkill was made navigable from Port Carbon near Pottsville down to Philadelphia- a distance of 108 miles. Of this length, 62 miles were actual canal, the rest being so-called 'slack water navigation pools'- a series of dams rimmed by locks. The locks were necessary because the change in elevation from Port Carbon to Philadelphia was 588 feet, so 92 locks were built to overcome the gradient." She placed another folder in front of him. "This one has the specific details of the land around Frick's Lock, landowners and other information." She examined her watch. "It's getting close to

Noontime. Can I take you both to lunch?"

Jim was stunned. "That's extremely generous of you, but we wouldn't want to take up your time. I really appreciate that." He looked again into her hazel eyes, feeling the beginning of a new friendship. "We'll take a rain check. We may be up here again to do more research."

"Absolutely. You're always welcome. Those folders have some additional information on the canal and the various locks. Locks 54 and 55 at Frick's were part of what was called the Girard Canal. Many of the dams along the length of the structure are still intact. If you've walked around Conshohocken or Manayunk, you've probably seen them."

"I like Manayunk- kind of a funky little town." Natalie flipped through a few pages and started reading again.

"Any interesting footnotes to the story of Frick's Lock?"

"Well, a little known side story of the canal system involves the portion near the town of Auburn, Pennsylvania. There they built a 450-foot long tunnel through a local hill, the first tunnel in the U.S., completed in 1821, even though they could easily have moved the canal 100 feet to the West. The proprietors thought it would be a curiosity and attract visitors, which it did. Did you have any questions about the local property owners?"

"Actually, yes. Do any of these sheets list specific names with the old houses? I was looking to confirm one in particular."

"In that file they're listed alphabetically and you can match them with the spot locations of the homes. It should also indicate the most recent homeowner. May go back 30- 50 years before the location was abandoned, but at least you can get a name. There's a computer over there where you can search current tax records for owners or their relatives. I hope that's helpful."

"Very." He saw the small brown desk where the computer rested. As he took the folder into his left hand, he offered his right one. "That was great. Is it alright if we sit down and review these now?"

"Sure. I'll be at lunch for the next hour. Feel free to read through the files and go down the hall if you need assistance. I should be back before 1 p.m." Shaking his hand firmly, she gave him the same friendly smile that first caught his attention. "It's been my pleasure. If you're done before I get back, please contact me again if I can assist you in any way." She took Natalie's hand briefly before stepping past the desk toward the door.

"I've rarely met a person so accommodating."

"…and so kind." He thought about the smile as she grasped his hand. The new feeling was peaceful, almost serene. "A true professional... a welcome change from some other people I've met." He glanced back down at the folder and saw the list of homeowners. "Now… let's get to the letter L…." Inspecting the long line of entries, he shifted his attention to the computer. "Why don't you go over, log in and search for Larson while I check the house locations?"

"Will do."

He searched through the lengthy summary. "I think I have it here. That spot you visited. This corroborates that the last owner was Daniel Larson!!" He felt a tingle in his stomach continuing to read, flipping past the other names to the actual blueprint of the house site.

"Here it shows Daniel Larson is related to a Randolph Larson, the inhabitant of the house up until… the 1920's.

Must have been a great-grandfather or some other relation."
She focused on the next few paragraphs for up to date contact
information.

"Does it list the current address of the last homeowner?
That would be a real coup."

"Not yet… but give me a few minutes. There's a link to
current tax records for the township and it appears… they have
up to date addresses!!" She continued to scan each page slowly.
"Yes- Daniel Larson!! He lives at 428 Woodside Lane. I'll search
MapQuest and try to get directions from here."

"Love it. Beats pulling something out of the glove com-
partment. I figured out how to get stop lights to turn green."

"How's that?"

"Try reading a map while you're waiting for it to change."
He heard the Hewlett-Packard printer from across the room
clicking as it advanced each page onto the black holding tray.
"Let me know when you're done."

"Here goes. We have directions to his house!! Let's put
these files back and we can go." She strolled over and laid the
folder on the desk just as he returned from the printer. "Ready
Commodore?"

They went past the elevator and Jim kicked the door one
last time. "Couldn't resist" he said as they proceeded down the
stairs. "We could use the exercise anyway." Holding her hand,
the grip was as firm and kind as the one he felt thanking their
host, but the smile was even more inviting. "Trim the sails, this
should be a pleasant cruise."

The car made its way back down Route 724, the foliage
even more lush than he'd noticed near their home. "Where do
we turn?"

"Right at that stop sign, then a sharp left onto Woodside." She reviewed the addresses as they passed each house. "I say 428 is right around this bend." The car stopped as she noticed the flower boxes on the windows and small ceramic ornaments in each yard. "Cute neighborhood."

"It is. I'll introduce us. We're just checking out some local history- not discovering gold in the Klondike. Nothing about the box- got it?"

"Yes, sir!!" She rolled her eyes, stepping onto the sidewalk.

The doorbell was faint as they waited for the recently painted red door to open.

"Hello. Can I help you?" The voice came from a tall, slender man in his late 60's, very dark brown salt and pepper hair, graying heavily at the temples.

"I'm Jim Peterson. This is Natalie. We were just doing some research on the Frick's Lock area and spoke with Sherry Donahue over at the Township Building. She allowed us to search the records to find information about people who lived in the area and we saw the name Larson. Are you Daniel Larson?"

"I... am. What exactly are you looking for?" He stood firmly at the door, only three-quarter opened, his feet several inches behind the door guard.

"I hope we're not causing any inconvenience. I just had a few questions about the owners of a home there. We recently visited the Lock- the abandoned town- and saw some really interesting old houses." Jim waited for any sign of contempt, but saw a grin open up.

I used to have a house there years ago, but PECO owns it now- bought all of them before the 1980's when the power plant went up."

"Yes, the records indicated you were the last owner for one of them. It was the building that resembled a plantation style home in the back with beautiful architecture. Did you actually live there?"

"Yes… The house had been in my family since the late 1800's. My mother inherited it from my great, great uncle Randolph. I got it from her and lived there until PECO came along and bought everyone out. I really liked that small town." He remembered the phone call late on a Sunday night… "Got a call from a real estate agent years ago trying to steal the place. It wasn't an offer- it was an insult. Little did I know the power company had the area re-zoned…and we were *forced* to sell." He drifted off, lost in the memory… "I loved that house. Randolph was a great man…" He looked at the old photos along the bookshelf. "I think he's still there… walking around, not ever wanting to leave…"

Jim spoke loudly to get his attention. "I know how you feel. My mother just turned 90 and was so reluctant to leave the home she'd lived in since 1949. She had to- for her safety. It's sad to see the 'For Sale' sign. What did you know about Randolph?"

"Not much, really. Just stories, pictures. Died before I was born. He lived there until the mid-1920's. My mother used say he was a very interesting guy. A genius actually. Kind of a miser, too. Saved every cent he made. Probably stashed a fortune away somewhere, but we never saw it." His attention drifted toward the kids playing across the street for a few seconds, then he stepped back from the door. "Would you like to come in?"

"Yes, thank you!!" Jim stepped gingerly on the narrow oriental throw rug in the foyer and followed him into the living room.

"Here, please sit down." He stood as they both settled on the couch. "Randolph Larson died a few months before my mother brought me into this world, so I never knew him, but felt like I did when grandmother told her tales. Mom had a few of her own, too. He lived there for almost fifty years. What were you looking for? Is there some reason you're asking about the house?"

Jim tensed up as he hoped Natalie wouldn't start to talk. "We're just fascinated with the story of how locks were part of the transport system in the area, before the railroads came through. We enjoy exploring old sites, abandoned towns and just wanted to learn more about Frick's Lock. We thought the prior owners could give us a real sense of what it was like living there before the town was shut down. What did your mom tell you?"

He hesitated as he tried to determine Jim's sincerity before responding. "Mostly she talked about how interesting a guy he was- maybe more interesting than the story of the locks. My grandfather used to tell her that he was crazy- couldn't understand half of what he was trying to say, babbling on. My mother told me she thought he might have been a genius because he was very gifted working with his hands, a tinkerer with machinery, all kinds of tools. He'd make things in his little shop and give them to his family, to help them in their daily chores. Apparently Randolph was extremely creative- could fix anything and had a sharp mind- up until the end." He glanced at the Berber carpet and remembered the last time he saw his mom. "She said they eventually had to put him in a home- for his own good."

"Why? What happened to him?" Natalie leaned closer.

"In his later years, he got a bit confused. I remember mom said she heard that his neighbors would take my grandparents aside and tell them he was hallucinating. I guess he started having these grandiose illusions, like he was some famous person that nobody recognized. Got to the point where he was losing touch- didn't pay his bills, wouldn't eat for days and couldn't take care of himself. They finally had to put him in Pennhurst State Hospital. That was around 1925. He died there in 1940- just short of his 95th birthday. My mother visited him often. Told anyone who would listen that he was an amazing guy, even if he was a bit… strange." He exhaled, then stretched his arms.

"Sounds like he was a fascinating man."

"He was. Wish I could have known him myself. Something tells me I would have learned a lot from him. That house was built in the early 1800's. A lot of those houses are over 200 years old. It's a ghost town now."

"Yes, a Pennsylvania rarity. I love exploring places like that!" Natalie touched Jim's hand, indicating she was ready to leave.

"Can I get you two some iced tea? I haven't had anyone ask me about him in years. You brought back some nice memories…"

"Oh, that's very kind of you, but we must be going. You've been really helpful." Jim started to get up.

"Not a problem. It's too bad I can't walk around the old homestead whenever I want. The place is off limits now because of the power plant. I'd love to visit some of the spots I knew so many years ago."

"It would be interesting to explore. Thanks so much for your time." They both made their way to the door, waving as they left.

"Thanks for coming." Daniel heard the plane over head and thought of him again.

They walked quietly back and got in the car. "Pennhurst? I think they shut that place down back in the 1980's. I remember seeing reports about it on the national news."

"Yeah- not good ones." The tiger lilies formed a thick orange line along the road as they approached the on-ramp to the highway. "A tinkerer, huh? My dad loved to work with his hands. Could fix *anything* in the house. Drove my mother nuts because he would never let her buy any new appliances- said he could repair everything!! I remember our old refrigerator kept breaking down. He'd keep tinkering around with the broken parts and always got it to work. One day the door latch broke and it wouldn't stay closed. We thought finally- a new refrigerator! YEAH!! Not dad. He rigged a bungee cord to the back pipes and attached it to the handle. We even painted it pink to match the kitchen when the wallpaper was changed. Quite stylish- a pink frig with a bungee cord! All us kids remember it. An extremely intelligent guy, though… and very creative. Anything mechanical he could fix, like it was part of him, his… soul."

"I'm glad technology allowed us to get together."

"Yes, Yahoo Personals had its benefits- you!! I've always wondered what our lives would be like if just a few of the inventions we now take for granted didn't happen. Without the car or the telephone, people would probably never have spoken to or met others who lived hundreds of miles away. Whole families might never have existed. Remember the most important invention of all… Post-Its! Used one to write down your phone number from the first message you left me. "

"Almost home." He reduced the speed to 50 as they approached the dated building. "Hey, check that out... The Hillside Motel. Sign says they have 'Color TV'!"

"Fabulous. I'll cancel our suite at the Waldorf Astoria."

"Didn't we have cocktails on the calendar tonight over at Jackie's house?"

"My God, I almost forgot!" She glanced at her watch. "It's already 5. We're supposed to be there between 5 and 5:30. Let's just go straight over."

"Good plan." He drove toward old Kennett Pike before cruising slowly up the long driveway to the three-story home. "Nice place." He walked along the winding path of flagstones, neatly laid within lush gardens.

"Hello you two!! Glad you could come!! We have cocktails ready. What would you like?" Jackie's pleasant demeanor warmed him as she leaned forward to hug them both.

"Chardonnay for me. You, Jim?"

"Perfect. We just got back from an interesting encounter."

"What was that?" She brought them both filled glasses as her husband Steve walked into the room.

"Hi guys! Hope you had a fun day."

"Steve, good to see you. Yes, we did some exploring. Went up toward Phoenixville and searched some municipal records of people who lived around Frick's Lock. Then we got to meet a guy who's the great, great nephew of one of the original homeowners there. Interesting conversation."

"An excursion back to the 18th century. Well, what did you discover?" He took a small sip of wine as he watched Jim's expression.

Natalie answered first. "Well, his ancestor was apparently

very creative- smart, but a bit crazed. Eventually they had to put him in Pennhurst."

"My God!! I've been to Pennhurst!! I went there as a Girl Scout. We had to do these training sessions to earn our merit badges. One involved going to Pennhurst and 'assisting' the residents with their daily chores." Jackie took a sip of wine and rolled her eyes.

"What was it like in there?"

"Oh, a bit weird. I mean- most of the people there were O.K… but some of the old men were, might I say- *overly friendly*. I was always watching my rear end when I was there."

Natalie laughed. "How old were you?"

"Like, ten years old!! I remember one guy touched me strangely and I screamed!! To think I wanted to make social work at Pennhurst my profession- at least until my dad said 'No Way'. Now I know why he told me that."

"Tough way to earn a merit badge. Why didn't you just sell cookies?"

"Not for a merit badge. Hey- I almost forgot!! Did you want to see some of my paintings from Frick's Lock? I brought a few up from the basement."

"Yes, definitely!!" Natalie stood up as Jackie dashed into the adjacent sitting room.

"Here they are. I brought up my three favorites, even though I can't really look at them now. They're so… elementary."

"I think they're lovely. Those old houses… so stoic, their chimneys punching up toward the clouds." Jim studied each painting, admiring the details.

"Oh, I don't think so. They'll probably never have value for anyone, except maybe a consignment shop owner."

"Check this out. This house looks just like the one I was in!!" Natalie held the oil painting up close. "Yes, that's the same place. I know it!! Looks like there's... something on the cornerstone of the house. I can barely read it." She held it out for Jim and Jackie to see.

Jim squinted, then grabbed his reading glasses from his pocket. "Lasik is great- except I need these all the time now for up close." He put on the glasses and moved his eyes within two inches of the canvas. "I see 'G... e...?' Can't make out the rest of the word- it's too faded. I do see what looks like a date. Says '11... 19... 63'. Looks like someone carved in something during the early 1960's, almost twenty years before they closed the town."

"I remember painting that house!! I could barely read the inscription myself. Do recall that date, though. Seemed interesting."

"Well, we can toast to your latest adventure! If you discover anything else about Frick's Lock, be sure to let us know." Steve held out his glass and clinked it against Jackie's, then Jim's and Natalie's.

"I really like this painting, Jackie. The inscription has me intrigued."

"Look, for being such good friends- I'm *giving* it to you!! One of my early 'plein air' creations. I'm glad someone likes it."

He peered closely at the cornerstone again and felt a prickling all along his neck, then picked up his glass to take another sip of wine. "To good friends- and newly discovered gems from your basement."

Chapter 6

"Inventing is a combination of brains and materials.
The more brains you use, the less material you need."
--Charles Kettering

He pulled the cord for the beige blinds lining the corner window near where Linus and Lucy were already perched, awake for a new day watching blue jays and finches outside. He loved the first chirps of the morning, bringing energy into the room, flowing through the entire house. "Really? You saw *three* cardinals yesterday? As I recall, they were doing recon work for fallen seeds. Some of those will be sunflowers soon, giving you two a nicer view." He lumbered back over to the pot where the water was already boiling. Pouring the steaming fluid into the cups, the aroma enveloped him as he looked at the January Angel his father had given his mother as a gift for Jim's birth. He touched her wings gently. "I was her 36th birthday present... It's good to have angels close by." The moment turned to minutes as he remembered her grin the day she told him the story as he made her breakfast after church that Sunday. He grabbed the two mugs and heard Natalie's voice.

"Who were you talking to?" She moved up behind him and put her hand on the edge of his maroon robe.

"Just giving some guidelines to the troops."

"That was nice- you have my cup ready. Meet you in the Conservatory. You can let the kitties up." She passed the pewter Lincoln bust along the Southwest wing where the watercolor painting of Cathedral Rock near Sedona graced the wall. Moving slowly toward the gleaming black Grand piano, she glanced outside and saw their furry friends coming in for their morning snack.

"Here we go." He put both mugs down on the brown leather coasters and joined her at the window.

"Must have left the bowl out last night. Bear and Dadcat are down there munching already."

"Well, they got an early snack." He wrapped both arms around her before they moved back toward the steaming mugs.

"I was thinking about, of all places, Pennhurst."

"That's the first thing I think about *every* morning."

"I'm serious. Jackie reinforced something I thought earlier in the day."

"That some people *we know* should have been put in there?"

"Stop!! No, when Daniel Larson mentioned his relative was in Pennhurst. It's subtle, but I was just feeling something a bit... strange. What's the chance that two people we'd talk to in the same day would have experience with a notorious mental institution?" She brought her nose close and breathed in the aroma.

"You're right. It's improbable. I still say we could have made a few recommendations for enrollees..."

"Be serious."

"I am serious. I have five names on my list and I bet good money they'd all have been admitted, no question."

"As I recall, Pennhurst started out as a well intentioned institution for people who couldn't take care of themselves. Through the years, it served the area pretty well, but due to inadequate funding and neglect, the place deteriorated badly. Then we started seeing stories in the newspapers."

"I'm sure most are far worse than what Jackie told us. A lot of hidden secrets behind those walls." He took a full gulp.

"I'll bet we'd find some interesting things walking around those buildings, but the place has been closed like Frick's Lock and abandoned for years. I'm going to do a web search. If we can somehow get in, I'd like to spend some time in there."

"Like 3-5 years, with time off for good behavior?"

"I promise- we won't get in trouble. If the signs say 'No Admittance'- we stop right there. The place was also mentioned in 'Weird Pennsylvania', so there might be some unusual things to discover."

"Let's not end the day in a police line-up."

"I'm going to my computer. Pour me another cup." She strolled through the French doors toward the foyer. Sitting at her desk, she started her search just as she heard her cell phone ring. "Who would be calling me this time of the morning?" She flipped it open and put it up to her ear. "Hello?"

"Natalie, this is Jack. Jack Clark. I hope I'm not catching you too early. I figured you might be a morning person."

She glanced over at her office door and stood up, nudging it mostly closed with her foot. "Oh, hi. Not a problem. I'm up. What's going on?" She whispered, peering out through the crack in the door to make sure Jim wasn't on his way in.

"Just wanted to say how much I enjoyed our lunch. You looked great. I'm checking on your case and have a call in to the sheriff's office. Should be able to get back with you soon." He started to plan their next meeting as he waited for her to respond.

Natalie glanced again at the door and lowered her voice further. "Yes… lunch was nice and thank you. That is good news."

"What about lunch later next week? My schedule's fairly open."

She felt the pressure in her temples build as she tried to find the right words. "Oh, well… I'm in a bit of a rush right now. Let me check my calendar… Listen, I really have to run… keep in touch!!" She closed the phone and put it quickly inside her desk just as she looked up to see Jim opening the door to her office…

Inside the FBI building, Jack shook his head as he put the phone down. "Cold feet? Doubt it. Just bad timing. She likes you, buddy. Be patient… It'll happen." He opened one of the case files on the desk and started writing the summary…

Jim didn't say anything for several seconds, watching her moves as she sat up straight in her chair. "Who was that and why did you have your *door almost closed?*" He stood next to her at the desk, agitated awaiting the response.

She felt a stab in her stomach and swiveled slightly in her chair as her mind raced wildly for an explanation. "Oh, you remember that FBI guy who interviewed us with Frank Rawlins- his partner, Jack Clark? He said back then that he'd follow up at some point. He just called to check and make sure everything was OK. I thanked him and said we were fine."

He studied her face and stayed silent for several more seconds. "I remember him. Why is he calling you now- on your *cell phone?*" His eyes were glued to her expression, recording any change.

"Remember how scared I was about those Mob thugs possibly following us? He just wanted to make sure we'd be safe, so I gave him my number. I'm sorry, I didn't mention it to you. You know those FBI guys- always working, following up on cases." She turned and tried to focus on the computer. "Got right to an interesting website!! Says the place was built in 1903 and was called 'The Eastern State Institution for the Feeble-Minded and Epileptic'. The original buildings were completed in 1908; 'patient #1' was admitted on November 23rd of that year. The facility was fully established by 1921 with several buildings to house and care for the mentally disabled."

He continued to scrutinize the side of her face, staying silent as she spoke, sensing what he'd just heard was only half true.

She watched as he put the cup in front of her and tried to get Jack out of her mind. "Thank you." Turning back toward the screen, she started reading again. "They divided the people into three groups based on IQ. At that time they used terms like moron, imbecile and idiot to describe them, but over the years, those words were regarded as degrading- though they became common slang. Later categories were mild, moderate, severe and profound mental retardation." She didn't look up at him once.

He thought back to the lies he'd gotten from women over the years, disregarding the pain while trying to enjoy their beauty. "How many times did I pay more attention to a beautiful smile- and a great figure- than what I knew was going on behind my back? Too many" he thought as he watched her scanning each page. He wanted to know it was true... hoped it was true... "I can't do this. I won't accuse her of cheating on me without any hard evidence. You're being way too critical, Jim. Too many years analyzing financial statements. She's not a balance sheet. Give it a break... and give her the benefit of the doubt. That's what mates are supposed to do." The turning in his stomach subsided and he relaxed as he saw her smile up at him.

His thinking turned to her description of the patients and he felt the sadness envelop him. He recalled the mentally disabled children and adults he'd seen at shopping malls over the years led around by a caregiver, their smiles at him a gentle reminder of the dedication to a cause they believed in. At the same time he'd felt despair when he looked into the eyes of the patients, getting blank stares from faces who never knew what it meant to be independent and free. The last time he saw those faces, he started supporting the Special Olympics. "Society has never been comfortable dealing with those who can't take care of themselves. To call ourselves truly humane, we need to do a better job of that."

"You're right. Apparently conditions got so bad, they did a news special in 1968 called 'Suffer the Little Children'. All the patients' there- whether they were eight or eighty- were called 'children' due to their dependence on others."

"I think I recall that. Reporter had a unique name... Ballini?"

"Pretty close. It was Bill Baldini and he did a four part report, interviewing patients and caregivers, filming scenes which shocked many people. The documentary illustrated what were by then degrading, unhealthy practices and living conditions, even though many of the staff members interviewed- including the doctors- felt things were just fine. The official capacity was about 1,900 persons, but they had over 2,700- without enough personnel to handle them all in a responsible manner. I think the documentary really opened the eyes of the public, building support for the place to be closed down."

"What caused them to finally shutter the operation?" He leaned on the back of her desk chair, squinting to read the print on the screen.

"A class action suit was brought to court in 1977, claiming violations of patients' constitutional rights. Allegations of beatings, assault and extended isolation were argued before Judge Raymond Broderick. It took many years and a process of de-institutionalization to get all the residents transferred to other facilities where they could get adequate care. Some patients were just released, left to roam homeless in the nearby town. Pennhurst was eventually closed in 1987."

"Sounds like a nightmare that lasted for years."

"Some claims *were* exaggerated, with people saying patients were being tortured in dungeons, which didn't occur. Yet, an entrenched establishment perpetuated what most people knew was a horrible situation until enough citizens came forward to stop it."

"The only thing necessary for bad things to happen in this world is for good people to do nothing."

"Why does it take tragedies for us to learn?"

"We rarely alter our behavior based on subtle changes. It's only when something drastic happens- or is about to happen- that most of us sit up and take notice."

She clicked on the next story which had several photos. "Take a look at this- it just *looks* ominous." She pointed to the shots of the aged, red brick Pennhurst Administration Building and some of the structures on the Lower Campus, vines growing through cracked windows. "Here it gives the names for each building; men were separated from the women. Looks like the ones for males were labeled 'Q', 'T', 'U' and 'V' which were 'cottages' for boys. Randolph Larson must have been in one of those buildings. God, I'd love to check those out!!"

"You might find some things you don't want to see."

"I know the place was a disgrace, but it would be fascinating to get in there and walk the corridors, see the rooms where the patients were kept…"

"Against their will, some tied to bedposts, others on the floor alone in the corner, beating their heads endlessly against the wall…"

"Bad things happened. We can't change that, but maybe by going to see the place for ourselves- we might get some insights." She cringed as she viewed the images of young children crying, lying in fetal positions on their beds, their hands wrapped around their ears. She was near tears as she saw one young boy, stripped naked, standing in the corner, his back revealing bruises and welts. "My God!! How terrible that must have been." She shook her head in horror at the scenes.

He said a prayer in silence. "Maybe we can both learn something from all this. Let's make a promise. If we somehow get in there to take a look around, we're going to bring back something of value- like a greater empathy and understanding of the mentally disabled. Maybe Sherry Donahue knows more about the place. I should call her. It's just a couple of miles south from Frick's Lock in Spring City."

"OK, but next time we visit her, let's use the stairs." She watched as he went over to her phone and dialed the number.

"East Coventry Township- Records Division."

"Sherry, Jim Peterson. How are you?"

"Wonderful. I hope you're well and that you both found some useful information here."

"We sure did, thanks so much. We have a side project going. What do you know about Pennhurst?"

"Touchy subject, but an interesting one. Place was started back near the turn of the century to help those who couldn't take care of themselves, but over the years, due to neglect, it became an embarrassment to the state. A few horror stories…"

"Well, could we take you to lunch and discuss it sometime in the next few days?"

"That's the best offer I've had all morning!! When did you want to stop by?"

"I didn't want to interrupt your work. Tell me a good day and we'll be available."

"You can stop over tomorrow any time after ten and we can take it from there."

"Let's make it 11:00 a.m.- we can discuss some of those little known stories and then have lunch."

"Great. I'll pull together some information for your research. See you then."

Sherry put the phone down and looked over at the grey file cabinet at the very end of the room. She'd avoided opening it for years. Taking a breath, her right hand grasped the latch unlocking the drawer, pulling it toward her. Bright red stickers announced "CASES: PENNHURST" as she glanced down at the thick row of folders. "God, do I *really* want to see these again?" She took another deep breath and put her hands at the middle of the stack where she knew it was filed. Pulling out the folder, she shut the drawer, walking to the nearest desk to sit down. Waiting several seconds, she flipped the file open and saw the horrors come to life... The blood-stained backs of the men from the beatings, children lying in a fetal position on the floor amongst their own vomit and feces... children who hadn't been out of their cribs for years. The woman, face black and blue after being left alone for an entire day in an isolation room, beating her head endlessly against the wall until she collapsed unconscious. Breathing harder, she flipped to the back of the file- the photos of bodies taken away from the premises after 'unexplained accidents'. "There were too many of them to be *unexplained!!*"

Her mind raced back to the day in 1986, the year before Pennhurst was closed, when her curiosity forced her to push a close friend to allow her in to see the 'special rooms' where no visitors went. She shook at the memory- the screams, the moans of agony, the old man who leapt out and grabbed her, begging to be freed... She thought of her cousin and saw her picture amongst those on the table. "I'm so sorry it happened to you, Bernadette. I... should have done something..." She returned the photos and closed the drawer. "I can't look anymore..." At her desk, she put her right hand on the phone, wanting to call Jim back to cancel their meeting...

Jim glanced back at Natalie, who was eagerly reading the next story. "We're there tomorrow at 11."

"Sounds good. We're lucky to have met her. It would be

great to find a way inside those walls... check out the abandoned rooms." She continued to focus on the images on the screen. "That looks like a tunnel. They had miles of them between the buildings. I bet they're filled with bats and wild animals now, maybe some ghoulish relics from the asylum." Her eyes widened as she viewed each scene, the dark corridors, buildings falling apart, weeds consuming the structures.

"Something tells me you were the one in your family who wanted to ride the roller coaster five times in a row at Lenape Park."

"No, just liked to lay on the grass under the tracks looking up at the cars as they raced down the first big hill. Cheap thrills."

"At least you lived to tell about it. I need to head over to Wal-Mart to pick up a few things. Should be back in less than an hour."

"Fine. That'll give me time to do more research."

He smiled and gave her a quick hug before heading to the car.

—————————

"Do you think she knows much about Pennhurst?" Natalie asked.

"She seems to know a lot about *everything* in this area. It must take years of research to get to that level." He studied the sky as he brought the car to a stop. "Stratus clouds. Could be a front coming in the next 24 hours."

"Where did you get your knowledge of meteorology?"

"Broke open a lot of meteors with my rock hammer when

I was a kid. I'll get your door." He ignored the elevator as he followed her into the lobby, past the bulletin board with municipal announcements and went up the stairs.

"Hello, Sherry."

"Hi there!! Glad you two could come by. I gathered some files on Pennhurst. You can spend some time viewing the state archives on-line. Be prepared. Some of the photos are a bit shocking, although you may already have been exposed to a few of them."

"Overexposed. We did a search and found some scenes which were quite disturbing. I can't believe they treated people that way."

"Some of the more lucid patients became irate, claiming they were being held against their will. Due to lack of funding, conditions eventually became deplorable. They spent more money on animals at the Philadelphia Zoo than they did on these people! It was horrible" Sherry exclaimed.

Natalie cringed as she opened the folder and saw the images- worse than the ones she'd viewed at home. "Oh, my God!! Look at them- they're like skeletons! Did they stop providing meals?"

"No, just cut them to a minimum. Many had to be hand fed and there wasn't enough staff. Also, they used electro-shock treatments on the patients. It was a brutal test of a new theory-that you could 'shock' people into submission and 'acting right'. The doctors who administered the therapy would talk nonchalantly about the screams, the agonizing seconds as the volts passed through, how they'd flinch at the sight of the patient's eyes rolling back with each jolt, sending many into convulsions. At that time, some of the doctors didn't fully understand what they were doing. It's sad to think that hundreds of people may have suffered needlessly. People were malnourished, unsupervised and unable to fend for themselves."

"These photos remind me of survivors from Auschwitz." Jim stiffened as he examined them. "What's worse than this?"

Sherry hesitated for several seconds. "Well, the most controversial things are in the official records- and they're all sealed. Only law enforcement personnel or medical examiners are allowed access. So we'll probably never see the *really* bad stuff, but I can tell you a few stories I've heard over the years from people who were in a position to know."

Natalie immediately closed the folder. "What kind of stories?" She moved closer to Sherry and leaned on the edge of the metal desk, its rubberized rim giving her a small cushion.

"Not sure what to make of this, as it's about a ghost who's supposed to roam the halls there. Story goes that back in the early 1930's one of the female residents was so distraught about having to live the rest of her life in the asylum, she hung herself in the bathroom with the cord from her robe. Workers for years used to swear they'd hear weird sounds at night, moans, like a dying woman wandering the halls. One maintenance guy who'd worked there for over 30 years said he couldn't take it anymore. Apparently he saw her several times. One night he said he found her body actually hanging in the bathroom. Quit on the spot and left for good."

"Did anyone else see the ghost?" Natalie inquired.

"Staff up through the 1980's claim to have seen her walking the halls, cord dangling from her neck. Hangman's noose. Not just the maintenance crew- I'm talking some of the management team. People who ran the place."

"I'd like to get in there. Ghosts are my specialty!" Natalie stood erect, like a soldier preparing for an important mission.

"Hold on. The place is closed, correct?" Jim waited for Sherry's confirmation.

"Yes- totally off limits. A local company owns the property. It's been in private use for a composting business. If you really want to learn more, you should go speak with someone who used to work there."

"Like who?"

"I do know one guy, actually. Name is… Abraham Olson. He was on the staff from the late 1930's up until the place closed. I believe his grandson was also an employee. Abe lives not too far from here."

"Is there any way we could go meet him?"

"I don't know why you couldn't. He's an old man now- around 90, maybe 91 years old. Grandson lives with him. He's in his mid-fifties. I may actually have his contact information in a listing of former Pennhurst employees." She proceeded to a tall file cabinet and flipped through several folders. "Here it is- and he's…. there on the list. Says they live at 231 Wayland Avenue. It's about five, six miles from here. Easy to find. Just off the main road."

"I'm writing that down" Natalie said as she grabbed her pen and leaned onto the desk. "Mind if we go through these and check on the computer a bit before we go eat?"

"Not at all. Take your time. I'll be over here if you have any questions."

"Thanks so much. We'll just run a few searches, then we'll do lunch." He went to the computer and clicked on each tab, showing images of the workers, the buildings and the patients, then more ghastly scenes, with people huddled in corners, tied to beds, lying in their own urine. "Oh, my Lord… not sure if I want to go through all this… Maybe I'll stick with the written descriptions."

"Some of the scenes are a bit gruesome" Sherry remarked as she tried to focus on the papers in front of her. "There was one small consolation. Patients who'd been used to homes with dirt floors and seeing at night with kerosene lamps got a dose of the latest technology- incandescent lights, all powered by Pennhurst's own onsite electrical plant. They had hot and cold running water, which for many was a luxury, along with a central ventilation system. Pretty advanced for the early 1900's."

"So, even in their misery, they enjoyed benefits from recent advancements. Interesting." Jim continued to page through the screens, reading each one for details on living conditions. "I think I've seen enough. How about a break?"

"I'm ready. Natalie?"

Natalie looked up from the stack of files in the folder. "I am, too. Let's go." They walked to the door and down the hall past the elevator. "Any other spooky stories before we eat?"

"I've heard so many. You just don't know which ones are even near the truth. The one I told you is probably the most accurate."

"Do you believe it?"

"I certainly do. Worked with some of the people who claimed to have seen her. These are serious, no-nonsense professionals. They wouldn't make up something like that."

Walking into the pub, Jim saw the expansive bar, with the 30-foot wide mirror and pieces of Americana hanging all along the wall. "Nice place. I'd be here for Happy Hour every week."

"I wish I'd seen her myself- then I could say I've actually experienced a ghost. I'm one of those non-believers, but I put a lot of weight on what my friends said. Kind of eerie to me."

"Right in my zone. Now I *really* want to go there!! Wish we could sneak in at midnight."

Sherry laughed. "You're a real adventurer. Wonder if Jim shares your enthusiasm."

"Discretion is the better part of valor. Plus, I'm drowsy by 9, so ghost hunting at midnight would require a double espresso." He ate slowly. "Let me get the check."

They dropped Sherry off, then headed back. On the drive home, Jim's thoughts ran from ghosts to suffering patients as he tried to understand how things could have gotten so bad. "Maybe there's a lot more people don't know about that story."

"What, the ghost? Oh, I believe it completely. Remember what happened to me that time we had lunch at The Ship Inn?" She looked at the car ahead of them, the bumper sticker 'If you don't like this life, the next one's not that hot either' facing them as they pulled onto the side road, cruising up in front of their garage as the door opened.

"She never actually saw the ghost- just relying on what other people said. Who knows what really happened?"

"Makes you want to curl up on the couch with a mystery novel, which is what I recommend."

"Fine, but no mandatory toe rubs while I'm reading Hemingway. It ruins the intensity." He grabbed the copy of "Islands in the Stream", flopping onto the loveseat.

As they read, photos from the files flashed before both of them, disturbing the normally lazy afternoon's relaxation into an agitated daydream… Jim made it to page 138… then flipped back as he realized the last five hours he'd had his eyes mostly closed, dreaming of the horrific scenes he'd viewed earlier in the day. He looked up at the clock. "Hey, we both nodded out. It's too late for dinner. Not really hungry after that lunch, anyway."

"Let's just go to bed. You can fall asleep again reading there." Climbing up the steps, she noticed the moonlight had replaced the rays from earlier in the day. After their normal bedtime routine, they settled under the sheets, picking up where they left off in their books. Just then a loud rumbling noise rose from the side of the house. "What was that?!!" Natalie concentrated, trying to listen.

"I'm heading down right now." Grabbing his bathrobe, he quickly descended the back stairs, nearly missing the last step.

Floyd ran into the garage after he managed to force the door open, the cylinders rumbling overhead. Sprinting toward her car, he saw the box on the floor and squatted down quickly, prying apart the flaps and rummaging through the contents. "What a bunch of crap!" He picked each piece up and tossed them aside, then looked up as he heard movement in the house. Grabbing a nearby wooden board, he stood beside the doorway, waiting…

Opening the door slowly, Jim looked up to see the middle garage door pried open. "What the…? " A heavy board came crashing down on the side of his head and he fell to the cement floor, writhing in pain. "Awwwwhhh!!! Shit… my head…" Just as he started to get to his feet, he saw a man running out the doorway, sprinting down the driveway to a waiting pick-up truck. Raising his hand up to check the wound, he flinched as he touched it, the area throbbing. "There'll be a lump, but don't see any blood." The truck screeched down the street as he stood erect, walking over to the middle of the garage. Jim scanned the area, but didn't see anything out of place. "Hard to tell if anything's missing. Wait... here's the box. Stuff all over the place, but... looks like... they didn't take much- if anything. Strange... Better get this mess off the floor or she'll have me on a cleaning spree in the morning." He glanced back up as the truck rounded the corner at the end of the cul-de-sac. "Wait a minute... that truck... looks like the one I saw up there with those two guys at Frick's Lock!!" The taillights glowing in the night were firmly in his mind. "I think I know who those guys are..." He put all the items back in the box, closed the garage door and turned out the light, still shaking, moving slowly as he went back in the house.

The muffled tone of a cell phone permeated the silence. Realizing it was Natalie's, he trotted over to grab the phone from her purse. Flipping it open, he saw the caller ID. 'Jack Clark'. "HELLO?!" There was only a dial-tone. He threw the phone back into her purse, cursing as he stomped up the stairs to their bedroom.

"Looks like we had a break-in... and I think I may know who did it." He slid under the covers.

"Who?"

"Can't say for sure, but I recognize the truck. Sounds strange- but I think it could have been those same guys- the ones we saw up at the Lock."

"What??!! Why would they come all the way down here?"

"It doesn't make any sense, but I think they wanted something in that box we took. There were things scattered all over the floor. Strangely enough, I don't think anything was missing." He brushed his hair back, feeling the bump rising before he settled onto the pillow.

"Let's call the police. NOW!!"

"What, so we can tell them about the box you stole- and *lied about*? No way!!"

She stopped to think for several seconds. "You're right, we can't call the cops. We'll just have to stay quiet on this. It's pretty shocking. Someone breaks into your house and you can't even report it... "

"We can't change that, but we'll have to be extra careful now. Watch the house and where we go more closely. Never know, if those guys came all the way down here, they probably have a pretty good reason. We may see them again." Picking up his book, he tried to envision the man's face. Then acid churned in his stomach as he thought about the phone call. "Why was Clark calling her *again*- and at this hour?" He clenched both fists around the edge of the book.

———◆———

Dexter sat in the truck as it sped away from the cul-de-sac. "Did you get *anything?*"

"NO!! It was just a bunch of junk. Dead spiders and old cans of chewin' tobacco."

"What now, Floyd? We were thinkin' we'd get some things- maybe sell 'em at the auction and make a few hundred bucks each." He watched the trees float by in the dark as the truck sped back onto Route 1 North.

"Don't worry, I got some ideas… Somethin' tells me there's money to be made, one way or another."

"Next time, let's just make sure there's nobody home. We got these god-dang cell phones- let's use 'em!"

"OK already!!"

Chapter 7

"It has become appallingly obvious that our technology has exceeded our humanity..."
--Albert Einstein

"Natalie, it's been well over a week. Remember we said we were going to try to visit that guy, what was his name- Olson- who used to work at Pennhurst?" Ozzy caught his attention near the top of the tidal basin mowing his lawn, then Jim noticed their own lawn was overdue for a trimming. "Hey, our guy didn't come yet this week, did he?"

"Yes, I remember and would like to go- and no, the lawn guy hasn't made it here yet. It rained for two days, so he's probably backed up."

"What's the itinerary?"

She closed the dishwasher next to him, now fully loaded and pushed 'START'. "I want to talk with Olsen. I'm sure he has some interesting anecdotes to share." She folded the sage green towel and placed it neatly next to the chopping board along the sink. "Let's stop by to see if we could meet with him. We have his address. If we leave now, we could be there before 2:30."

"Shouldn't we call first?" Jim asked.

"I tried to find his number. It's unlisted."

"Let's do it."

"Should be a great day, not a cloud in the sky."

"I'm curious what we'll find out, if anything, when we meet this guy. He's 90 years old, so he may not remember a lot." He grabbed his car keys from the table.

"My grandmother lived to almost 98 and was sharp up until her final days. Advanced age doesn't have to be a prescription for senility." She recalled their trip up to New York to see her, Elaine and Joe, wandering around their magnificent home decorated with exotic sculptures and expensive furniture. "I'm glad we saw her. She was gone less than a year later."

"It was a pleasure meeting her and the rest of your family. I'll always remember how your grandmother looked up at the sky as we were talking with her. I wonder what she was thinking… Joe and Elaine were quite hospitable."

Turning down the air conditioning in the car to 'Level 2', the memory of Joe giving Jim a personal tour of the house came back to her. "Grandma was just thrilled we came. Made her very happy. You were a hit!! She thought you were the 'perfect WASP'. She didn't know you were Catholic. I think Joe was surprised I'd managed to find such a nice husband."

"You *were* lucky to get me. I had five offers on the table that day."

"That's the turn off." The SUV arced onto the side road rimmed with Summer lawns in their green splendor, bathed in the intense sunlight.

"There's the sign- Wayland. Was it…231?"

"Correct. I see the house." The façade revealed a home

built in the 1940's with the trademark square brick frame and small front porch with a brown metal awning. "Hope they let us in."

"I'll use my powers of negotiation." The car proceeded just to the side of the pavement and stopped. "They say life all comes down to a few moments."

"Relax. We're not interviewing the Pope." She followed him to the door and watched him press the buzzer.

"Uh, yeah??" The man in his early fifties threw open the door, revealing his beer belly hanging over the edge of heavily faded jeans, a Flyers T-shirt worn at the shoulders. He scrutinized Jim's face intensely.

"I hope I'm not disturbing you." Jim put out his hand, but the man ignored it. He gazed around him to the furniture in the family room, hearing the TV blaring loudly.

"Depends. Wudda ya' want?" He burped, then glanced at Natalie, pulling in his gut as he checked out her curves.

"We're doing some exploring in the area. We've done some research on Pennhurst and stopped in to visit the local municipal building where the historian gave us some information. She told us Abe Olsen used to work there." Jim waited as the man stood motionless, still focusing on Natalie and could tell from the odor he hadn't showered in at least two days.

"Yeah, what about him?" His tone was harsh as he gazed past Jim, noticing the shiny black SUV glistening in the sunlight.

"Well, we were just hoping to say hello and maybe speak with him for a few minutes about some of his experiences there." He could feel Natalie's shoe press against the back of his, her 'Maybe we should be going' sign. "I promise we won't take long." He felt another kick at his ankle.

"Oh, I don't think so… he's old and gettin' a bit senile." He turned around and peered into the family room, then looked back at Jim.

"Who is it, Richie?" The voice was barely audible over the TV.

"Pops, some guy wants to talk to you about Pennhurst. I told him 'No'." He scowled at Jim and started to close the door.

"Let him in! I'm fine. We can talk for a bit." He got up slowly off the couch and entered the small foyer. "Who's visiting?"

"It's Jim- Jim Peterson. Are you Mr. Olson?"

"I am. Who is that lovely woman behind you- and why are you letting her just stand there? Come on in!!"

Richie frowned and shook his head, then stepped back to let them both through the doorway. "There's a game comin' on soon, so you can't stay for long." The female announcer on ESPN was detailing the upcoming Phillies/Mets game, her soft voice a pleasant change from the often gruff tones of their other personnel.

"Shush!! They're our guests and they're welcome here as long as they want to stay." He put his hand out toward Jim. "I'm Abe Olson. This is my grandson, Richie."

Jim shook his hand and felt the surprisingly strong grip. "Good to meet you." Natalie reached forward as she stepped toward him.

Abe took her hand in both of his, bringing it to his face, kissing it gently. He brought her wrist up to his nose. "I love your perfume. What is it?" Then he glanced over at Jim. "Where did you find this beautiful woman?" He held her hand for several seconds before letting it go, grinning.

"It's Chanel Number 5. Glad you like it."

"I met this wonderful lady almost ten years ago. We live in Kennett Square." Jim smiled as he noted Abe's eyes locked on Natalie.

"Well, come in!! Richie said you wanted to talk about Pennhurst?" He settled down slowly and waved his left hand for them to rest on the loveseat across from him.

"Yes, we've been doing some research on the place and heard you worked there."

"Forty-nine years." He smiled at Natalie. "Can I get you some iced tea?"

"Actually, that would be nice." She sat back and noticed Richie scowling.

"Richie, get these nice people some iced tea- with lemon. Love it in the Summertime." He concentrated on Jim. "What was it about Pennhurst you wanted to know? Lot of memories inside those hallways…"

Richie shook his head, looking at the floor as he went back to the kitchen.

"What was your impression of the place? How did you like working there?" He waited, noting Abe's grin disappearing as he looked down at the oval brown throw rug.

"Good and bad. Pennhurst was started way back… and it was a good idea- to take care of people who couldn't take care of themselves. You can't fault the government for wanting to do that, even though government usually screws things up if you give 'em a chance." He laughed, then stopped abruptly. "You're probably wondering about all the stories you've heard."

"We've read a bit, but decided firsthand knowledge would be best. Perhaps you have some personal things to share."

"I want to say right up front- all those stories about beatings and abuse- I never saw it myself. Worst I saw was they grabbed some of the guys- and a few of the women- who were getting out of hand. They had to. You can't let people just go wild and maybe hurt others." The smile was gone.

"We know they had to detain people who sometimes were a threat to others. You never experienced anything... violent?"

"Here." Richie handed them each a glass three-quarters full and stood next to the couch. "What are you tryin' to say- that my grandpop hurt people?"

"Richie, calm *down*!! These are nice folks." Abe relaxed and spoke softly. "Look, some bad things happened there. A few people got out of control and had to be put in special rooms, away from the others. Yes, I did see some of the 'children'- that's what we called them- who had marks on them- their backs, sometimes around their wrists. Did it look like they'd been hurt? Perhaps. I didn't see it happen, but I did notice the signs. Hey, as overcrowded as it was, it was bound to take place. Bad things sometimes occur when too many people are put in a facility that can't handle all of them." He glanced up at Richie. "Turn that thing down, will you?" nodding over toward the TV.

Jim set the glass on the table, hoping their stay wasn't over. "Oh, I didn't mean to bring up bad memories- just wanted..."

"You wanted- to do what?!" Richie interrupted, hovering over him at the edge of the chair, with a furrowed brow and glare in his eyes.

"Richie, enough!! These people are *my* guests." He shook his head as Richie stomped away, back into the kitchen. His eyes met Natalie's. "Are you sure you want to hear about that place?"

"I do."

"Well, let me tell you. When I first started there... back in 1938, the place was spotless. Spic and span. Well run, too. They had staff for everything they needed. I started out in maintenance and worked my way up to assistant nurse. I was more interested in finding out about the patients- why they were there, what made them 'different'. They were different, all right. Most weren't able to do the things that you and I do on a daily basis- make their own meals, bathe themselves, take care of their rooms. Some couldn't tie their shoes without my help. That was... sad." He gazed out the window up at the clouds and breathed in deeply. "Then there were the 'problem' kids. You never knew what they were going to do. Hurt themselves or lash out at someone else. Some would fly into a rage, scratching and kicking... others pounded the walls with their heads."

"Did you ever get injured working there?" Natalie sat up, nervously rubbing her forearm.

"Almost. We were coming back from lunch one day, and this guy- he was in his late 20's, big, strong young man, well over six feet tall- he didn't want to go to his room!! So I said 'Look, lunch is over. You need to return to your room'- and he takes a swing at me!! Luckily, I ducked and grabbed him in a bear hug until a security guy came and restrained him. Could've had a bad shiner on that one."

"Did you ever see a revolt- a group fighting to get away from the staff or try to escape?" Jim cleared his throat before taking a sip of iced tea.

"Oh, yes, several times, but it never amounted to anything. They had a whole security detail there- 20, 30 guys- who were called at the first sign of trouble. No doubt things could have gotten out of hand, but those guys took care of it right away."

Natalie set her drink down on the stone coaster. "We're doing some research into people who were patients there and found the name of a gentleman named Randolph Larson. We think he was at Pennhurst from around 1925 to 1940. He would have been an old man by then. Did you ever meet him?"

He looked out the window again. "Larson... I don't know. There were so many. Hard to remember them all."

"Randolph Larson would have been about 80 years old when they admitted him, so when you started working there, he was about 93. People say he was a very intelligent, but highly eccentric man. He'd say strange things all the time. People thought he was just crazy, but supposedly he was quite sharp- intellectually." She waited for his next words as if an announcer was reading the winning lottery numbers.

"You know, I do recall a guy- an old man who was admitted just before I started- and yes... I think I actually met the gentleman! Very strange man. I recall one day I was with him- this would have been in 1938- and Randolph heard an airplane overhead. This was before World War II, so we didn't see too many planes flying around back then. Randolph saw a plane outside and said 'I was there.' I had no idea what he was talking about. He'd say strange things all the time. I figured he was batty, you know, from old age." He looked beyond the window and observed the sky just as a 767 passed overhead, the roar causing him to pause before he started again. "Then later that same day- I'll never forget- this guy Randolph was focusing on a light bulb above his head. He must have stared at that thing for two hours! I finally went up to him to see if he was okay and he said 'That's part of me'. I thought he was nuts and didn't pay any attention. He'd either mumble to himself all day long or rant about some thing or another. It was driving the other patients crazy- and for most of them, it was a short trip." He chuckled, then looked at Natalie's blue eyes. "Can I get you some more iced tea?"

"I'm fine, thank you! I'd love to hear more."

"For you sweetheart, anytime- but only if you keep showing that lovely smile of yours. Now it's coming back to me... This guy Randolph, he did seem to be pretty intelligent, but he'd say all kinds of nutty things!! One day he kept yelling the same crazy phrase- again and again. Started screaming it at the top of his lungs! Scared the hell out of me. I called security, but by the time they got there, I had him calmed down. Gave him some mints. He really loved mints. Seemed to quiet him a bit. He did things like that all the time. Got to the point where I didn't make anything of it."

"Was he coherent?" Natalie was on the edge of her seat.

"Not really. Couldn't make sense out of what the hell he was saying!! He'd mumble different things over and over. Started to annoy everyone. It got so bad, I just wanted to keep my distance from him, even though he wouldn't hurt a fly. Nice gentleman, just crazy."

Richie came back into the room, intentionally brushing up against Jim as he passed the chair.

Jim tried not to look up and watched Abe sit forward on the couch. "There must have been a lot of strange people there."

"Plenty, but this guy Randolph, he was... different. There

was something there- you could tell, something working away in his mind. I'd go up to him and he'd appear to be in a trance. Then for a few seconds he'd snap out of it and actually communicate normally with me. I mean just pleasantries like 'How are you?' and 'Hope you're doing well'. Yet, he was… apart from the rest. I could tell there was something exceptional about him." He glanced up at Richie, shaking his head to him in a warning to behave.

Natalie touched Jim in a signal to leave. "We probably should be going." She rested the near empty glass on the table.

"Yes, we should." He leaned forward to shake Abe's hand. "We really appreciate this. You've been very kind." They both headed towards the entrance as Abe got up and followed. Richie was already at the door, ready to escort them out.

"You know, it just came to me!! One day he shouted 'I flew with the Wright Brothers!!' Wouldn't stop yelling it- almost had to put him in a padded room. We thought he was going bonkers and might hurt someone. Finally he calmed down, but never stopped repeating the same lines."

"Can you remember any others?" Natalie asked.

"Hmmmm… No, but he used to write things all over the walls. Day after day- he'd write stuff. Happened so many times, we finally gave up trying to clean 'em off. Probably still on the walls there for all I know. Gosh, I remember like it was yesterday…"

Jim's eyes widened as he nudged Natalie, then noticed Richie was opening the door.

"Do you remember the buildings there? Where did he stay?"

"Listen, it's time for you two to go!! You come in here

snooping around, asking lots of questions. You can leave now-and don't come back."

"Richie, shush!!" He focused on Natalie. "You have the most beautiful blue eyes. Makes a man my age want to be younger." He let out a chuckle as he straightened his pants, tugging at the belt buckle. "I do remember, worked in those buildings for so many years. It was Quaker Hall where he stayed- on the second floor in the back, near the stairway." His eyes turned to look out the window again, lost in the memory. "Can't believe I can recall all this. Guess the old noggin' is still pretty sharp."

"You've got a great memory for someone your age." Natalie took his hand to thank him.

"Many people my age aren't in too good shape, but what's age? Just a number!! I say, make each day count. Stay active, read, keep your mind workin', that's the key. A sharp mind and a healthy body. I exercise three days a week right over there. Richie got me these hand weights. See?" He curled his left arm up, making a muscle, a very slight bulge lifting his shirt. "Want to arm wrestle?"

Jim laughed. "No, I'm sure you could beat me!!" He put his hand on Abe's arm as his own muscles tensed instinctively. "Jack La Lanne was going strong up until he was 96... and he could put men thirty years younger than him to shame."

"I like the guy!! Remember when he turned 60 years old. He wanted to show the world that you can still be strong and active- so he swam New York harbor with his wrists tied- *towing 60 rows boats all the way!!*" Now that was amazing!!" He let out a deep belly laugh.

"I recall seeing that on TV. Truly incredible. It shows that you don't have to accept what many people say is inevitable."

"At 70 he did another equally miraculous stunt. People thought he was going to kill himself, but he proved them all wrong. Yessirree- age is a state of mind- and if you focus on living a healthy, active life you'll be in good shape. I love that song... 'Accentuate the positive... eliminate the negative...'"

Natalie put her hands around Abe's, then pulled him closer for a hug. "You're probably in better shape than I am. You're an inspiration for us all!!"

He kissed her hands and then tilted his head up at Jim. "Come on!! Betcha' a dollar I can beat you in arm wrestling!! Let's try it- just once!!"

Jim laughed again and put his arm around Abe's shoulders. "Abe, you're living proof that the soul is ageless. Your spirit is uplifting. My hat's off to you."

"My father used to tell me 'Use your head for somethin' other than a hat rack!!' That cracked me up... Well, I got a good mind, still- and your coming here has just cheered me up. I'm going to do some exercising later on."

"Excellent!!" Natalie kissed his cheek. "Thank you so much!!"

"Abe, here's my card. If you think of anything else, please call me. I'd love to talk with you about Pennhurst. It's got my phone number and e-mail on it. I don't know if you use a computer." Jim put it into his hand just as Richie grabbed Jim's shoulder, pushing him toward the foyer- then nudged him firmly into the doorway. Jim tried to push back, his anger building. His pulse raced as he wanted to take a swing at him, but stopped as Natalie pulled his right arm.

"Time for you to go!!" Richie glared at Jim as he stood erect grasping the doorknob in his left hand, his right one clenched firmly into a fist.

"RICHIE, STOP!!" Abe scolded, then looked back at Jim. "Yes, of course I use a computer. Great way to share information- the Internet. I'll say, whoever came up with that idea was a true genius. Think of it, being able to access information at any time, from anywhere on the planet!! Now that was a technological breakthrough!! People with ideas like that- they change the world. I use e-mail all the time... get photos sent to me from my grandkids." He shook Jim's and Natalie's hands. "You two have a wonderful day", waving as they went toward their car.

When the SUV pulled away, Natalie glanced over at him. "You could have gotten us into trouble back there. Almost started a fight."

"He pushed ME!! I didn't start it." He focused on the traffic coming up to the stop light, trying not to let the thought distract him.

"Yes, but you wanted to."

"I did!! He was way out of line!!"

"Calm down, Rambo. We have other battles to fight- like trying to figure out a way to get in there."

"Where?"

"Pennhurst."

"You *really* want to check that place out, don't you?" The light turned green and the car sped onto the intrastate.

"In a heartbeat!!" She thought about what Abe had said and could feel the excitement grow. "What would it be like to roam around those buildings- all by ourselves? We could investigate the dormitories, discover hidden secrets- maybe even find where Randolph stayed!!"

Back in the house, Abe looked down at Jim's card to read

the name, but felt it being snatched away.

"I'll take care of that." Richie grabbed the card and put it in his shirt pocket.

"You need to let it go, Richie. That was a long time ago. I know you didn't do all those things people accused you of."

"I just don't want people snoopin' around, tellin' lies about that place... and me. I hate it!!"

"Look, who says they're telling anything?? They were just asking some questions about my experiences. You did the best you could with a tough situation. Hell, it was tough for me when I worked there, too. Plus, I was the one who got you the job."

"Don't you think I remember??!! I'm not senile, like some old people I know..."

"Now, wait just a minute!! I won't have you speak to me like that! I am your grandfather. I've done a lot for you." He glared at Richie, but Richie turned away, shaking his head.

"I don't want those memories any more..." He thought about the years there, cleaning up after every 'accident'- the moans throughout the night, patients sitting in pools of their own vomit. "I did my best, but it was never enough. Hey, I know the bathrooms didn't sparkle. The beds weren't always made. The kitchen was a mess most of the time. What could I do? We were way understaffed. It got so bad, I didn't want to go to work anymore, but I had to. I needed the money. So what happened? When they finally closed the place, some camera crew comes right up to me- shoves a microphone and their camera right in my face. This reporter wouldn't go away- starts asking me questions. 'Why was Pennhurst such a disaster?' and 'Why didn't you and the other people there work to make it better and help the patients?' Like I was the cause of the problem!! Well, I tried to help, but management wouldn't listen. It's not my fault!! This reporter keeps pushin' the camera in front of me and I just said 'There was nothin' I could do.' Then I walked away and heard him talkin', sayin' stuff like 'Folks, that's the sad story about Pennhurst. Even the people there didn't do anything to help and in some cases may have made things worse. You heard it right here…' Richie looked down, clenching his fists. "I'll show 'em…"

"Now, Richie- you calm down!! That was over 20 years ago. Remember, I helped when you had nowhere to go. You were in that gang- even got arrested- and had no job- nothing!! When you started working there, you seemed to perk up!! It was the first decent job you'd had in years. I think the place did you some good."

"The hell it did. All I ever got out of it was people comin' up to me- accusin' me of hurtin' little kids, beating people… One time a guy at the grocery store pushed me and said 'You're the one who caused all that trouble at Pennhurst. You should be in jail!!' I almost decked him right there!! There were people in the neighborhood, ladies with little kids who'd walk, almost run away when they saw me- didn't want me near them. I could tell they were sayin' bad things about me- lies- all lies!!! No matter what I said or did- nobody wanted to hear the truth. I couldn't take it any more!!"

He tramped toward the back of the house into his room, sitting down at the computer as he looked at the card. "I'll make sure they never come back here." He thought again about the room where they were forced to hold the 'children' against their will, in straight jackets, yelling, crying. The intensity shook him as he tried to log on to check his e-mail. Opening up Outlook, he placed the card onto the desk as he started to type in the address. Then the pain came back, a dagger into his chest- the people on the street accosting him, saying 'You're the guy we saw on the news at Pennhurst!! You were part of that mess!!' and the phone calls into the late hours of the night, no voice on the other end, just someone breathing, then the hang-ups, week after week. The stress caused him to fall forward, but he pushed against the sides of the desk and sat up straight. He finished typing the e-mail address and crafted the message.

'Get out and stay away!! Don't ever come back!!!! Stop butting where you don't belong!' He inserted the images- the eerie skull… the dungeon… then added audio- clips of people moaning, screaming.

'A H H H H!!!!…. O O O O O O H H H H!!!!!!…. AAAHHHHHHHHHH!!!!!!!' Skulls all around the dirt floor, cracked open, blood and pus pouring out of the eye sockets. He shook as he felt the screams inside himself, night after night walking the halls of Pennhurst. He couldn't get away from the moans, the sorrow… the horror… Then he looked down at the keyboard and clicked 'SEND'.

━━━►((◉))◄━━━

"You ready to relax?"

"Yes, but that was very interesting. I'm sure we could learn a lot more from Abe. He's a total gentleman. I bet there's some amazing memories inside his head."

"His grandson wasn't exactly Mr. Personality" Jim noted.

"Forget it. We won't let him ruin the experience." She

walked into the kitchen and saw Linus and Lucy on their perches.

"I'll get us a glass of wine and we can discuss it more comfortably over here." Jim opened the bottle of Sobon Estate Reserve zinfandel and poured the ruby liquid into the crystal glasses. "You can smell the lushness from here." He took a glass into each hand and wandered past the Remington statue to the couch.

"What would it have been like to be there, with him and Randolph, back in the 1930's?" She gazed up at the starfish, pectin shells and seafaring memorabilia lined along the cherrywood bookcase.

"I wouldn't want to be a patient" he declared, putting his arm around her.

"The sad part is, *nobody* wanted them. That was the only place they could go." She sipped the red wine and kicked off her shoes, closing her eyes for a few moments. Upbeat jazz tunes flowed out of the speakers, soothing them as they discussed the recent encounter. "Long day. I think I'll finish this and go to bed." She kissed his cheek and got up.

"Be there in a minute. I want to check out a few things up in my office." He took the last sip and walked toward the back stairway. In his office, he saw the smiling, white-bearded face, the air of a man who'd lived many lives- cub reporter for the Kansas City Star, war correspondent, world traveler, amateur boxer, award-winning sport fisherman, big game hunter, Pulitzer and Nobel Prize winning author. "I'd be lucky for this adventure to even approach the ones you had..."

At his desk, he turned on the computer and went directly into Outlook to check e-mail. "A lot- 28 just today. This one doesn't look… familiar. Don't recognize that address." He clicked on the note and haunting sounds emanated from the speakers, mysterious at first, then ghastly human voices, the moans accentuated by what flashed across the screen. "Oh, my God… What is… this?!!" He braced himself in the chair, trying to move away, but he couldn't take his eyes from the horrid scene unfolding in front of him. Skulls cracked, blood oozing from the eye sockets… rats gnawing on dead bodies, cockroaches piling over one that still appeared to be alive. Moans again, louder with each second, cries of pain and suffering unlike anything he'd ever seen in a horror film. Then came the sound, electronically muffled, yet clearly a human voice- sharp, terrifying. "Get out and stay away!! Don't ever come back!!!!!!!!!!!!!!" A grey-green skull hovered above the scene… hollow eye sockets set above a toothless smirk… then disappeared as the message faded.

He sat for several seconds not knowing whether to call Natalie or end the nightmare. "DELETE." He was in a cold sweat as he pondered who the message was from- rat231@hotmail.com. The scenes of mayhem played again and again in his mind. "Nobody I know. That's a deranged lunatic!! They went way over the line- criminal even." He shook his head and tried to come to grips with the chilling message- and the psycho who sent it. "If you try to make sense of the irrational, it'll drive *you* insane. I can't tell Natalie. She has enough troubles right now." He turned off the machine and plodded back to the Master Bedroom.

"Done in your office?" She started to fold the two sides of the book together and smiled up at him.

"Overdone" he thought, leaning towards her to get under

the sheet and light Summer pastel-colored blanket. "Yes, just wanted to check a few messages."

"Anything interesting?" She looked back down to begin reading again.

He watched her gentle face, the curl of her pink lips and the delicate nose above them. "Nothing much. I'm tired. Ready to turn in. You can read for a while. I need some rest after a long day. Good night."

"Good night, love. I won't be up long."

He turned onto his right side, away from the light and pulled the blanket over his shoulder, falling into a deep sleep within minutes… The scene was different this time. He entered the old building at night. Darkness dissipated as light streamed through a window from the full moon hanging in the sky behind the huge sycamore tree. The beams were so bright it drove him away, toward the far corner of the dimly lit space- and into the bloodied body of a man, writhing in agony, screaming, his voice echoing off the walls. "God!!!! Get me outta here!!!! Save me…"

Then the room turned completely black, his eyes unable to focus for several seconds. His first visions revealed round, pale grey globes at his feet. "What in the…?" He bent down to touch one and shuddered, backing away from the skull glowing ominously in the darkness. "Oh… ohhh!!! God, please… please…!! Please, will you… stop??!!" He slipped and fell backwards. "What is this?! Good Lord!! There's blood everywhere!" Shaking, he blinked several times before gaining the strength to stand up. "PLEASE!! TAKE ME OUT OF HERE!!!!!!!" He ran into the hallway where ghastly figures emerged, bony fingers outstretched, reaching to grab him, their clothes mere rags, torn sheets bloodied, dangling from their skinless arms. One of them got within inches of him, then plunged, wrapping itself around Jim's waist. Jim screamed out in terror. "HELP ME!!! HELP!!!!!! GET ME OUTTA' HERE!!!" The creature left smudged blood stains on his pants as Jim turned, running through the hall filled with shadows- directly into the chest of a looming beast, the smell of rotting flesh piercing Jim's nose. "AHHHHH!!!!" His voice echoed down the hallway... and throughout the building, bats diving from their perches, flying haphazardly around the ghoulish scene... their high-pitched shrieks agonizing as he searched the darkness, desperate for a way to escape. The last sounds he heard were moans in the distance growing louder... enveloping him, leaving him para-lyzed. He squinted and found himself flat on his back- then felt his legs and arms tied firmly to the bedposts surrounding him. AAHHHHHHHHHHHHH!!!!!!!!!"

He awoke, shaking, unable to move his arms or legs- then glanced over and saw the glowing face of the digital clock dis-playing 2:31 a.m. "Oh, I can't *breathe!!*" He sat up and noticed Natalie was sound asleep as he gasped to catch his breath. "Good. I hope she didn't hear any of this... ohhh... dear Lord... Please... don't ever let that happen to me again..."

Chapter 8

"The century of airplanes has a right to its own music."
                                    --Claude Debussy

The faces on the cat calendar beamed at her from the wall. "Gosh, already June 25th!! Hard to believe this month is almost over." The orange and ochre striped kitty's grin glowed above the dates. "Super cute. At least *you* have something to smile about." She dwelled on the notice which would arrive any day now from the court- what it would say, the charges against her, seeing it official- in writing. "You're a criminal, Natalie! It'll show in black and white. What if some clerk screws up- and posts it to the Internet?!! Or tells their friend over drinks- and they KNOW me??!! Oh, my God!! Natalie, calm down!!!!" She shuffled to the edge of the terrace, leaning on the railing, the irises bowing gently in the light breeze. Her cell phone rang, breaking her brief reverie. "Whoever that is, it better be good news. I don't need any more of the other kind." She ran back inside, reaching into her purse, flipping the phone open by the third ring.

"Hello?"

"Natalie, this is Jack. How are you?"

Air rushed from her lungs, her breathing strained. She inspected the phone, re-verifying the caller. "Oh, fine I guess. How are you?" She waited for a positive inflection, any signal that the next words would be what she wanted to hear.

"Doing well, thank you. It took a bit of effort, but I have some good news. I discussed this with my immediate supervisor- Frank Rawlins, who you've met- and we agreed that your assistance in the antiquities case was essential in getting those mob guys put in jail. I explained to Frank what happened to you at Frick's Lock and although he was shocked, he felt- as I do- that it would be a needless use of the court system to have you charged and tried for such a minor crime. He agreed to contact the local sheriff and pull some strings from here in the Bureau. No guarantees, but I have a good feeling about this." He glanced down at his Day Planner, the next several days all open for lunch.

"Well, that sounds great!! Did he actually get in touch with the sheriff? Will I hear something soon?"

"Again, I can't put this in writing, but when Frank calls in a favor- he usually gets it. Since we have superior jurisdiction in these cases, his word usually is the final one."

"So, what should I do now? I was expecting a notice from the court with the official charges. Are you saying they'll be dropped?"

"Natalie, remember this is all 'off the record'- OK? Nothing guaranteed. I just did my best for you, because... I care for you. I wanted to help you any way I could. Let me just say there's a very high probability that the charges will be dropped and you'll be cleared- completely." He waited several seconds before hearing her voice again.

"Jack, that was *so kind of you*!! Thank you!! How can I ever repay you for this?"

"You could have lunch with me on Thursday. My day is pretty open." He started writing "Lunch- Natalie" as he waited for her confirmation.

She felt the anxiety again, but it was a different feeling. The stress in her chest was a dull ache, not the stabbing pain in the sheriff's chair. "I was afraid this was going to happen!! Now what??" she thought as she held the phone and walked back outside onto the terrace in the afternoon sun. The mixture was spiraling- elation that the charges would be dropped, then the apprehension of pursuing another encounter rimmed with the excitement of a brief fling with a gorgeous man. "Natalie- STOP!!!! This is where it ends. I don't care how good looking he is. Shut this down, right now!!" she resolved before speaking again. "Oh, Jack- that is so nice of you. Jim and I have a pretty full week ahead- in fact, the next few weeks are really booked. I'm sorry. I appreciate the offer. You're such a gentleman and I owe you so much." Soft sunlight warmed her cheeks as she leaned back onto the railing, lifting her face to see the leaves fluttering in the wind.

"Back off, Jack. She's telling you something. Are you listening?" He erased what he'd just penciled onto the page. "Not a problem. I just thought it would be nice to celebrate your... victory... together. Well, I understand. Listen, you should be getting something in the mail in the next few days- good news. If there's anything I can do for you, or if you want to get together for cocktails, give me a call."

"I sure will, Jack. Thanks so much!! Take care." The glow

on her face enhanced what she felt inside. She raised her head and felt the breeze caress her. "Mmm… that's one kiss from a gorgeous man I'll never have, but the fantasy's worth savoring for a while." She turned to go back in through the glass door and saw Jim standing there. "Oh, hi!! Isn't it nice out here?"

"Who was that? I heard you talking on your cell phone." He didn't move from the doorway as she approached him.

Two clouds rolled by quickly overhead, a grey shadow falling across the scene. "Oh… umm… that was… Jack Clark. Remember, the FBI agent on our case?"

"I remember. I know who he is. Why were you talking to him- again?" His voice raised a few decibels as he stepped onto the terrace in front of her.

Natalie froze. "I can't lie to him. I took a vow to be faithful- in all I do" she thought, trembling two feet away as the sun disappeared behind the clouds. "Umm… I… I had to see him- just to ask for his help!! I swear!! It was nothing romantic." Tears appeared as she tried to take his hands in hers, but he resisted and stepped back.

He glared at her, his fists clenching as he continued to back away.

"No, Jim!! I swear to God!! I didn't do anything with him- nothing!! I just wanted his help!! I thought… he could pull a few strings…and get me out of all this…" She started to cry as she tried to prevent him from going inside. "Please!! Believe me!!" She sobbed as he rushed away from her, pushing her hands from his waist.

"Get away from me!! You're having an affair… I never thought this would happen. I trusted you!! You're no better than all the others." He went quickly toward the garage door, grabbing his car keys from the counter.

"NO!! Jim! PLEASE!! Believe me, it was nothing. I just wanted his help!! I swear to you. I never had sex with him. Never even kissed him!! I didn't want to." She ran up to him and wrapped her arms around his waist. "Don't go!! Let me... explain. PLEASE."

He looked into her eyes for some proof of what he'd just heard. "You can always tell by the eyes and the touch" he resolved, remembering the times it wasn't there and he'd been cheated on. Tears were flowing onto her cheeks as he felt the strong grip of her arms around his waist.

"I love you!! You're the only one I'll ever love- or ever want!! Please, Jim- believe me. I'm sorry!! I didn't want you to get jealous, so I didn't tell you about having lunch with him."

"You had *lunch* with him??!! That's why he's calling you all the time." Pushing her hands away, he opened the door and walked outside, veins burning with rage. Each step felt like weighted cement as he tried to rush to the edge of the forest, sending three deer sprinting away into the trees. Hardly able to breathe, his chest was pounding with anger, the strain nearly causing him to collapse. Then he stopped without looking back. He watched as three Canadian geese glided effortlessly above the treetops, their wings outstretched against the blue sky. Leaning down, he picked up a large stone and threw it at the birds, its trajectory far below theirs as it arced back down into the woods. "I should end it here, right NOW!! If she wants to have an affair- the HELL with her!! It's OVER!!!!" Shaking, almost unable to control himself, his left foot nearly tripped over some discarded brush. He saw her in Jack's arms, kissing him- and he had to stop. His forehead was flaming hot, temples throbbing. "I'll show HIM!!" he exclaimed, his fists clenched so tightly, his nails cut into the palms of his hands. Then came the sounds again. He peered up toward the sky and the three geese were circling back directly toward their house, the lead one calling out, it's drawn-out honks soothing. Jim noticed the lead goose looking down right at him, honking again, its voice pleasing, gentle, leading the two others slowly away toward the horizon. His arms relaxed and he started to breathe more easily. "Maybe... a sign of peace?"

He followed their path as they flew toward the edge of the forest, the lead one turning back once more to look at him. The fury was dissipating and he smiled as he felt a slight breeze take the heat from his cheeks. He recalled all the times in his 20's and 30's when the anger had overwhelmed him, but found comfort, far away from the rage... a different place to dwell. "Too many times you've wanted to do something rash, but when you cooled off, you felt... serenity. Don't do it, Jim. Step back... from the cliff." He turned toward the house and started walking, looking up to see her face, her eyes red from crying.

"It's NOT what you think!!! Please, Jim!! I had lunch with him to ask for his help!! That's all- nothing more! I have no interest in him. I just want you. I want YOU, Jim!! No one else!! Please... believe me. Please..." She fell to her knees and sobbed, her face toward the grass, reaching to clutch his hand.

He observed the lovely strawberry blonde hair around her shoulders and felt the soft touch of her fingers. He wanted to leave- as he'd trusted his instincts so many times before, but a different feeling flowed into him as he stood there, watching her curled at his feet, crying. "You didn't do ANYTHING??!!"

"I swear!! Nothing. I promise you. I just wanted his help!!

That's all." She raised her head as she felt his arms around her.

"You know, when you've been lied to as many times as I have, you start to doubt everyone- even yourself." The battle was still raging inside, torn between rationality and sheer emotion as he contemplated all the women who'd lied through their teeth, smiling at him. The gorgeous ones... the 'trophy' dates... "Guess it comes with the territory, Jim boy. You play on the wild side, you get burned, just like the rest of 'em." Then it came back to him- the day he proposed, overlooking the ocean at sunrise, the rays bathing them both in a sacred light. He'd wanted now to forget it, but couldn't, fighting as he did, failing to suppress the intensity he'd felt in that instant and ever since that day. Starting to smile, he pulled her toward him and felt her hands around his waist. "So, tell me- why should I believe you?" His eyes were locked on hers, then he glanced briefly down at the lovely malachite pendant around her neck he'd given her as a special Valentine's Day present years before.

"Because you're the only man I'll ever love- and ever want to be with. He means *nothing* to me!! I swear- we didn't do ANYTHING!! I just wanted some help, that's all. I didn't want to be a criminal with a record for the rest of my life. I thought, in some way- he could fix it. Nothing more." She looked up at him as the last tear ran down her cheek.

He stood motionless for what seemed like an eternity. The lies of the past were behind him and he wanted to feel the warmth of her grasp, her arms around his waist pulling him firmly toward her. "I think... I'll need some... reassuring. I've been through this before, so it'll take a bit of effort to get me on solid ground again."

She pulled his face toward hers. "You'll get much more

than that." She pressed her lips against his, holding them there for several seconds, her arms firm around his back. "I think I have some 'making up' to do. I'm so sorry I wasn't totally honest with you, but *I promise-* I always will be." She kissed him so strongly, he almost fell over.

"Wow!! I haven't felt that since our first date."

"We didn't kiss on our first date, although you tried."

"The second date made up for it." He smiled for several seconds, putting his left arm around her as they stepped slowly toward the lower patio. The last cardinal flew away from the bird feeder as they approached, replaced by two humming-birds, silvery green and blue, calmly hovering in front of them near a thicket of sage as they neared the garden.

"I'll get the mail." She wiped the last tear away as she strode toward the end of the driveway. "Hope there's some good news." She opened the black metal door and pulled the mass of envelopes from inside. "Kaolin Mushroom Farms must have fertilized again" she thought, wrinkling her nose as she flipped through the items in her hands on the way back to the house. "National Geographic and Islands... Uh-oh- this looks... official- for ME." The tension from the sheriff's chair gripped her chest again, a feeling she'd tried to forget since she talked with Jack. "I have to open this."

She placed the rest of the pile down on the counter and ripped the envelope slowly edge to edge. Breathing in deeply, she opened the letter. "Criminal Court... official proceedings against you..." She stopped breathing, her arms stiffened to lifeless stumps as she read down on the page. 'It is the decision of the sheriff's department of Spring Lake, after careful deliberation of your case, to drop any previously noted charges against you.' "YES!!!!" She saw the sunlight again, felt it pulling her outside. "God- THANK YOU!!!! Woo-hoooo!!!" She ran back out onto the terrace and scanned the sky, smiling as two yellow finches came toward her at the bird feeder. "Hey, Ray Ban!! Haven't seen you in a while. Welcome home!!" She laughed as the two started pecking hard at the food cylinder, lost in their feast. "Enjoy, guys. I've got something to celebrate, too. I got a second chance." She held the letter in front of her again to make sure she hadn't misread any of the words along the page. 'You will not have to appear in court. This case is officially closed as of June 30th, 2010. If you have any questions, you may contact this department at the number and address listed below'.

Pressing the page to her chest, she closed her eyes, elated... the same feeling she had years ago, dancing in her fathers' arms... The calm enveloped her, stress dissolving from her hands. "Thank you, Jack. I hope you'll understand. I won't call... I can't- but I want you to feel this, right now. A genuine, heartfelt thank you for all you've done for me. You've given me my life back." She smiled as she went inside and saw Jim walking toward the table.

"Anything interesting in the mail?"

"I have some good news- for us." She held the letter out in front of him, putting her right hand on his shoulder as he read.

"Well, that IS good news. I guess he came through after all." He glanced at his palms, where his nails had dug into his hands. The redness was gone.

"Don't worry, I'm NOT going to contact him... ever. If he calls me again, I'll simply thank him. That's it. Nothing more.

Please don't have those thoughts about something going on…
There isn't. There NEVER will be."

"I believe you." The words he'd wanted to say and feel permeated his chest, his hands at rest, shoulders relaxed. He gazed
at the lines on the letter again, then down at the Smithsonian
Magazine on the table. "Did you see this latest issue? They have
an around the world trip- goes to Machu Picchu, Easter Island,
the Galapagos Islands, Stonehenge, the Great Barrier Reef- even
the Taj Mahal and Angkor Wat." He saw the calming flecks of
green again in her eyes as he rose. "I can't think of anyone I'd
rather be with on an around-the-world trip than you."

She stood on her toes to kiss him, wrapping her arms
around his neck. "Sounds like a good idea to me. What got
you started planning that trip?"

"I found a new place… a bit more serene. I needed it. A lot
nicer than where I'd been before…" He kissed her and held her
tightly against his chest. "All those places should be fascinating.
We've talked about a worldwide trip, but never planned one.
I've also wanted to do more exploring ever since we met Abe.
For 91- he's so full of energy! We'd be blessed to have half his
vigor when we're that age." He thought back to their visit…
his voice… 'accentuate the positive…', his grin so infectious.
"Some of the things he said were intriguing, like Randolph raging on about the Wright Brothers. I'm going to check into that
story. I've always wanted to go to Kitty Hawk, though seven
months out of the year it's just too hot."

"I don't mind it hot. Anything under 90 degrees is fine
with me."

"Well, from May through October it's pretty torrid there.
We'd have to go around November… or maybe wait until next

Spring. I'm still going to check that out. I think I have a few books on the history of flight in my library."

"Go to it. Maybe we can have an early evening snack after you've done some reading. I'll be in the garden weeding…"

———◦《◎》◦———

Richie drove with his hands clenched tightly around the steering wheel to his favorite spot to brood, taking the back roads to Pennhurst, grinning as he saw the mangled stumps of once vibrant trees scattered, lying dead along the edge of the blacktop. "I don't believe anything they say in the papers… but if this is true, somebody's got hell to pay…" He slammed on his brakes as he saw the line of cars entering the gravel road into the complex toward the Administration Building. Getting out, he ran up and flagged the next car to slow down, standing in the middle of the blacktop as the truck stopped.

"Hey- what the hell are you doin'??!!"

"What are *you* guys doin'? Isn't this place supposed to be closed?"

"Read the newspapers- they're gonna' open it up again- for a freak show!! Should be good…"

"Whuddya' mean?"

"New owner's gonna' open it up for Halloween. Ya know- all the horror and shit…like it was back in the day… People gettin' tortured… you know the story…"

Richie's veins were on fire as he held back from running up to the window and pulling him out of the truck. "So it's true- this is gonna' be a Halloween horror exhibit?"

"Sure is- and they pay *pretty good!!* I'm gettin' 25 bucks an hour for this crap!! Not bad for scarin' people… Hey- get outta' the way… I need to drive in there…"

Richie stood fuming as the truck passed, the sun starting to go down, casting a shadow over him and his car. "They're gonna' pay…they'll all pay… I'll get 'em…" He jumped into the car and floored it as the wheels slipped on the edge of a pile of leaves leading toward the center of the complex. He glanced back, making sure the gun rack was still mounted as he came to a stop in front of the far edge of the development. Getting out, he checked to see there were no workers along the landscape. "Nobody around… too bad I can't nail anyone… BASTARDS!!" He grabbed the rifle and walked slowly toward the antiquated building, overgrown with vines. "Here's something for your FREAK SHOW!!" Three shots rang out, shattering two windows near the top of the structure, putting a deep bullet hole in the crumbling shutter nearby. "Good one!! Now let's hit somethin' that'll make a difference…" He scanned the horizon- and saw it. A silver truck painted with a large decal on its side. 'PENNHURST SECURITY'. He lowered the barrel in line with his target and saw the driver's side window in the center of the sight. "Too bad nobody's sittin' there I can take out…" The window shattered, releasing a crushing alarm which pierced the enveloping twilight. "Oh, SHIT!! Gotta' get outta here…" He ran back to his car and yanked the door open just as he heard a siren coming in the distance…

———◉———

Jim headed up the back stairs to his library and scanned the bookshelves for volumes related to the topic. "There's one and … here's another." Strolling to his desk he clicked on the computer. "A quick scan on-line could save me a lot of searching elsewhere. Kitty Hawk... Wright Brothers... manned flight." He perused the screen. "My God- over 4,000 entries. It'll take me forever to go through the first five pages! Well, I've got to start somewhere, might as well have at it." He read each story slowly, then one caught his attention. 'Henry Ford Museum, Greenfield Village- Wright Brothers shop.' "What is that?" He clicked and read through the nearly 12 pages quickly, moving faster as he felt the excitement building. "Henry Ford was a huge history buff!! Built a whole museum to cover the history of business and technology in America. Now that's... interesting. Even took their bicycle shop- piece by piece- and re-built it at the museum- along with Edison's lab from Menlo Park!! I can't believe this!! Now that would be a great place to do some... exploring." He read the last page, then headed downstairs.

"Hey Natalie, did you know that outside Detroit there's a place that has the story of America, the Wright Brothers and Thomas Edison- all laid out in a museum?"

"Oh, sure. It's called Greenfield Village. I went there years ago when I lived in Bloomfield Hills. Pretty neat place."

"I think we should go. Besides, we'd told Dianne that we wanted to come for a visit. Why don't we make it a trip to spend time with her and check out Greenfield Village? We could probably spend several days exploring all the exhibits. They even give a tour of the nearby Ford plant. It would be fun!!"

"I'm always up for an adventure. I'll check with Dianne and make flight reservations."

He opened the first book he'd grabbed from his library. 'The Wright Brothers- A Biography' by Fred G. Kelly. The dedication page caught his attention. 'To the Brave Flyers of the United Nations Fighting All Over the World for Humanity and Decency Against the Forces of Barbarism.' Glancing at the adjacent page, the small print came into view: first printing, 1943. "The world was at war, one that shook the foundations of society as the globe was engulfed in a desperate struggle with Hitler, Mussolini and Tojo. We almost lost. The air war and the atomic bomb dropped from a B-29 ended that one and saved us from tyranny. Thank you Wilbur and Orville for your dedication and perseverance." He started reading and got through the first ten pages quickly. "Their father was a Bishop!! Must have kept them in line. He gave them a toy helicopter made by the Frenchman Alphonse Pinaud, who invented miniature versions of flying machines- and it captured their attention. That looks like the start of something big..."

Holding the book, he entered the foyer. "Hey, did you know the Wright Brothers got their start from a toy helicopter?"

"Really? Didn't know helicopters existed before airplanes. We can get a decent round-trip fare to Detroit for under $250. Not bad. I'll book it after I talk to Dianne."

"We'll be benefiting from the Wright Brothers' ingenuity going to see your sister and checking out Henry Ford's monument to them. Imagine what they'd think of the Space Shuttle, which is about to take its last voyage."

"Another chapter in the history of invention. Any other tidbits to share from your reading?"

"Well, from a very early age Wilbur and Orville apparently were fascinated with anything mechanical. Even though famous engineers and scientists had been working for many years to build an airplane- they'd all failed. Some, like Lilienthal in Germany and Pilcher in England, had been killed trying to fly some of the early gliders. A guy named Maxim spent $100,000- a hell of a lot of money back then- and gave up. The French government supported various flight experiments including something called the 'Ader machine', but finally called it quits. So the Wright Brothers, without even a high school diploma, were against heavy odds. Strangely enough, their sister Katherine did graduate from Oberlin College, a rarity back then, but the lads were too engrossed with their research on flight to want to take time off to get an 'official' education."

"Well, most people didn't go to college back then. My mother never did."

"Neither did mine. It was 'expected' that girls would pursue some kind of a trade or become secretaries, legal assistants. I'm a huge proponent of higher education, but some of the most successful people in America never got a diploma. Bill Gates was a Harvard drop-out. Not bad for a man who would later become the richest person in the world through Microsoft."

"Wouldn't these guys have been successful at whatever they pursued? I mean, they all seem to have had exceptional talent, immense curiosity and a strong drive to succeed."

"A diploma may be the formal 'stamp of approval', but it never takes the place of personal initiative and hard work. Calvin Coolidge used to say it all the time... 'Perseverance and determination are omnipotent'. Wonder what the topic will be for the next set of visionaries. The airplane, the automobile, the Space Shuttle- then what? Will we see new modes of transportation allowing us to travel in ways we've never dreamed of?"

"What is unimaginable today will be commonplace tomorrow."

"The most important discoveries will come from a deeper understanding of the capabilities of the mind itself. Einstein said he felt he only used 10% of his intellect. Now that's Einstein. Where does that leave you and me??!! We're flying pretty low to the ground…"

She laughed and shook her head. "The brain is an amazing thing– and we've only scratched the surface in our understanding of how it works."

"Someday, thought itself will literally take us places, allow us to see in new ways that we weren't aware of. A hundred years from now, brain waves will actually transport you to a different place, physically."

"Beam me up, Scotty. What are you looking at?"

"Maybe our skies will be filled with cars as they rise from garages into the 'high speed commuter lane' to work. Better yet, our minds will allow us to accomplish *everything* from home, in the comfort of our den. There will be no need to commute."

"We have that today, or perhaps you didn't notice. It's called the Internet. Lots of people work from home now." They sat down to eat as the sky darkened outside.

"No. I mean EVERYTHING we do. The next 'evolution' of technology will make the last one look archaic by comparison. Moore's Law- technology doubles its capabilities and capacity every 18 months." He finished eating and started taking the plates to the dishwasher. "I'm heading upstairs for an early night. Ready?"

"Hold on, Mr. Wizard. Just finishing up here and I want to get through reading 'Weird Pennsylvania'. You can have it after I'm done." She put her plate down, following him up the stairway.

"I'll be asleep in ten minutes. Wake me for any good parts before you check out for the night." Opening his book, he saw the famous photograph from December 17, 1903- Orville flying in the first man-made, power-driven, heavier than air device successfully over the dunes at Kill Devil Hills, on the beach in South Carolina. Wilbur is standing off to the side after holding the right wing to prevent it from flipping over and his younger brother is lying flat on his stomach, facing forward as he achieved a breakthrough that changed the course of history. "I wonder what was going through their minds at that very moment... if they realized they had turned the world on a new course." He was there... on the beach... the wind blowing 20 miles per hour... sand spraying up into his face, running behind the contraption he was sure would collapse at any moment... Then he saw Natalie was already asleep. "Eight minutes. Thought I was the lightweight." He put his book down on the nightstand, getting up out of bed to turn out her light. "I'll be out soon, too." Climbing back in bed, he flipped forward and saw the images of Huffman Pasture outside Dayton, Ohio where they conducted flight tests and the patent office certificate dated May 22, 1906 for their 'flying machine'. "Time to hit the hay." He drifted off, recalling the photo of the first flight again, sharper than before, etched in his mind, the wind on his face...

"Ohhh... NO!! Get away from me!!!!.....Ahhh!!!! Oh, my God- HELP!!!!! Help me!!!!" Natalie was shaking as she tried to get up, the images in front of her terrifying. "STOP!!!!!!!!!" She sat up abruptly, almost falling off the side of the bed. Looking around, she noticed Jim had awoken and started to get up.

"What... happened? Are you all right?" He rubbed his eyes

and watched as she leaned back against the baseboard, eyes wide open with fear.

"I don't know. I had a… horrible nightmare."

"The usual? You're back at your old job, working for free and fighting with your boss?"

"No, this was terrible. It was ghastly!! I felt like I was under a spell. I was… in a dark room… and saw skulls lying on the floor… blood everywhere…then the scene changed to some kind of a dungeon. Creatures were coming up to me, grabbing me. Oh, Jim- it was horrible!! I tried to get away, but couldn't!! Felt like I was tied down… couldn't move my legs. That's when I screamed. Lord, it was unbelievable!!"

Jim looked down at the blanket around his waist and felt the blood pulsing in his arms. He started sweating, breathing harder and shook his head to snap out of it.

"What's wrong- are *you* alright?" She touched his hand under the covers.

"Natalie, I had that *same dream* just a few days ago. The way you described it- the skulls, blood, not being able to move!!"

"Are you serious? The same… dream? That's very strange…"

"I can't explain it, but I swear to you, that was my dream- almost exactly as you said." He rubbed his eyes again. "Somehow, we both experienced something very shocking. Maybe it was realization that Barney Frank might be running the country someday."

She pushed him, then became serious again as she leaned against the headboard. "I saw that strange-looking skull at Frick's Lock… do you think they're related?"

"I don't know, but I promise you we'll find out- even if we have to do some investigating around there on our own…"

Chapter 9

"I do not think there is any thrill that can go through the human heart like that felt by the inventor as he sees some creation of the brain unfolding to success."

--Nikola Tesla

Stella jumped onto the bed and licked her face again in the early morning light. "Oh, you bugger!!" Sue pushed the furry tabby away. "That's enough. I'm clean now." She got up and put on her bathrobe. "Looks like a nice day- good for gardening." She peered out the small window above the kitty portal. "You should be outside!! Go!!" Nudging Stella out the door, she watched her pad her way toward the banks of the Brandywine. "Ready for a cup of tea." She was startled by the sound of the phone.

"Are you up yet??" Natalie chuckled as she glanced out across the hillside to the Civil War-era stone barn almost hidden by the lush foliage.

"Yes. Stella thought I needed a facial, so she licked me awake. What's up?"

"I have a lot to talk about!! Why don't you come over and

we'll go out for breakfast at the chicken?"

"Oh, don't tell me… You talked with that sexy FBI agent!!"

"Yes… and it turned out pretty well. In fact- great. He got the charges dropped!!"

"I knew it!! Holy crap, you have to tell me all about it over breakfast."

"How soon can you be here?" She glanced at the walnut rimmed clock hanging next to the Cunard White Star poster at the edge of the breakfast room.

"I just have to find my sandals. I should be over in 20 minutes."

"You may want to put some clothes on. Don't want to scare the kitties. See you soon." She turned and saw Frankie and Francis parading slowly toward her. "Well, it's time you bums woke up!! Want to go out??" As she said the last word, their ears perked up and they followed her to the glass sliding doors along the terrace. "Go ahead… it's nice outside. Go climb a tree, but no fights with Dadcat- he's a bruiser."

"Are they all out?"

"No, Mom's sleeping in her favorite spot. She'll get up soon. Sue's coming over- we can all go to the chicken for breakfast."

"The chicken?"

"You know, the Sunrise Café in Kennett. They have that giant chicken out front. Sitting outside at a table will be nice." She went around him toward the staircase. "I'm getting dressed."

"It's a wrought iron rooster. Must be a 'girl thing'. I'll be up in a minute. Just wanted to check the headlines in the Daily Local. Greece is about to go under and it could take half of Europe with it."

"Serious? More financial trouble?"

"Yep. Decades of spending on failed welfare projects and overpaying their public workers is coming home right now- and they won't be the last country to feel the heat. They're having riots in the streets there because the government wants to raise the retirement age from *55 to 57*?!! Interesting thing is, some of their finance guys knew it wouldn't work all along. They just didn't want to rock the boat. Now the boat's taking on water- and there aren't enough people to bail."

"What do you think will happen?"

"Big European Union players like Germany will throw them a lifeline, temporarily- so they'll have to make drastic changes or default on their debt. If that happens, they become like Third World countries- no one will trust them anymore."

"What some states here are experiencing- like California."

"California is at the head of the line. The eighth largest economy in the world could go under- and take the rest of us with them."

"They won't let that happen!"

"It's happening now. California is running a $20 billion deficit. With overregulation and ridiculous rules for setting up a business- you have a recipe for disaster. It's sad that such a beautiful state is in a huge mess."

"Did you like living there?" She saw him slowly start to smile.

"Loved it… Riding my bike around Mission Bay… The Hotel del Coronado for brunch on Sunday. Croce's down in the Gaslamp… the Old Town Mexican Café, the women making fresh tortillas on the grille right in front of you. I miss those things…"

She heard the car in the driveway. "That's Sue. I'll be dressed in two minutes."

He saw the door open. "Hi Sue!!"

"Hello there. Where's Natalie?"

"Upstairs getting dressed. I was reviewing the global economy with her. Nothing too serious. Just a few minor calamities. I have to get changed real quick. Feel free to grab a cup of tea-the water's already boiling."

"Do you have Lipton? It's my favorite. I almost had a cup made when she called."

"We have plenty of Lipton. I prefer Earl Grey. Tea bags are in the pantry. Make yourself at home."

"Thanks!!" She poured the steaming water into the cup while dipping the bag slowly down several times. Moving toward the birdcage, she noticed Linus and Lucy backing to the rear of their perch. "Hi gang! Hope you're enjoying the day."

"Hey Sue!! Grab your tea. I have a lot to tell you" Natalie announced.

"Oh, I can't wait!!" She took the cup and sat across from her at the table. "Let me guess. You're not a criminal anymore."

"Exactly! I got a letter clearing me. Charges dropped."

"GREAT!! Did you get me a date?" Sue took her first sip as Jim neared the table.

"Nope… I forgot. Big news is- no trial. I'm so relieved. We also made plans to visit Dianne. Going to spend some time with her and then hit Greenfield Village."

"Been there. The place is pretty neat."

"Should be fun. The whole complex is dedicated to the history of America and they have exhibits on some of the most important inventors- Edison, the Wright Brothers. I took dad there once and he loved it."

"Wish I could go with you!!"

"Actually, that's where you come in. Can you stop over and take care of the ark? We need you to check in every two days to feed the clan- kitties, fish and birds. Make sure they don't have any wild parties."

"I know the drill. Just bring me back something interesting."

"You bet. Let's go to the Sunrise before it gets too late…"

————))•((————

"The pilot has announced preparations for our descent into Detroit. Please put your tray tables up, turn off all electronic devices, make sure your seat belts are fastened and bring your seats to their vertical positions. We should be on the ground in about 15 minutes."

"I wish they wouldn't say 'On the ground'. You can *crash* and be on the ground. How about 'We'll be landing…'"

Jim glanced across the aisle to the young Asian man in his 20's with his girlfriend- and the game he'd been playing on the notebook computer for the last two hours. "Clink!!… Clink!!" Every time he got the correct answer, the game simulated two glasses clinking together in a toast. It was driving Jim nuts. "At least I won't have to listen to that any more."

"Hush. He may have heard you!!" Natalie took his arm and squeezed it gently.

"I don't know how intelligent people can be enthralled with these mindless electronic gadgets. Can't they just enjoy relaxing with a good book?"

"They're not mindless. Some of the games they have now

are extremely interesting- and challenging. Sue gave me one to play at home and I love it. It's not easy- in fact, it gets me stumped most of the time, but it's really fun to play and helps stave off Alzheimer's."

"I enjoy simple pleasures. A good book. A sunset."

"Bookstores may be on their way out. Did you hear the news about Borders?"

"Very sad. Bad sign for the book business. Everything's going electronic. Holding a book in your hands is becoming a thing of the past."

"Not really. They have Kindle and several options for E-books now. Look, people between 15 and 35 are more comfortable with a laptop and a cell phone to get information. Books have just moved into a new medium. No more printing all those pages, killing all those trees."

"Gutenberg would not be pleased. It's a great feeling, holding a leather-bound, hardcover book in your hands, lying on the couch. They'll always be on the shelves in my library."

"Welcome to the 21st century. A lot of things are changing, but technology is taking us to places we'd never been before." She heard the last 'Clink!!' and noticed the Asian man closing his computer, putting it into the case below his knees.

"Ladies and gentlemen, we'll be landing in a few minutes. Tray tables up and seats belts fastened…"

Jim pulled the silver Lincoln Town Car up the small side street. "These are a bit more expensive, but worth it. Ford makes great cars. We'll be doing a fair amount of driving on this trip.

Lincolns are spacious and really comfortable. Besides, I like the Moon Roof."

"They're called Sun Roofs."

"To me, they're Moon Roofs. I enjoy opening it up at night and seeing a full moon overhead…"

"Well, its only 10:30 in the morning, so you won't be seeing a full moon anytime soon."

"Actually, tonight *will* be a full moon. Good for adventures."

"… and werewolves." The car came to a stop and they got out. Walking up the three wooden steps to the house, she tapped gently on the white painted door and waited.

"Nice big boulder in the yard. Must weigh a ton." He turned as the door opened.

"Hello!! How are you, Dianne?" Natalie gave her a firm hug.

"Great. Good to see you both! I'm so glad you could visit. Come on in." She walked past Cloe, who was lying comfortably against the stuffed snowman she'd gotten months before as a Christmas present.

"Hi Cloe!! How are you, little kitty??" Natalie bent down to pet her, just barely touching the fur at the edges of her paws, getting a swat in return. "She's getting up there. How old is she?"

"Almost 19. Slowing down quite a bit. Old age- it's affecting all of us." Dianne groaned lightly as she knelt down to pet the cat, keeping her distance. "She's still pretty finicky- doesn't like to be touched too much. Just a gentle rub- that's enough." Dianne stood up. "Can I get you two something to drink? Coffee? Iced tea? A Martini?"

Jim laughed. "It's five o'clock somewhere, but I'll take an

iced tea. Cloe looks like she's in good spirits. She didn't even hiss at me when I got near her. My sister Paula who lives in Naperville, outside Chicago, had a Siamese cat named Garfield for almost 20 years. She and my brother-in-law also had a Bassett hound named Toby who lived for an exceptional 14 years. They were like their children- and devastated when Garfield died. She was so close to the cat, said they had a special bond. Even claims she occasionally sees the cat walking around the house to this day... kind of eerie."

"Sounds like 'Pet Sematary'!!"

"She's a totally rational person, but swears the cat sometimes comes for a visit... strolling around the living room. I believe her. If pets are in your life for that long, they merge with your soul. Garfield became part of her."

"Well, Cloe is part of me, too. I can't think about not having her." She glanced down at the auburn fur around the edges of Cloe's face, the grey whiskers brushing against the edge of the snowman as she lay there. "You'll always be with me, Cloe."

"Frankie and Francis are our kids now. Who would have thought feral wildcats would make such wonderful pets? Momcat- she was ferocious. Wouldn't let anyone near her. She's even calmed down, but still ornery now and then." Natalie put her fingers to the edge of Cloe's paw, touching her fur gently.

"They adopted us. They're more indoor than outdoor cats. Now they run the place. Frankie's got her own library. Francis is playing my Brubeck records." Jim put his hand onto Cloe's head, her eyes indicating he should stop right there.

"Do they all get along?" Dianne set the two iced teas down on the table.

"Mostly, but Momcat takes a swipe at them and us

occasionally. Must be in-bred from her years in the wild, having to fight off predators. She's mellowed enough where she lets Jim pick her up without shredding his arm."

"Well, let's all go out back to the terrace. I built a new trellis and portico I want you to see." She led them through the kitchen to the back door, which opened onto a lovely stone patio shaded by solid oak beams, flowering vines interweaved along their edges providing a gentle break from the sunlight.

"Very nice!! I could see myself relaxing out here every afternoon." Natalie sat down and took a sip of tea.

"Your poppies are in full bloom. I'm going over to get a few shots- the light is perfect." Jim meandered past the multi-colored pots, hand painted by Dianne, towards the back of the yard, where dozens of gold, ruby and peach-colored poppies swayed, faces pointed into the sun. "They look happy out here." He took several photos in succession, angled to catch the edges of the petals in perspective, sunlight revealing their translucence.

"We had a nasty Winter. It was bitterly cold for so long- all the flowers are celebrating. So, do you folks have any specific plans for the next few days?" Dianne sipped her drink as she put her feet up onto the small buff-colored wicker ottoman.

"We just wanted to spend some time re-charging… this is perfect for today. Plan to go to Greenfield Village tomorrow. So much to see there. We could probably spend all week." Natalie watched as Jim knelt in front of each stalk, catching the light from several different angles.

"I haven't been there in a few years, but it would be interesting to go back. Didn't you take dad there years ago?"

"Yes- he loved the place! Being an engineer, he was in

his element poking around Edison's lab, the Wright Brothers shop. I could sense his mind deconstructing each item- how he would have built it, what he would've changed. We had to remind him three times the place was closing before he agreed to leave!! That was a great day with him."

"When I was at Bucknell, one of my professors had us read 'Zen and the Art of Motorcycle Maintenance'- a story about a man and his son who take a cross-country motorcycle trip and find themselves becoming 'one' with their machines. It was written at a time when many people were rebelling against the intrusion of technology in our lives. I loved it."

"Well, tomorrow we'll all go to Greenfield Village to see Henry Ford's vision. I think they open around 9, so we can get an early breakfast and head over there." Dianne leaned forward to see Jim's camera as he held it in front of her to view the shots on replay. "Those look superb."

"Used my trusted, old Pentax SRT 101 for almost 30 years, but most of those photos don't come close to the ones I get from this digital. We can also enhance them manually on the computer. It's light years ahead of what I used to be able to do."

"See, you're embracing technology. You finally admitted that your old camera doesn't hold a candle to the new gadgets." Natalie winked at Dianne as she took another sip from the glass, beads of condensation falling down the sides.

"Had to experiment a few dozen times before I liked it. I was in the dark. Hey- Edison worked by candlelight and kerosene lamps starting out. After several years and over 1,000 tries, he found the perfect filament. It just took me a while to come around."

"Why don't we continue this conversation over lunch?

There's a cute little place in downtown Birmingham. Nice outdoor patio, too. If we leave soon, we can get a good spot."

———————⋙《◉》⋘———————

The bar at the Devon Seafood Grille on Rittenhouse Square was starting to fill up with the early Happy Hour crowd, even though it was only just past 5:00 p.m. Jack was working on his second Tanqueray and tonic, keeping Harry busy in conversation.

"You know, I've been pretty lucky. I've met a lot of girls- dated some gorgeous ones... but there's one I just can't figure out. I mean, I know she likes me. I can see it in her eyes, but she's keeping her distance."

"They all do that, Jack. It's part of the game." Harry dried off two more mugs and put them in the line on the counter behind the bar.

"Yeah, but this one's different."

"That's your first mistake- thinkin' the game has changed- just for you. It hasn't. Women, especially good lookin' ones, do it all the time. They know the farther away they push you, the more you want 'em. It's how they get what they want."

"Don't worry, I won't get played. I've dated some pretty hot babes- 10's. Didn't have any problem getting them to come my way." He took a long sip, watching the ice cubes swirl back to the bottom of the heavy crystal tumbler.

"OK. You're a handsome guy. Doesn't matter! Look, before I was married, I dated a lot of women- and yeah, some real lookers, too. Even got a proposal from one!! She told me how much her father was worth and said 'If you play your cards right, you'll come into a lot of money some day'- like she was tryin' to buy me."

"What happened?" He finished the drink and pushed the glass forward toward Harry, standing at the register.

"That was our last date. I'm not for sale- I don't care how much money they have. Another one?"

"Yep. I hope she was at least good lookin'!!" Jack held a wide grin as he waited.

"She was... let's see, on a scale from 1 to 10, she was about a 6 1/2... maybe a 7. Her best features 'preceded her'. That part was a 9."

Jack laughed and pulled the now filled glass toward him. "Know the territory. Dated one girl in Denver- she had some mountainous terrain. Man, was she great to watch in aerobics class!! Then she tells me- *after* we were in the sack- she was in love with *some cop* who was livin' in Dallas!!" His words were becoming more slurred and he took a long sip before looking back at Harry.

"So, what did you say?"

"Waiter, check please!!"

Harry let out a deep laugh as he put two wine glasses in the metal framed cabinet. "That's one nice rack I'd have to pass on, too!!"

"Hey- in your *professional* opinion, what's the best vodka on the market? I say Ketel One, but some of my buddies say it's Belvedere or Grey Goose."

"They tell me Grey Goose is the best, but it doesn't matter. I can't afford any of 'em. That stuff's for the high rollers- or maybe me, when I win the Pick Six!!" He shrugged as he placed three more wine glasses in the cabinet, the 'clink' barely audible.

Jack let out a long laugh, then felt his head starting to droop. He shook himself and sat up straight, glancing over to see two couples approaching the far end of the bar. The room was starting to move slowly around him, but he took another sip. "I just can't get this one outta' my head!! Met her on one of my cases. Too bad… she's married."

"That's not a diamond you want to play baseball in. Move on."

"I can't!! You're right… now I want her even *more*… and I won't let up until I get her!!" He took a long sip and felt the buzz down into his chest.

"What's this babe's name, anyhow?" Harry gazed over at the two couples and nodded. "Be with ya' in a second."

"Natalie… Ohhh… Natalie… where *are* you tonight??" His head was starting to spin and he put both hands on the bar in front of him. "Ooohh… maybe my last one" he thought as he tried to focus on the other people coming up to the bar.

"Natalie, huh? Nice name. I still say leave it alone. Hey, I gotta' serve those people down at the other end. You want another one?"

"No, I'm done. I gotcha' covered." He took out two $20 bills and put them next to the small bowl of peanuts sitting in front of him. "That's way more than enough. Extra payment for the… sagely advice." He downed the last of the gin and slammed the tumbler on the bar, drawing the attention of two attractive women in their late 20's sitting at the small table across from him. "Sorry, ladies. Have a good evening!!" Jack slid off the black leather barstool and slowly plodded toward the door.

"Hey, Jack!! Thanks for comin' in!! You take care."

"Thanks, Harry." He pushed the heavy door open and lumbered toward his car.

Harry watched him through the side window as Jack reached the silver Porsche 911 Carrera. "Well, he doesn't live far from here. Should get home OK." He scanned the length of the bar and saw a few new arrivals waiting for drinks. "Can I help you?"

Frank Rawlins pulled the maroon Ford Taurus into the lot and came to a stop. "Well, it's been a tough week. I deserve a quick one before I head home." Walking through the doorway, he waved. "Hey, Harry- how are you??" Frank took one of the stools at the far end of the bar.

"Good. Busy tonight. One of your guys was just here."

"Who was that?" He watched as the last seat was taken by a pretty woman in a business suit and Frank nodded as she gazed up at him for approval.

"Your guy, Jack. Just missed him. What'll it be?"

He thought for a few seconds. "Ketel One martini- very dry. Just put the vermouth bottle nearby."

Harry laughed and started making the drink. "Good choice. Yeah, Jack was sittin' right there. Talkin' about some hard to get babe."

"Well, he's a single, good looking guy, young, having some fun. Comes with the territory." Frank reached forward as the glass was put in front of him.

"Sure, but he's all tied up in knots over this one."

Frank took a long sip, rummaging in his pocket, feeling for the vibrating cell phone. "Sounds like he was a little shook up over it." He noted the number, then turned it off.

"Oh, yeah. Couldn't stop talkin' about her... Some

older woman he knows from one of the cases you guys solve… Married, no less… named Natalie."

Frank's eyes opened wider as he heard the words. "Natalie… no- can't be. I only know one Natalie from our cases… Jim Peterson's wife." He took a long gulp and held the tumbler in front of his face for several seconds. "Did he say her last name?"

"Nope. Just Natalie… but he's got his eyes on her, big time. She won't give him the time of day, so he wants her even more… you know the routine."

"I do." He thought about the words he wanted to say to the woman 15 years ago, hoping she'd become his wife. He could still see her face- the freckles, rimmed with blonde hair, falling to her shoulders, her contagious smile. "I wonder… could it be- Natalie Peterson?" he pondered. "Well, Natalie is a common a name… but… I can't recall any other women named Natalie we've had a case with in over… three years." He thought about his deepening friendship with Jim since last year, sharing insights about their travels out West, their lives. Taking a long sip, the pleasant burn of the vodka gave him a tingling sensation as it made its way down. "If it's her, he's do-ing recon in some dangerous territory. I should look into it" he decided as he watched Harry serving two women standing about 15 feet away. Frank put a $10 bill on the counter and hopped off the stool. "Harry, thanks. Have a good night."

"You too, Frank!!"

Frank acknowledged the two women as he passed. "I hope you're both having a pleasant evening," giving them a wide grin as he nodded his head, smelling their pleasant perfume waft through the air.

"Oh, thanks. Yes, we are!!" They both giggled, then meandered toward the first open table in the corner.

"Women... the sexier the smile... the more trouble I get into. Just keep your head down and your nose clean..." Harry thought as he noticed the form-fitting dresses around their voluptuous curves. He picked up two more glasses to clean...

⟞⟞⟞•⟨()⟩•⟝⟝⟝

Dianne and Natalie got into the Town Car as they gazed down the street of 1960's-era single homes with their small manicured front yards and wooden porches. "Seems like a nice, quiet neighborhood."

"It is. Been here for 15 years. Comfortable- just my style." Dianne fastened the seat belt as Natalie closed her door.

"I read that Henry Ford started Greenfield Village in 1929- right in time for the stock market crash. Wonder if he had second thoughts about spending all that money." A line of neatly trimmed azalea bushes guided them out onto the main street.

"He came along when the Industrial Revolution in America was going full force. It actually started in Great Britain around the year 1750. By the early 1800's, inventors had developed things which changed the way people worked. Some of the biggest ones early on were the cotton gin and the steam engine. Not many people know that it actually started with agriculture- then moved to more 'industrial' pursuits that we're now more familiar with. When Ford came along, gasoline engines were relatively rare. It was actually Edison who told him 'Young man, that's the thing; you have it. Keep at it...'"

"I'd never heard that," Natalie remarked as the car glided past a strip mall.

"Edison was his hero, so Ford took that as a stamp of approval. Even wrote a book titled 'My Friend, Mr. Edison'. By the mid-late 1920's, Ford was already very successful, but you're right. The year 1929 was not a great time to start spending lots of money on hobbies. Despite the questionable beginning, it's endured. The museum celebrated their 80th anniversary just over a year ago and has expanded many times."

"I never asked- why did he build the place?" Dianne watched the traffic pull ahead as they got onto the interstate.

"Ford honored the inventor on the 50th anniversary of his development of the incandescent light. Edison was about 82 years old, having been credited with hundreds of patents and inventions. Ford wanted to remind Americans that our heritage is precious- too important to be confined to books. He desired a home for the special things and places in America which meant something to him. Had a strong tie to his roots outside Detroit and wanted to reflect the 'beginnings' of American business as he remembered them. Ford became an avid collector of Americana. If he were around today, he'd be collecting some of the first space rockets and microchips- maybe have Steve Job's first personal computer on display."

"I'm guessing some people thought he was just a rich industrialist who wanted to show off his collection of Model T's."

"... and A's..." Jim chuckled.

"Don't be bad!!" Natalie quipped.

"Even though automobiles are featured in one of the exhibits, the museum highlights everything from the courthouse where Lincoln practiced law to Edison's laboratory, the Wright

Brothers' bicycle shop and the home where the famous song-writer Stephen Foster lived. You could argue that Ford himself is really a minor part of the museum. He had a simple goal- to reproduce life as it was lived, so people in future generations could come there and understand firsthand what it was like."

"A worthy goal. Helps to have millions of dollars to play with!!" The sign up ahead pointed the way. "We're here. Henry Ford Museum- Greenfield Village."

The car came to a stop amidst dozens of vehicles. "Good sized crowd" Natalie observed.

"We often ignore how lucky we are. Ford didn't. He took advantage of our heritage. Governments which allow their citizens the freedom to become productive, successful entre-preneurs will always be the dominant players on Earth. Those which don't will enter the dustbin of history. By 1979, the 50th anniversary of Greenfield Village, they'd already had over 40 million visitors here! It's a testament to our success as a coun-try." Jim strolled briskly toward the entry gate. "Three adults, please." He took the tickets and turned to Natalie. "Where should we start? Maybe that exact replica of Independence Hall right over there?!!"

"We have to check out the Menlo Park lab and the Wright Brothers' shop. Booklet says the dedication banquet for this place included luminaries from around the world- Madame Curie, Thomas Edison, Orville Wright, John D. Rockefeller, Herbert Hoover and Will Rogers, among others. What a party that must have been!!" Natalie flipped open the pamphlet as they went down the lane. "There it is- Edison's lab." She read the description as they entered the building. "Look, they're showing some kind of machine. Let's get closer."

"This is how Thomas Edison made his first recorded sounds. He used this cylinder, turning it while speaking into this tube. The sound waves made impressions on this sheet of tin, which is wrapped around the cylinder. As you speak into the tube, the vibrations are recorded onto the sheet, making indentations. When you play it back, you can hear the sounds. Watch as I demonstrate." The man rotated the cylinder as he yelled into the tube "Mary had a little lamb!!" Then he reversed it, rotating the cylinder and playing it back. The high-pitched voice came through as kids watched, their eyes wide with amazement.

Jim felt goosebumps all along the back of his neck as he leaned closer to see the demonstration again. He squinted as he studied the metal plate, forcing his way up to the very front of the crowd. The sensation intensified as he heard the voice again and turned to see the excited look on her face.

"That was pretty neat!! I've never seen that before" Natalie remarked.

"Did you see the metal sheet he was rotating? It looks just like some of those you found at Frick's Lock!! Those weird ones with all the imprints. I say they're the same."

"Hmmm… Could be. I didn't take that close a look. Let's head upstairs to see his lab." She followed the line of people slowly up the steps to the second floor, where the room opened wide, exposing shelves lined with hundreds of multi-colored bottles holding various chemicals- cobalt blue, amber and milky liquids.

"Folks, this is the restored Menlo Park laboratory of Thomas Edison where he worked on many of his most famous inventions. Edison believed in conducting several different projects at the same time. He felt insights gained from one experiment helped him and his team on other things they were studying. Notice the chair. That is in exactly the same spot Edison left it in his original lab. When he came here for the opening celebration, legend has it he felt so at home, he looked out the window and told one of the people with him he recognized the house of one of his workers- forgetting that he was in Dearborn, Michigan- not New Jersey. Take a few minutes and look around at the workspace of the most famous inventor who ever lived."

The man resumed speaking as more people entered the room. "Edison's 1,093 U.S. patents remains unsurpassed. His experiments explored several different areas of science- electricity, light, sound, even mining and synthetic materials like rubber. His work in power generation became the foundation for companies like General Electric, Consolidated Edison and Detroit Edison. Henry Ford actually got his first serious job at the Detroit Edison plant. Most people don't know that Edison didn't actually 'invent' the light bulb. He discovered and then patented the first commercially successful light bulb by developing a viable filament which lasted far longer than the existing ones. Above all else, he was a very practical man- always striving to do things more efficiently."

Jim examined the walls, peering at each bottle. "I wonder how many critical experiments each one of these had a part in..." Then he saw an arm poke through the edge of the crowd in the distance- a middle-aged man grabbing two metal devices from the edge of a table 20 feet away from the tour guide. "That guy just stole some of Edison's inventions!! I don't believe it!!" The guide was talking with an 8-year old in front as Jim nudged his way ahead, keeping Natalie's hand with him as he made it toward the front of the group. She gave him the "What the hell are you doing?" look as he started to lean in toward the tour guide. "Hey, I don't mean to interrupt, but that guy over there just stole some things from your exhibit."

The guide's eyes opened wide as he stared over at the man, then grabbed his cell phone and whispered, despite his tense voice. "Security. Incident here in the lab." Within moments, two blue-uniformed guards ran into the room, watching as the guide pointed to the suspect.

"Sir, please step outside!!" They grabbed his arms and pushed him through the door, struggling as the man slipped loose and threw a punch, bringing one guard to the floor. "We need back up, NOW!! In the Lab!!" the second guard yelled into his wireless as he wrenched the man's arm behind his back and detained him, struggling wildly to get him into a neck lock. "Stop now or *we'll have you arrested!!*" He pulled him outside as the crowd gawked, children in the front giving each other a high-five. His yells startled the parents as they all tried to focus again on the guide.

"Sorry for the interruption!" The one security guard regained his composure as he got to his feet, touching the edge of his nightstick, wishing he'd used it as he followed the suspect outside.

The guide tried in vain to regain his composure. "Ahem… We're glad you visited Greenfield Village- and Edison's Menlo Park Laboratory…"

"I can't believe he actually tried to steal something from here!" Natalie watched through the window as the man was led away toward the Visitor Center.

"Uh… I recall a box that was removed from a site that was

off limits… Let he who has no sins throw the first stone…"

"Well… That place was abandoned!! It doesn't *really* count…"

He shook his head, then thought again about the metal sheet, rotating around the cylinder and the high-pitched sounds emanating from the device. Glancing over as they left the building, he noticed one brick in the far corner with an inscription. Stepping closer, he read it. "It's barely legible. R… L?" He squinted, then moved to join the two others.

"Let's go down to the Wright Brothers Bicycle shop- it's off of Bagley Avenue." Natalie walked quickly as they proceeded down the path to the street.

"That demonstration we just saw- I can't get it out of my head. I'm telling you, that tin sheet he played- it's identical to what we have in that box!! Those weird dents, the impressions- I think something's recorded on them."

"I believe you. Maybe somebody from the 1920's got inspired and used some contraption to record a bedtime story for his kid. There's the Wright Brothers shop. Let's go in."

"Did you know Edison got his first job as a telegraph operator? Back in the 1870's they needed interpreters to log in the Morse Code, so his skills were in demand. Nicknamed his two kids 'Dot' and 'Dash'."

"At least he had a sense of humor." She went through the doorway and weaved around the small display. "This bicycle shop proves that humble beginnings sometimes lead to great accomplishments."

"How did Wilbur and Orville become interested in flight?" Dianne asked.

"They were both intensely curious about mechanical

things. Orville took a keen interest in kites and started building them to sell to his friends. The nation was also taken with a bicycle craze by the 1890's and they started building, selling and repairing bikes- honing their mechanical skills. In 1895, they learned about a famous inventor who was doing glider experiments and were fascinated by the idea that man could someday fly. About this time, a friend of theirs had actually built the first 'horseless buggy' to ever run on the streets of Dayton. Orville felt the new invention might be big and perhaps they should become builders of these contraptions. Wilbur disagreed, saying 'You'd be tackling the impossible. Why, it would be easier to build a flying machine!!'"

"A twist of fate."

"It took years of experiments with gliders, then small motorized machines to get the right 'mix' that finally enabled them to fly. That was after dozens of failures- and near fatal accidents- on the windswept beach at Kitty Hawk. They made their first airplane right here in this bicycle shop. Who would ever have guessed that could happen? It'd be like me building a Space Shuttle in our garage. They had to get the perfect combination of length, angle and tilt for the wings and fuselage. Clearly trial and error mechanics, but it worked!! Remember, even the most highly trained engineers at the time hadn't been able to get a plane up in the air for an extended flight. Most people said they were crazy and could get killed!! It takes a special type of individual, an inner strength to persist in that environment." Jim watched as re-enactors in period garb walked across the street.

Dianne was putting on her Wayfarers as she gazed around the edge of the complex. "How did they do it? I mean- what *is* the 'creative spark'?"

"The light within us all…"

"…but it's one in a million, coming up with a truly new idea. Many never see it."

"Most people never look. It takes one candle to lighten a darkened room…" He opened the map showing all the locations where each inventor worked. "This place is filled with interesting things to explore. Did you know they re-built every structure from its original foundation in the exact same detail as their former location? They've got a pioneer log cabin from the 1700's, a Cape Cod windmill, memorial to George Washington Carver- even a re-constructed 1600's-era home from Great Britain. Amazing."

"Too bad we can't spend more time! It's a wonderland for history buffs." Natalie scanned the small lane in front of her and pointed. "Let's go over to the Lincoln Courthouse. You'll like that."

"Brochure says it's the place where he presented many of his cases. Lincoln liked to use humor in his arguments. One famous case involved a young man accused of murdering both of his parents. Lincoln argued for the prosecution, joking that the defendant would ask for leniency based on the fact that he was an orphan!"

"He's regarded as one of our top Presidents, isn't he?" Natalie put on some Chapstick as they wandered the paths around the complex.

"Some feel he's the greatest because he kept the Union intact during the time of its biggest crisis. He's right up there with Washington, who'll always be the first for ushering in an age of democracy and freedom. You could argue that Washington and the other Founding Fathers made all this possible. Without a stable government that respects the rights of its citizens to run their businesses in peace, many great inventions may never have occurred." He studied the building's facade. "So this is where Honest Abe worked."

"We can take a quick walk inside- then let's move on. There's no way we can get through this place in a day. The Rouge Factory tour starts in 30 minutes. I've never seen an auto plant."

"You know, Ford failed twice in his attempts to start a car company, but finally succeeded on his third try- in 1903- the same year the Wright Brothers triumphed at Kitty Hawk. His gift was persistence- and structuring the car-making process to become fully automated- the 'assembly line' method, which was far more efficient than the small factories. His methods were copied by all the major manufacturers- and it helped spawn an industry which changed our society. Fast forward. GM and Chrysler had to take government bailouts. They said it was mandatory or they'd go under. Ford was the only one which didn't. Now Ford's in the best shape of them all. Henry's vision is alive and well." He watched as the group filed out of the courthouse onto the path.

"The F-150 is still the best-selling pick-up on the market, as far as I know. Has been for years" Natalie exclaimed. She reached for her sunglasses. It's time for the Rouge Factory tour. Let's head over."

"Ever notice that most cop cars- marked and unmarked- are Ford Crown Victorias? They're pretty good cars. Talked with a PA State Trooper at the Wawa in Kennett Square recently. He said they're replacing them with the Ford Taurus starting in 2012. I loved the two Fords I had- Lincoln Town Cars. Smooth ride, luxurious… Did you know they used old Ford Model A's to pull the Wright Brother's planes around to each location for the air shows?... There's the line to go in."

"Folks, please follow the walkway and do not lean over the railings. This is for your safety. You'll be taking a tour through an actual working Ford assembly plant. The people you see in front of you are putting together one of several models which will be rolling off the line later, into a showroom near you. This plant is designed to utilize the process Henry Ford put in place a hundred years ago in building his famous Model T and other cars which became fixtures on the American landscape. Please keep moving."

Jim watched as the overhead robotic arms swiveled back and forth to each worker, their movements calibrated to achieve the most efficient use of time and materials. "Ford's assembly plants have been regarded by some analysts as the most efficient of the Big Three."

"That's probably why they didn't go bankrupt- like GM- and become a burden on the taxpayers" Dianne interjected.

"They were also efficient in their use of cash. They kept large reserves to tide them over through the downturn. GM and Chrysler didn't. Not bad for a company that's over a century old, which some people called a 'dinosaur'."

Dianne gazed down onto the shop floor, seeing dozens of workers attending to their own workstations. "It's incredible how they use those robots throughout the process. You'd think that humans and robots wouldn't always mix that well."

"They have it down. Computers tell them exactly what they need, when and where they need it. Henry would be proud. There's the exit. Let's go over to the museum store. I'd like to get some books to take back with us." The odor of engine grease drifted up from below.

"Not too many. We'll have to lug them around in our suitcases." Natalie walked through the scattered group of parents and small children to the other building. "I want to see some of their historical logos- like from the 1930's. I'll be over there."

Jim went immediately to the first shelf of books and saw the wide selection. "This looks good- 'Edison- A Life of Invention'." He flipped quickly through the pages and saw two others nearby on the bookcase. 'The Wright Brothers' and 'The People's Tycoon- Henry Ford and the American Century'. "Well, why not get all three? They should keep me busy on the flight back." He walked to the counter.

"Will that be all?"

"Over 1,300 pages. That should hold me for today."

The girl chuckled as she gave him his change. "Enjoy. Thanks for visiting Greenfield Village."

He located a small couch off to the side and sat down. "Lot of walking around. Tired." His mind wandered back as he saw the photos in the book on Ford, the workers at the Highland Park assembly plant in 1914, the Model T's lined up outside the factory- and the advertisement "Buy a Ford- and spend the difference!!" He paged through, seeing Henry's face grinning as he stood next to Edsel with the new Model A at a 1928 exhibition. He contemplated the images from the 1940's and 1950's… and he was driving on old Route 66 outside Holbrook, Arizona… the Wigwam Motel… the Jackrabbit Trading Post, signs flying by, feeling the cool November breeze on his face, the 1953 Ford Fairlane convertible humming along. The Old Mother Road… the path to the sea… a treasure of out of the way towns and forgotten cafes…

"Anything interesting?" Natalie nudged him over slightly as she sat down.

He focused again on the tour of Greenfield Village and how the automobile changed America. "He ushered in the Consumer Age- making a car affordable to the average person. A trend was sweeping the country- the move from the farm to the factory. Ford was at the forefront of that revolution. At the time, most of the country was content to either work on the farm or in a local business, without even thinking about exploring faraway places. He even doubled the wages of his employees. People said it was a stunt. Henry believed that if you paid people well, they'd be loyal. His workers earned good wages- which they used to buy *his cars*."

"Pretty savvy. Who knew back then that by putting a bunch of guys together on an assembly line, they'd change the world?"

"He knew that he was altering the way we lived and worked. Did you know both he and Edison lived to about 84?"

"Interesting coincidence."

"Edison made it a few months past; Henry died just a few months short of his 84th birthday, born a few weeks after the Battle of Gettysburg, in July 1863. That was a ripe old age for men back then."

"Hey, you two!! Ready to go?" Dianne had a small bag in her left hand.

"What did you buy as a good worker-consumer today?"

"Oh, just some refrigerator magnets. Scott likes them. I may keep one."

"Let's head back…"

—◦◦❁◦◦—

Sitting on the back patio, Jim sipped another iced tea. "The auto industry was a dominant business in the U.S. from the 1940's through the 1980's. The old saying 'What's good for GM is good for America' *was* true, but the industry here became complacent. Then labor unions flexed their muscles. Did you know that the union was able to get GM to guarantee each worker 95% of their salary even when they were *laid off*? No industry can survive being run that way. Japan and other countries produce cars far more efficiently than we do. GM and Chrysler weren't looking in their rear view mirror."

"I love my Beemer." Dianne sipped at her drink.

"Interesting footnote. Samuel Gompers, a major force in the AFL back then- opposed the liberal socialist tide washing across the country. He was actually a conservative!! Do you *believe that*?!"

"Nixon went to China."

"Unions did play an important role in building many industries in the U.S., eliminating dangerous working conditions and unfair labor practices, so they had a very positive influence early on. In recent years, they've gone a bit too far."

Dianne shook her head as the fountain grasses swayed in the light breeze.

"A bit sad. I've owned American cars and foreign cars- and enjoyed driving them all. U.S. companies can build the best cars in the world- and retake the lead!! We'd been doing it for decades… but we lost our way. Maybe we don't want to be the best anymore…"

Natalie nodded in agreement as she heard a cardinal chirping nearby.

"A dedication to excellence may just save us in the end... but only if we want it badly enough. If not, we'll *all* be wondering... what happened to the American work ethic?"

Natalie heard his voice trailing sadly lower as she paged through the book he'd just bought and saw the photos of that famous 'first flight'- Wilbur running behind the plane as it flew above the sand. She flipped back a few pages and the caption underneath one photograph hit her. 'Wilbur and Orville discuss aerodynamic problems with R. Larson, known mechanical expert in several fields'. She read it again to make sure it was there. "Jim, look at this!! It says right here- R. Larson!!"

He was silent for a few seconds. "Larson, the relative of Daniel Larson? Couldn't be." He sat up and leaned over to look at the page.

"It very well could be!! This was around 1900. Randolph would have been in his early-mid 50's... and the photo is of a man who looks... about 50." She examined the picture for several seconds as Dianne approached to see the photograph.

"Who's R. Larson?"

"We think he's an inventor who owned a house at Frick's Lock, where we did some exploring. He was later admitted to Pennhurst. We talked with one of his relatives and a guy who used to work at Pennhurst back at that time. Supposedly Larson was an eccentric genius. Apparently everyone thought he was a total crackpot."

Jim recalled the initials carved into the brick on Edison's lab. "Larson's a fairly common name. Could be just a coincidence, but... I didn't say something back there."

"Say it now." Natalie swatted a fly off of her arm.

"As we were leaving, I saw an inscription on the edge of the Edison building. It was pretty weathered and faded away, but I swear I could make out the letters 'R. L.' etched into a brick."

"Remember all those things Abe Olson said? It's *got to be the same guy!!*"

"We need one thing."

"The most valuable commodity?"

"Exactly." He heard Cloe purring as the last rays dropped below the line of bushes at the edge of the yard, giving one final glow to the flower petals. "Happy Hour. Any wine for a toast to a wonderful day?"

"Certainly. I'll be right back." Dianne went into the kitchen, then came out after a few minutes with a bottle of chardonnay on a small pewter tray. "Here you are. Why don't you pour us all a glass?"

"To the innovators." He touched his glass to hers and Natalie's. "Clink!!"

Natalie laughed, remembering the Asian man on the plane. "I won't say it!!"

"Now, if we could just invent a machine that would vaporize those idiotic games that go 'Clink!!'"

⸺⫸‹‹❍››⫷⸺

"Ladies and gentlemen, we are now at a cruising altitude of 28,000 feet. Feel free to move about the cabin as necessary. We'll be coming through with our beverage service shortly…"

"A nice trip. Good to see Dianne… and the Village

was fascinating." She flipped through the US Air in-flight magazine.

"It was good. Piqued my interest in all those early inventors and what was happening around the world at the time."

"What do you mean?"

"Art was going through what would become the major movement of the late 19th and early 20th century- Impressionism. Monet, Cezanne and Van Gogh were turning the art world upside down. Music was also reflecting new ideas with Debussy, Ravel and Stravinsky. Listen to Debussy's 'Prelude to the Afternoon of a Faun'- then look at Monet's 'Rouen Cathedral, Morning'. You'll see and hear things changing dramatically from what had been done before."

"Excuse me, I couldn't help but overhear your comments. I teach a course on the history of technology and popular culture. We actually do cover how art reflects changes in science. Your point about Debussy and the Impressionists is accurate."

"I appreciate that. Where do you teach?" Jim leaned closer to hear him.

"A small community college outside Detroit. I have a background in science, but I also try to highlight non-scientific changes that were occurring during each period."

"Have you ever been to Greenfield Village?" Natalie asked. The oval window fogged as the plane passed through a cloud.

"Wonderful place. I mention it in my course. Ford did us all a great service by preserving those important structures and presenting the story to each new generation."

"We really enjoyed our visit there. We're on our way back home, near Philadelphia. I'm Natalie, that's Jim."

"Bob Cantrell. Good to meet you both. I'm actually on my

way to Philadelphia to see some family. I hope you were able to walk around most of the Village. A lot to see."

"We tried, but the place is huge!! It was amazing just seeing all the important buildings. Did get some books- a lot of reading to do." Jim took a sip of the ice water and watched as the stewardesses pushed the carts further down the aisle.

"Glad you got a chance to visit the place. Here's my card. Perhaps we could keep in touch. Have a nice trip."

"Absolutely!! Thanks for your comments." Natalie noticed the people across the aisle taking sandwiches and chips from their carry-on bags. "Maybe the airlines will figure out how to run efficiently enough to have flights with free meals again- without an extra $25 charge for each checked bag. That'd be a breakthrough we could celebrate."

"I mentioned what was happening in art and music around the turn of the century and realized they were mostly Frenchmen. Another famous Frenchman set up his business right down the road from us."

"… and that was…?"

"E. I. du Pont. Started on the banks of the Brandywine back in 1802. Made gunpowder that helped protect America in every war from the War of 1812 to World War II… Du Pont scientists invented nylon, Teflon, Corian, Kevlar, Tyvek and StainMaster carpeting. It's hard to think about products people use in the average home today without mentioning Du Pont. They gave us some of the greatest consumer products the world has ever seen."

She noticed spots of iced tea on her blouse. "I wish they'd invent StainMaster clothing. Now *that* would be a 'Miracle of Science.'"

"Perfect for spaghetti and red wine dinners... where I do the most damage."

"People sometimes forget all the humanitarian contributions of successful businessmen. The du Pont family built Longwood Gardens- along with Winterthur and Nemours, superb displays of early Americana. Add in the Du Pont Hospital and school outside Wilmington and you have many great deeds which have helped society..."

———— ‹‹()›› ————

"Good to be home." She pulled open the blinds as she watched Linus and Lucy flutter around the cage. "Hi guys!! Hope you behaved. Jim, if you bring in the bags, I'll get us a drink. Dinner will be on soon."

"Will do." He strolled over to the door just as the phone rang. "Hello?"

"Hi. This is Abe- Abe Olson. You came over to my house recently and we spoke about Pennhurst. I hope you don't mind me calling. You did leave me your card."

"Oh, of course!! Hi Abe. Not a problem. What's on your mind?"

"Well, I really enjoyed your visit, but I wanted to apologize for Richie's behavior. He was... a bit rude, I think. He can't help it sometimes. Look, he's had a rough life. His father was an alcoholic... and his mother wasn't the best role model, either. Went through a wild phase- got a bunch of tattoos... chains, demons, skulls... When he reached 16, he got a motorcycle and joined a biker gang. Those were troubled times... He eventually moved in with me and straightened out. Got his

G.E.D. I was able to get him a job at Pennhurst. Things were going fine- until he lost his job when they closed Pennhurst. People started calling him all sorts of names- even accused him of hurting patients there!! It changed him... and he's been depressed ever since..."

Jim wanted to accept the apology, but stopped. The skulls in the nightmare floated before him... "Abe, it was nice of you to call and share that with me. I'm not sure how to comment. Maybe I should speak directly with Richie."

"Oh- NO!! He's... I didn't tell him I was calling you. I just wanted you to know I appreciate your coming over and talking with me. I don't get a lot of visitors... Brought back some memories... most of them good. I didn't want you to take away a negative impression."

"Not at all. Thanks for taking the time to speak with us Abe. Have a good evening."

"You, too- and please give that beautiful wife of yours a kiss for me."

"I sure will." He hung up the phone slowly.

"Sounded like you had an interesting discussion."

"Abe wanted to apologize for Richie's behavior. It was a... strange call."

"How's that?"

"Richie was in a gang for a while... troubled kid... got a bunch of tattoos. One Abe mentioned in particular caught my attention. A skull. He said it shocked him when he first saw it- kind of demonic looking. Now that I think back, Richie did have tattoos on his arms- and I did see an eerie looking skull!!"

"Yes... and...?"

"Remember? We both had the same nightmare- filled with skulls!! Skulls, dripping with blood... and there was one *just like that* on his left forearm!! I know it!!"

"Relax. Gang members don't choose images of Mother Theresa."

"I can't quantify it, but I can feel there's a link..."

Greenfield Village (Henry Ford Museum)- Dearborn, MI

Wright Brothers First Flight at Kitty Hawk, December 17, 1903

Ford Model A at Eagle Gold Mine- Julian, CA

Edison's Menlo Park Lab, restored at Greenfield Village- Dearborn, MI

Thomas Edison and his phonograph

Chapter 10

"In the field of observation, chance favors the prepared mind."
--Louis Pasteur

"I think it's time to go through *everything* in that box. Greenfield Village really piqued my interest. Hard to believe we've been back from our trip for over three weeks!! Where has the time gone?"

"Yes... mid-August already. I agree. We only did a quick glance the last time, though it looked mostly like a bunch of junk. There could be some other interesting things in there after all, aside from the metal sheets. I'll do the dishes while you bring it in from the garage."

"I want a second look at those. I'll get it now." Stepping into the garage, he saw it sitting next to the old croquet set and a Blue Rhino propane tank. He squatted down and put both arms around its edges. "Won't make that mistake again. No more leaning over to pick up something heavy. Last time I could barely move for two days." Lumbering into the kitchen, the box tilted in his arms, he dropped the heavy load onto the counter, the items inside rattling from the impact.

"Jim!! Careful… you might have broken something in there."

"I think I broke something out here." He massaged his lower back. "Mom used to always say 'That's what having six kids'll do for you'. Now I know how she felt."

Natalie pulled back the heavy cardboard flaps, stained with soot, grease and mouse droppings. "Here's that scrapbook!! I never went through the whole thing…" She placed it on the counter and started slowly flipping the heavy, foot long pages. "They made them different back then. These must be an eighth of an inch thick, like the matting we used in Arts and Crafts in fifth grade."

"In Catholic school, that's what we used for our science projects. Remember- the drawing of the wires from the 12-volt battery, hooked up to the frog?"

"We did different ones. Ours were more lady-like."

"Used to watch the frog jump. Today you'd get a citation for that." He grinned as he moved the cylinder aside and pulled the metal sheets from the box, dust falling to the floor.

"Look at this!! I didn't get to the back. It's a tribute to Lincoln on the 100th Anniversary of his birth: 1809- 1909. Says 'To my dearest grandpa- a celebration of the birthday of our greatest President!! Love, Annabelle'. This is really cute!! Notice the drawing of Lincoln- looks like a collectors' item itself." Natalie sneezed as dust rose into the air.

He peered over, squinting as he eyed the detail in the picture. "That's the same drawing used for the penny. Did you ever notice that Lincoln is looking to the *right* on the face of the penny, while Jefferson on the nickel and all the other denomination coins have the figure looking to the left? Wonder if the designer was a Conservative."

"Never paid any attention. It's the analyst in you."

He took out the rusted cylinder and placed it to the side as he glanced down at the metal sheets. "Hmmmm… just as I thought." He gently laid them down side by side and studied each one. "These *are* similar to that sheet the guy played at Greenfield Village. I think they may be early recordings."

"Now we just need to find out what's on them. How in the world could we ever do that?"

"Come back to my laboratory, madam- and I'll show you…"

"Cute. Look, here's that weird light bulb." She held it up to the rays coming in from the window. "Actually, it doesn't look anything like the bulbs we use."

"This guy was a tinkerer. Who knows? Maybe he was trying to design something unique and gave up." He studied the lines of indentations on each metal sheet, bringing the surface to within an inch of his face. "You can tell whatever was recorded had some variation. Maybe a song- or someone speaking loudly, then more softly." He picked up the last sheet and compared it to the other three. Etchings at the bottom left corner of each one were barely visible… 1/4… 2/4… 3/4. "I think these were all recorded together, in a sequence. They're a set, whatever they are."

"Sounds possible. What is this??" She held up a heavy black piece of metal, about three inches long with a rounded center.

"I… think I've seen that somewhere before. My buddy Dave in high school was a car nut. Back in 9th grade at Ardmore Junior High he was the only kid in the history of shop class to take apart an entire transmission and reassemble it- without any help. When we got our licenses, he'd drive me to junkyards around the Main Line to find old car parts. We'd be sifting through piles of rusted debris, then he'd yell 'I got it!!' That, I believe… is what's called a 'dog bone' radiator cap. They used them back in the 1930's. Shape made it easier to twist off. More than I can say for things in cars these days. Aside from replacing the windshield wiper fluid, you have to be an electrical engineer to figure out what's under the hood."

"I would never have recognized it." She glanced down and picked up another oval-shaped piece of rusted metal. "Appears to have an inscription."

He took the item and placed it under the kitchen light. "This looks interesting. I can barely read it… Says 'For…' The writing's mostly faded. 'Ford… Motor Company, Detroit, Michigan, U.S.A.' This must be a metal hood ornament from an old Ford!! Probably circa late 1920's or 1930's. Definitely a collector's item."

"That's pretty neat. My dad always drove Plymouths."

"My sister dated this guy Sammy back in the mid-1960's whose dad owned a construction company. We all thought he was rich. One day he drove up in a long, black Lincoln Continental and let all the kids get in it. It was great!! I'd never seen a car that had electric windows… I'd play with them, raising them up… then letting them down… raising them up again. To me it was something from the Space Age. That was the first time I was in a car made by Ford." He held the ornament in his hands, the rusted metal edges of the oval sharp against his fingers.

"What in the world is this??!!" Natalie pulled out a 10-inch section of heavy beige material, rimmed by decaying wood.

He grabbed the cloth and inspected the surface for several seconds, flipping it over to see the underside, which was badly weathered and frayed, holes throughout its length. "Appears to be heavy canvas matting- for something." Then he thought about the other thing Abe said about Randolph. 'I flew with the Wright Brothers!!' He stared at the surface again and it hit him. "If I didn't know better, I'd say this could have been used in some kind of a kite or large glider."

"Well, if it was a glider or even an airplane- weren't they all made of metal?" She gazed at the piece of material again, then up at him. "Maybe a sail from a boat?"

"It's impossible to tell, but I know from old photographs that the earliest airplanes used heavy canvas backing rimmed with wood, kind of similar to this."

"Well, Mister analyst, exactly what evidence do you have to support this theory?"

He held the section of canvas up again to the light. The scene came back to him... wind swirling sand up in the air, running down the slope toward the shoreline as the sun glistened on the edges of the wings, the thrill of seeing the plane up above the ground for several seconds... "The Wright Brothers had gliders and later, powered planes using reinforced canvas- many of which crashed into the beach. I know they tried to recover the equipment, but some of it may have been unfit for further use." Then he held the canvas up closer to his eyes. "I see something hand written in the corner, but it's almost completely gone. Let me get the magnifying glass." He went to the desk and opened the drawer. "Here. Now I can see a bit better. Looks like... a K and... it's very faint... maybe an... H?" He thought for several seconds. "This is a leap, but many of their flight experiments were at Kitty Hawk."

Her eyes opened wide as she studied the canvas under the glass. "Oh, my God. Could that possibly be?"

"Remember that picture in the book you saw while we were at Dianne's? Caption read 'R. Larson.' Might be a coincidence, but I doubt it." He held it up and felt the wind across his face again…

"Who knows? A link to the past…" She peered again into the box, both hands now picking up clumps of debris. "Mostly rotted paper, couple of old pencils… and of course, another dead spider. Here's that tin of chewing tobacco you couldn't open. I don't want to try."

"Uggh!! This is rusted shut. I'll try tapping the edges and putting it under hot water. That usually does it." He walked to the sink and let the water run over it until steam rose to his face. "Here goes…" He grabbed the circular rubber friction pad from the drawer and breathed in, twisting hard with both wrists. "Owww!! I don't want to break a few metacarpals just to see some rotten tobacco. Forget it."

"No! There could be something in there."

"What? Bugs from 1902? Who cares?"

"Just try once more."

"It actually does feel a bit heavier than the others. OK- one last try." He inhaled for two seconds, then put all his weight into his grip. "Ugghh!!... Opened it!!" He laid the top on the counter and saw the masses immersed in the decomposing brown strands. "What are these?" He picked up the first one and brought it over to the faucet. "Whatever it is, it probably hasn't had a shower in a hundred years…" As the water flowed over its surface, his mouth dropped open.

"What is it?" She came up next to him at the sink.

"Recalling my mineralogy courses at Bucknell, I'd say that's a diamond. A HUGE one. It's gotta' be three carats!!"

"Too bad you didn't find it before you proposed."

"Do you know what this is worth? I haven't a clue what diamonds went for back around the turn of the century- but today the stone itself is worth at least $15,000. With gold near $1,500 an ounce- right off, I'm holding $20,000 in my hand."

"Very nice!! Can I have it now?"

"I saw something else in there. Let me check it out." He grabbed the tin, dumping it onto the counter, two more items rolling along the edge toward the garbage disposal.

"Grab them!!"

"I got it." He put the next one under the water, its surface glistening red. "My God!! That... is a gorgeous ruby!! It's got to be two carats for sure- maybe three. Look at the delicate gold pattern around it. They don't make 'em like this anymore..."

"They don't make much of *anything* like that anymore. What's the other one?" She picked it up, trying to avoid the decaying shreds of slimy tobacco wrapped around its base.

"Let water do the trick. Always helps things- young and old- to get a bath. That's what my mother always said." His eyes widened as the brilliant green shone through in his fingers. "This... is an emerald. One of my favorite gemstones. It's HUGE!! At least five carats... Check out the gold base, with the intricate design. What a beauty!!"

"Well, Mister geologist- what are all these worth?"

"I can't quote retail, but these three rings are clearly collector's items. The stones themselves have got to be worth $50,000. Add in the gold settings- and the historic value- we could be talking $75,000 or more…"

"YEAH!! When do I get them as gifts?"

"Never thought I'd find gems in old tins of chewing to-bacco. Whoever put them in here must not have had any other place- or anyone- to give them to."

"You can give them to me anytime. Let's see… my birth-day… our anniversary… Christmas. What's in that last tin?"

He put the rubber grip around it and gave it a big tug. "Owww!! That's it. No more exercise for today. It's really light. Feels like it's empty, anyhow… We'll open it some other time."

"So, despite all this gunk, we found something really valu-able!! What's the tally so far?"

"Well- we have some exquisite rings, a dog-bone radia-tor cap from an old car, a Ford hood ornament from the late 1920's, some dented metal sheets, a strange bulb… and some-thing which might take us into orbit if we get the right angle with the wind…"

"Let's toast… to re-discovered relics from a forgotten age."

"Anything that makes sense out of this mess will be wel-come. Might have to get those appraised."

"I see fragments of a bygone era… and a lot more to learn from this dilapidated old box."

———— ⟨◉⟩ ————

She walked out onto the terrace, enjoying the chatter of birds at the feeder, holding the Daily News in front of her. 'War in Afghanistan May Last Years'… 'Budget Controversy Has Dems Against Republicans'… 'Obama Mulls Possible Change

in Strategy As He Anticipates Mid-Term Defeat at the Polls'…
She gazed out at the tidal basin and saw the familiar buff colored groundhog nibbling at some low shrubs. "Hey Blondie!!
Haven't seen you in a while." Natalie turned her focus back to
the newspaper, flipping to the Entertainment section. "Let's
see… Movies… New Videos… Upcoming Events…" She read
the lines and froze. "Excellent! This is awesome. Halloween
Haunted House at Pennhurst!!" Reading down the page, she
saw the disclaimer. "The current owner of Pennhurst has indicated his intention to have a Halloween Haunted House at the
facility, but is facing legal disputes with some local residents
due to the controversy surrounding the institution. It is expected that the event will be approved, with the opening date set
for September 24th, 2010." She glanced at the calendar. "That's
only a few weeks away!! I HAVE to get tickets!!"

The phone rang and Jim headed slowly over toward the
counter.

"I got it!!" She grabbed the phone and saw the familiar
number on the caller I.D. "Yes…?"

"Hello… I wanted to tell you about the episode of 'Ghost
Hunters' last night!! So exciting!! They were in this Civil War
fort- at a place called Pea Patch Island… I think it's not far
from here."

"Oh, yes. Jim told me about it. It's called Fort Delaware.
They held thousands of Confederate prisoners there. Horrible
conditions. I also heard it was haunted…"

"YES!! The crew brought the cameras in and Natalie- I
swear- it showed something flashing across the screen. I know
it was a ghost! I'd never seen anything like it!! I mean on TV- in
front of my face. I always thought these shows were more for

entertainment, but this- I swear to God- was a REAL ghost!!"

"What did it look like?"

"It was kind of grey… more of a hazy shadow than anything else. One second it was there and then POOF… gone."

"Talking about spooky things, did you see the paper today? They're going to have a Halloween Haunted House at Pennhurst! I think we should all go." Natalie was pacing back and forth, unable to contain her excitement.

"Perfect! Count me in!!" Sue glanced down at Stella, poised in front of the bird cage, hoping to get a nip at Cassidy.

"If I can get tickets, I'll buy three so we can all go."

"I'm there." She strolled to the front door and opened it. "Stella, out!!" She watched as the cat stopped to sniff a rose petal that had blown in from the yard.

"What?"

"I was just telling Stella to get her butt outside. Let me know if you get tickets!! I have to run. I'm meeting Terry for lunch."

"Will do. I'll call you as soon as I know something. Have fun!!" Natalie turned and saw Jim standing three feet away. "They're going to open up Pennhurst for Halloween. We need to go."

"Well, it would be a chance to check out the place. I'm game for a reasonable adventure… without state trooper sirens."

"Exactly. I'm going on-line now." She entered her office and plopped down in her chair, swiveling around to face the screen.

"Get the best tickets. We'll want front row for the ghouls. It'll be a fun *and scary* start to the Halloween season." He walked out to get the mail and felt the late Summer breeze on the side of his face, turning his hair over. "Murphy's Postulate: If the wind is blowing, it will be perpendicular to the part in your hair, shoving it completely over to the other side. Editor's Note: Murphy was an optimist- and the wind never blows when it's extremely hot." He watched his neighbor Joe toss a ball to his little dog Ed… short for Edison. "Cute name for a pup." Edison brought the ball to Jim and he threw it back over toward Joe, smiling, then wiping the dampness on his pants. Watching several hawks overhead, he heard her voice.

"Yes!! I got tickets for Pennhurst!!" She came running out to the driveway, her bare feet avoiding the sunnier spots along the hot blacktop.

"Good job. We can see the place without jail time. What's the date?"

"September 24th. I know, it's a bit early for Halloween- but we'll be the first ones in!! It's opening night. Pennhurst hasn't been available to the public for over 25 years. Hey, let's call Abe Olson and see if he can give us directions to the building Randolph lived in. Quaker Hall, if I remember correctly."

He studied the smile lines around her eyes, sensing her elation… then frowned briefly. "Time out. It's a *guided* Haunted House, correct? There's bound to be monitors everywhere."

"Well, maybe… but if there aren't… perhaps we can slip away… down some dark corridors- into the patients' rooms. Let's at least be prepared in case we *can* sneak off safely. We'll post Sue on watch.

"Alright. I'll call Abe" he agreed, a bit reluctantly.

She tiptoed quickly back to the porch door. "Ooh!! Hot!"

Jim looked up Olson's number and picked up the phone to dial. "Natalie, how can he give us directions? Won't he need a starting point? What building is the event in?"

"Oh yeah, hold on." She hurried back into her office and Googled 'Pennhurst Asylum' again. "It's in the Administration Building."

"What?? My next invention will be a sound tube from your office to the kitchen so I can hear you…"

Natalie shrugged and walked into the room. "THE ADMINISTRATION BUILDING!"

"OK, already!! We're not at a WHO concert." Jim finished dialing, hearing Abe pick up the other end.

"Hello?"

"Hi Abe, this is Jim Peterson. Got a quick question for you about Pennhurst… and Randolph Larson."

"Sure. Shoot."

"Can you describe where the Quaker Building is in relation to the Admin building? Looks like we have an opportunity to see the place with a Halloween night there. Thought we might try to find his room."

"You're actually going to Pennhurst, huh? Read about it in the paper. Watch out- lots of controversy swirling around. Anyway, Quaker is just two buildings East. Right after Dietary. Good luck."

"Thanks. We'll let you know how the event turns out." Jim hung up and sat at the glass table recalling all the photos they'd seen at Sherry's office. The children in pain, helpless adults tied to their beds, the toilets with straps to restrain them.

"So, did he help with directions?"

"Two buildings over from Admin." The images flashed again before him. "Just be careful. We may get much more than the price of admission…"

"I'm open to whatever we see... I don't care how scary it is!!"

"Remember, there are going to be lots of people around-maybe hundreds- families who really don't want to experience this again. It was tough enough the first time- rekindling bad memories could be trouble. This won't exactly be a love fest. Be prepared for some negative feelings, perhaps even a run-in with the press."

"I'm sensitive to the issues. If they want to interview me, that's fine. I know the difference between a haunted house and real life atrocities..."

⸺⸺●⸺⸺

The uncertainty was smoldering deep down as he thought about Clark, the lingering doubts... whether she'd told the complete truth... and he felt it again. The emptiness... "Is there always a weak spot, a wound that never heals? Shut it down, Jim. The world's for conquerors, not losers. Can't let your emotions rule the day. Especially when it's about a woman. It's destructive... Wait!! This isn't just *any* woman. It's the one you've chosen to spend your entire life with... It's true... marriage is a series of compromises. More like a series of enormous bridge-building projects. I won't compromise my core values no matter what happens. If you do, you're no better than people who have none. If you stand for nothing, you'll fall for anything. Move on! Don't dwell in it. Go out. Get some fresh air! See an old buddy... Yes!! I haven't seen Frank in months. I should give him a call. I could use a new face to talk to." He moved over to the phone and dialed.

"Special Agent Rawlins here."

"Frank, Jim Peterson. How are you?"

"Great!! Jim, it's been a while. Good to hear from you. How are things with you and Natalie?"

He hesitated for a few seconds. "Doing well. Busier than ever, now that I officially 'retired'."

"Never thought I'd hear you say that word. Activity is your middle name."

"We're out and about. Doing a bit of traveling, some exploring." He thought about the incident at Frick's Lock. "Hey, I want to thank you for helping with Natalie's… *experience* with the authorities. Very kind of you."

"That wasn't just me personally. It had to go through the chain of command. Needed to persuade the higher ups it was worth it. I'd do it again. Anything for you two- you helped us a lot. Say, we should get together for a drink. It's been awhile."

"Read my mind. How about tonight… a quick one near you? Any watering holes close by downtown?"

"There are a few. Moriarty's Pub is a cozy place for a cocktail. It's at 1116 Walnut Street. Can you be there soon- around 5… before the Happy Hour rush?"

"Sounds great." He hung up the phone and grabbed the car keys. As he opened the door to the Ford Explorer, he contemplated the conversation he was about to have with a senior agent of the FBI. "How am I going to tell him that one of his guys was… trying to have an affair with Natalie? There's no easy way. Just… say it and let the chips fall where they may." He pulled out of the garage and headed up Route 1, veering to the right onto Route 322 East to get onto I-95. "With any luck, I'll beat rush hour." Going down the ramp onto Broad

Street, he turned and saw the sign. "There it is." The car glided under the 3-D 'PARK- BEST RATES DOWNTOWN' sign and he handed the attendant his keys. The sidewalk along Walnut Street was already starting to fill up with the business crowd getting out of work a bit early.

"Jim, good to see you!! Just got here."

"Great to see you again. It's been what- over six months? We need to get out for a cocktail more often." He glanced at the bartender who had come up to them, waiting for their order. "I'll have a Bombay Sapphire gin and tonic."

"Make mine McClellan's on ice." Frank put his hand firmly on Jim's shoulder. "So, how's life now that you can do anything you want and not worry about the time?"

"A lot busier than I thought. Never know how much there is to do until you stop working. Natalie loves to check out new places. We're always visiting museums, galleries, any place she hasn't been before. We could write a tour guide for the area." He grabbed the tumbler and took a long sip.

"Sounds like fun. Wish I could have that life of leisure. Must be very relaxing." Frank took a drink of the scotch, watching the ice cubes as the bartender nodded.

"It can be… but something's got me a bit… worried. It's not easy to say this… I think Natalie is getting some heavy overtures from one of your guys. I don't know what happened exactly. We talked and came to an understanding, but… I'm still not sure about the whole thing. It's driving me nuts… and I haven't been sleeping too well."

"You probably know we have a very strict code of ethics- and the Field Director frowns upon personal relationships interfering with our work."

Jim considered the situation for several moments. "It's Jack Clark."

The events started falling into place, his mind filling in the pieces of the puzzle he'd seen briefly only weeks before. After another long sip, he gazed at Jim. "Did you see or hear anything? Has he come over to the house?"

"No, not that I know of. We've gotten some phone calls. Natalie said he was just checking up on us- making sure we were safe after what happened with Caniletto and his crew of thugs... then he asked her out and she had lunch with him. For me, that took it over the line." He drained the glass and raised it for another to the bartender who was watching. "She says it's nothing, but I just can't let it go. Look- I know she asked him to get her out of that jam... and we're very grateful... but he's a young, handsome guy. I'm sure the women fall all over him. I don't know... he may even have called her a few times since then. I don't need that kind of aggravation in my life."

"Jim, I understand exactly how you feel. I don't know what happened, if anything, but I promise you this- I will find out and put a stop to it." He glanced over as the door to the bar opened.

Jack's eyes froze as he noticed them sitting there together and he tried moving away to the other end of the lounge. Seeing Frank waving him forward, he hesitated to regain his composure, then approached.

"Hello, Jack." Jim kept his hands at his sides.

"Hi Mr. Peterson. How are you?" he said, the lilting pitch of his voice revealing his anxiety. He sat down slowly on the stool, Frank situated between them. "Frank, good to see you." He focused on the brass railing at his feet for several seconds.

"Well, Jack- Jim and I wanted to finally have that drink we'd planned for a long time, since you and I worked on their case." Frank kept his eyes on him, analyzing any changes in his behavior as though he were a suspect.

Jim finished half the glass and put it on the bar next to the bowl of cashews. "I know you helped Natalie out of that mess. Thanks. There's no need to check up on her or me. Just want to let you know, we're *doing fine*. I don't think we'll need any more follow-up calls, *O.K.??*" He pierced Jack's eyes with his glare, daring him to turn away.

"Oh, I was just... umm... making sure you were both safe... no open issues. Good to hear that." He coughed and waved to the bartender. "Grey Goose martini, please. Very dry." He coughed harder, the groan much louder as he grabbed a light blue handkerchief from his suit pocket.

"Shaken, not stirred?" Jim imagined as he watched Jack wavering slightly on his stool. "I want to see him squirm- right in front of his boss" he thought, taking a long gulp.

Frank eyed Jack's expression and broke the silence. "Well, Jack- it's fine that you followed up on this case, but everything's resolved, so our job is *done*. I know you have a large workload to concentrate on. You don't need any distractions."

"Yes, Frank. I agree completely. There's a stack on my desk that never seems to disappear." He took a sip and tried not to look at Jim, who kept his eyes locked on him.

Jim stood up and put a $20 bill on the bar, a feeling of victory giving him a lift after hearing Frank's words. "Frank, this has been fun. I should be going soon. Natalie loves to make me her special lamb patties wrapped in bacon, sautéed in roasted sesame oil. It's my favorite. There's this great gourmet market down the street from us in Kennett Square called The Country Butcher. They have wonderful cuts of meat. Everything's fresh-veal, lamb, the best Rib-Eye's and Delmonico's you've ever seen. She spoils me all the time. I've become addicted to her pampering." He noticed Jack reaching out his hand.

"Mr. Peterson, great to see you. I'm glad you're both doing well."

He waited a few seconds before holding out his hand in return. "So am I."

"Jim, we have to get together more often. Maybe we can have dinner sometime at the Dilworthtown Inn" Frank suggested.

"I love that place, very rustic. Their tableside Caesar is great. One spot that's even closer to us has the best mushroom soup in the state. The Kennett Square Inn. Their menu is su-perb- beef tenderloins, crab and scallop Alfredo over Angel hair pasta, it's all delicious. Next time, we're there for cocktails and a feast."

"Sounds like a plan. Thanks for coming by." Frank got up and wrapped his arm around Jim's shoulder. "Let's do that soon." Frank watched as he went out the door, then turned his attention to Jack. "A great guy. We've become friends since finishing up that case. Friendships are precious. I treat them that way." He regarded Jack intently. "*You should, too.*"

"Oh, I will… I mean… I do, sir. I certainly will." He felt an arrow deep into his chest, thinking about his last call to Natalie, but started to breathe a bit easier as he saw Frank's grin.

"Make sure of it." Frank started to take out a $10 bill, but felt his arm being pulled down.

"I'll get this one, on me. It's a pleasure having a drink with you, sir. I always learn a lot."

Frank put the bill back in the black leather wallet and tucked it into his coat. "That's what life's all about." He turned and walked out the door as Jack gulped his drink down to the ice...

Chapter 11

"If it keeps up, man will atrophy all his limbs
but the push-button finger."
                                        --Frank Lloyd Wright

"Seems way too early to celebrate Halloween." He inspected his side mirror in the fading light as they approached the access road.

"It's not Halloween, but it'll get us in the mood."

He turned into the back entrance, the highly fractured blacktop evidence there'd been no maintenance for over 20 years. The narrow, winding road had been flanked by a thick overgrowth of shrubs and trees, recently plowed down, the rough-hewn limbs strewn about as if they were thrown by reckless vandals intent on destroying the landscape.

"This is AMAZING!! Starting to look spooky already!!" She glanced out her side window as the sun approached the horizon. "Bring on the spirits …"

"I prefer my spirits aged 15 years… single malt." The SUV weaved slowly around the turns on the back road leading to the complex, trees overhanging from both sides creating a dense, impermeable canopy, a bleak scene in the twilight. "Only 6:30 and it's already getting dark. Turns aren't too easy to maneuver, either. Can't imagine what it would be like driving here in the Winter after a snowstorm. That would have been a real horror show" he said as he slowed the car around every bend. He nodded as they approached the young man waving traffic on toward the parking lot.

"You know, this complex is enormous- 26 buildings spread across 100 acres, most of the structures connected by underground tunnels. When this place was in operation, there were delivery trucks coming and going 24 hours a day. With all that activity for so many years, I don't know why people are making such a ruckus about a Halloween exhibit. Seems a lot less intrusive than when the place was actually open." Sue peered at the trees still standing in the distance, ones which managed to survive the recent executions.

"I think it's more about the nature of the event- potentially a wild, gruesome display which some people feel pokes fun at the disabled and the pain they endured. Wait, Jim... slow down!!"

"What?!!"

"Over there... on the top of that building!!" She grabbed the camera and started taking shots.

"Looks like a big vulture. So ugly!! I think it's staring right at us- watching us go toward Pennhurst." Sue rolled down her window and leaned outside the car.

"Jim, remember that pack of vultures I saw at Frick's Lock? They seem to always know when something has died."

"Even vultures must have feelings. Remember that mother vulture who sat on the white plastic baseball out on the edge of the tidal basin day after day, thinking it was the egg she'd lost? Hard to equate her with the ruthless ones."

"You're right. All God's creatures have a place. I was sad when you took the ball away, but I know it was to keep our kitties safe. See that building over there? The roof's almost gone… windows all broken, too." She gazed out both sides of the car as they passed the row of turn of the century buildings, long neglected, falling into horrible disrepair.

"I just hope the tour is through the more stable ones. Should have worn a helmet." He brought the SUV to a stop on the gravelly surface. "Ready?"

"Absolutely!" She shut her door and proceeded quickly as they approached the line heading into the complex. "It's already pretty dark. I don't know if we'll be able to take any decent photos. Might be blurry." She held the camera in front of her as they walked into the tunnel. "Neat! I wonder if there are any bats in here!!" The tunnel's red brick lining felt like a bloody garment draped around them. Darkness enveloped her as she noted the edges of the walls crumbling, plaster lying all along the dirt below.

"Let's get through this. I don't enjoy standing in dark tunnels. Gives me the feeling we're sitting ducks" Jim protested.

"For what?" She was taking it all in, scanning the scene for markers, signs of the past.

"Anything or any*one* who wants to take a crack at us. Keep moving."

"Oh, stop. This puts me in the right mood. Get ready for something different."

"There's something *different* up ahead. We're about 30 years out of date for this crew." He pointed to the long line of kids- all in their late teens and early twenties, many with tattooed arms and faces, nose rings, Mohawks with blue hair making their way up the path to the small trailer which served as a ticket booth.

"Kids like scary things. Anyway, I'm ready for my first Halloween tour."

"Those kids *ARE* the scary things."

"Glad we got here early. Looks like it could be packed later on." Sue followed within a few feet of them both, stopping to kneel and pick up scattered fragments of the bridge.

Leaves on many of the overhanging shrubs were already turning, a blend of apricot, ruby and gold creating a vibrant backdrop to the desolation surrounding them. "Where to?" Jim shouted to the guide as he saw the bend in the dirt path.

"Just up ahead- about 100 yards. Can't miss it."

Jim turned to make sure Sue was nearby. "Almost there. Looks like we present our passes at that trailer where the people are standing." He maneuvered around the ruts on the muddy path and saw the personnel stationed near the perimeter.

"I bought three VIP tickets, so we can go through the line without waiting." Natalie took the printout from her purse. "Look at that building with the boarded up windows and barricaded doorway, the dark stained walls all around it, crumbling into dust. Looks like a hallway scene from 'Murders In the Rue Morgue'."

"Let's not bring Poe into this. It'd scare *him* off." He observed the edges of the brick structure, its front porch near collapse bordered by a roof giving way to broken timbers underneath. Above the porch, a double window revealed one wooden frame caved in, its neighbor still intact. Flanking on both sides were duplicates boarded up with buff-colored plywood, themselves cracked and streaked from years against the elements. The window on the left seemed to be inviting him to peek inside. "Come closer... We have nothing to hide..." He felt a wrenching stiffness in his neck as he gawked at the adjacent building, many small rectangular glass windows shattered, a war zone of splintered beams below, half covered with overgrown vines. "You can't get away..." His shoulders began to shake despite the warm breeze.

"Here's your tickets."

"These are really neat!! The picture of the Administration Building surrounded by storm clouds... a ghostly presence hovering above the building. The Bates Motel and Chake Productions Presents 'Pennhurst Asylum- The Fear is Real'. Was this from that movie 'Psycho'?" Sue displayed a wide grin as she examined the ticket, then peered up at the buildings surrounding them.

"Could be. That was a great movie. We'll see how frightening they think they can make this place... I don't scare easy." She walked slowly along the path toward the entrance where enormous 100-year old oaks and sycamores lay uprooted, their grotesque, gnarled root systems pointing to the air, as if pulled from the dirt by a monstrous hurricane. "Good Lord! Check out those ghoulish trees" Natalie exclaimed as she pointed towards the giant trunks spewing their entrails.

"Up there. Must be... mountains of woodchip piles? This place is owned by a composting company- that's probably why they uprooted all the trees." Jim noted one lying sideways, its' twisted arms writhing out from the trunk, the mangled treetop its face, screaming in agony.

"This *is* a clip from a horror movie. Even the trees are grue-some. Very bizarre. There's woodchips everywhere!! They're piled up along the sides of those buildings, spilling into the windows." The scene had Sue and Natalie mesmerized.

"I see a guide up along the elevated pathway." Jim filed past the teenagers and stood next to the man in his late 50's, silvery hair down over his ears, a three-day beard surrounding a toothy grin. "Hi there. We're wondering about the history of this place. Anything you can tell me?"

"Sure. Worked here from the mid-70's until they closed. What did you want to know?" His steel blue eyes were pierc-ing, yet his voice was calm, friendly.

"That's interesting. You probably have a different perspec-tive from most of the other guides. Just curious- what was it like to work at the asylum?"

"Well, we didn't call it that. It was the Complex. Some people called it the Hospital. Had its ups and downs. I actually didn't mind working here. I was young- in my 20's back then. What do ya' know at 22? When you finally figure out that your drinkin' buddies aren't goin' to help get you a job and put money in your pocket, you start lookin' at life in a new way. The world's a different place when mom and dad aren't payin' the bills. I just wanted a decent paycheck, that's all. At first, I was a bit hesitant to work at a place that'd been in the news. You know, all the stories you heard, but it wasn't so bad, re-ally. I never saw any of the horrible things you may have heard about."

"What was your job?" Jim glanced back to see Natalie and Sue leaning over the railing to get close-ups of the adjacent buildings.

"At first, exterior maintenance. Worked the crew here for... oh, about five years. Then they needed some help inside with the patients- and those jobs paid a little better, ya' know? So I applied and they took me the next day!! I was an assistant to the main team which took care of the people."

"The 'children'?

"Yeah... the 'children'. Some of 'em were in their 40's and 50's... even had a few old ones in their 80's... They were all our children."

"Was it tough, taking care of the... disabled?"

His head dropped, concentrating on his worn boots, the old shine hidden by scuffs and dust, the soles thin from too many miles. "Ya' know, at first it wasn't too bad... but it got tougher the more I thought about it. I mean, ya' see these people- kids and grownups, who not only can't take care of themselves- some of 'em couldn't stand up on their own. Like... totally helpless." His eyes moistened as he wiped his nose on the back of his cuff. "I don't care if you're rich or poor, have a high-payin' job or live in the ghetto. When ya' see people who can't help themselves, you gotta' have a heart and try to lend a hand, you know?" He waited for a reaction, then turned away. Coughing, he put his hand to his mouth and looked toward the distant buildings of the complex.

"I'm with you. It must have been tough." He noticed the man was still focused away from him. "I'm sorry, my name's Jim."

He turned and straightened up as he put out his hand. "Bill."

"What were the hardest places to work here? Any of the buildings worse than others?"

"You see that one over there? That was the "Q" complex. Some of the worst ones were in there."

"What do you mean? Violent patients?"

"Not necessarily violent, although a few of 'em were. The guys in there were the furthest gone, if ya' know what I mean. Some of them spent their days in another world- and could get outta' control at times. Tryin' to figure out what was goin' on in their minds... drove me... nuts..."

"Ever have a run-in with them? Any fights?" Jim inspected the side of Bill's face and could see his jaws tensing up.

"Well... a few times we had to get the security team in there, but generally things weren't too bad. One time I do remember one of the patients was mouthing off to a security guard, sayin' things like 'I'm gettin' outta' here!!' and 'You can't keep me in here!!'- like he was gonna' break outta' the place."

"What happened?"

"I had to run up and jump the guy after he decked the security guard who was just a little dude. Don't know why they made *him* security! At any rate, I was all over this guy- and he was built like a bear!! I mean, his chest must have been 48 inches, thighs like tree trunks. I could barely hold him. Thank God two more security guys showed up. He would've thrown me, for sure!! This dude wasn't actually violent. He was just a big guy who lost it once. Had to 'cool' him for a while."

"What do you mean? Solitary confinement?"

"Yep. Padded room for a few days until he calmed down. I'm just glad he didn't toss me through a wall!!"

Jim nodded, then observed his eyes, sensing both caution and compassion. "You were brave, working at a place like this." Jim noticed Natalie wandering along the platform holding her camera up, ready for shots.

"When you're young and need to pay the rent, even a tough job is a good one. I learned a lot."

"About what?"

"Myself. Who I am as a person. I don't have a lot of money- and probably never will… but you can't call yourself a human being until you've at least tried to help someone in need, know what I mean? Don't have to be a creative genius to figure that one out…"

"You can be proud of that."

"Thank you. No matter what you heard about this place, the news reports and horror stories, just know that there were a lot of good people working here- taking care of good people who couldn't do the same. I can look at myself in the mirror every day and know I did the right thing."

"You sure did. The world's a much better place with people like you."

"You, too. Hey, enjoy the 'freak show'!!"

Jim chuckled as he spotted Natalie walking well ahead of him.

Sue and Natalie leaned across the railing. "This must have been a garden."

"Check out the antique birdbath." Sue stretched further to get a closer look.

"There was an old birdfeeder at Frick's Lock. Strange coincidence- what's with abandoned towns and birds?"

"Ask Hitchcock… bet *he* knew the answer."

Natalie surveyed ahead and spotted them- a swing set- with no swings. "Eerie. A place where children once played. Looks forgotten… like all the patients." She saw the 10-foot high metal slide, now completely rusted, its feet indented into the weeds below, the end of the slide pointing to a depression three feet wide in the soil. "Sue, that slide would take a few layers of skin off."

"Sign me up! My thighs could use a trimming."

"Hey, look over past the Jungle Jim. That sign says 'Dietary'. Abe said Quaker Hall was next to the Dietary Building. At least we won't have to walk far to get in there." Natalie re-focused on the Admin building just ahead as the three approached the asylum entrance. "Those ceramic plaques, aren't they beautiful? The colors, so vibrant. Quite a contrast to the dreary surroundings. They have an Art Deco look. That one- the slave women working in the fields- it's quite nice."

"Too bad someone chipped off her boobs and face."

"Sue, you're incorrigible!!" Jim interjected. "Too many horror movies- always looking for something gruesome."

Sue just shrugged and grinned at Natalie, studying the surface of the sculpture.

"The one over there looks a bit convoluted, almost like a psychedelic nightmare." Jim studied its pattern- teal blues swirling amongst yellows, browns and pink pastels. Small figures cowered in the lower corners amongst vases filled with flowers and... a yellow-eyed ghoul in the upper right corner. "Couldn't be. Was this how the patients saw their world?" he wondered.

"Perfect time to enter the 'nightmare'. Let's go!!" Sue declared.

Natalie stepped to the front and handed the guide her ticket. "Does the VIP pass mean we get an up-front seat with the ghosts?"

The young man in the Aeropostale T-shirt grinned. "Oh…
it'll be up front, all right. In your face in some spots. Enjoy the
tour." He ripped the lower half off at the perforation, handing
her the stub. "Keep this- or you may not be able to get back
in- or out…"

"Think this is the room with the history of the place- a
mini museum." Natalie proceeded to examine each item- photos of the facility from the 1930's- 1950's hung along the
scarlet walls. Men in suits wearing three-inch wide flowery ties
and brimmed hats stood admiring the latest technology just
installed- an intercom. They filed past the exhibit, noting the
dates of each addition to the complex. "Buildings were added
in several phases" Natalie noted as she reached her hand back,
making sure Jim was right behind her.

Jim studied each face on the wall, their 1950's grins the
same ones he remembered from Burma Shave commercials,
hearing their voices from decades ago. "We're glad you could
come… step through the entrance to the compound, please…"
Jim managed a tenuous smile as he proceeded forward.

She heard a scream from the adjacent room, feeling the
twinge of excitement as she crossed the threshold into the darkened foyer. A nurse sat at a large white desk, shuffling papers.
Then she gazed up at Natalie. "Please proceed to your left for
processing. All patients must go!! No personal possessions" she
instructed sternly.

"Notice anything unusual about the nurse?" Natalie asked
Jim.

"Yeah, half her face is gone!!" Sue howled.

Jim chuckled, then shook his head. "Gives new meaning to
the phrase 'I have half a mind to…'"

"Welcome to the Asylum!! Hah-hahhh!!!!!" A bloody ghoul jumped out, sending everyone scurrying as he tried to touch them.

Rounding the corner, a girl stood petting a live rat. "Yessss... everything will be OK... Don't worry" she whispered, leaning her face into the rats' pale fur. "BUT EVERYTHING ISN'T OK... AAAAHHHHHHHHHHHH!!!!" she screamed, running to the other corner next to Natalie.

"Whoa!!" Natalie jumped back, then laughed, avoiding the girl, keeping her arms against her sides. "That rat will probably need psychiatric care before closing time."

Jim watched as the scene turned to total darkness, ducking slowly past the metal chains dangling down in front of them. "I can't see anything."

"That's the idea" Sue smirked as she kept within two feet of him going into the blackness.

"WHO ARE YOU???!!!! YOU SHOULDN'T BE IN HERE!!!! GO AWAY!!!" A woman dressed in a shredded nurse uniform holding an axe approached him, swinging the weapon as she got near.

He pulled back sharply and his eyes could barely focus on the light arcing into the hallway from a side room as he stepped forward.

"You are now entering the asylum. You may not leave!!" He read the sign a second time as he filed past two other people gaping up at a bloodied body hanging on a hook from the ceiling. He slowly advanced into the next room, where a young man's body lay limp in a dentist chair, his face dripping with blood, the metal clamp stretching his mouth wide open.

"This is what happens to bad boys who bite!!" screamed the

man in the dentists' frock. He lifted the bloodied pliers in front of Jim, forcing him to step back.

Sue nudged past them both and stopped. "Gross!!" Moans emanated from the next room, where lights flashing on and off caused a scene of confusion, people before them hesitating to go forward. They filed down corridors filled with wandering zombies and screaming teenagers. Entering the morgue, she gawked at the long metal autopsy table where a body laid dissected, exposed ribs and entrails spilling over the edges, dripping onto the floor.

"Would you like to assist with my experiment? I could use a hand" the mad doctor asked, smirking as he held the patient's severed hand in front of him.

Natalie managed a half-smile and moved past him quickly. Sue edged by Jim to be next to her. "Hi there. Spooked yet?"

"Nope... pretty goofy if you ask me." A staggering zombie opened a door and pointed down the stairs. They descended cautiously to the underground chamber. "This must be the entrance to the tunnels. Way COOL! Looks like we can just wander around... Pretty dark... and empty, too. Time to make our detour. Sue, you stay here while we go a little 'off course'."

"OK... I'll bail you out later."

"That looks like a stairway over there" Jim indicated, pointing ahead. Moving swiftly down the tunnel, they stepped into an alcove and out of sight.

"We can go out up there." The cement stairs were streaked with rust, the decaying wooden balustrade creaking as they held on and climbed toward the back door. She hesitated. "What if the door is alarmed?"

"A possible jail sentence didn't stop you, but you're worried about a stupid alarm? If it goes off, we run back… okay? For now, let's keep moving." Jim breathed in, then pushed the door slowly, peeking outside into the night. "No spotlights or German Shepherds. Coast is clear…"

"Wait, hold the door open. I want to stick something in here so it won't lock behind us." She checked the nearby bushes and found a broken branch. "Here, this should do the trick."

"Let's hope no raccoons try to sneak in to nibble on these- or we're toast." He placed the wooden limb at the base of the door and let it close slowly. "Done. Let's go." He took the flashlight from inside his windbreaker and shone it ahead as they moved cautiously forward, weaving their way through the underbrush, twigs crackling beneath their feet. Natalie only saw part of Orion above amidst the blackness. Heavy clouds washed across the sky, an approaching thunderstorm rumbling loudly in the distance.

"Remember that episode on Ghost Hunters?" she asked, ducking under a branch, trying to keep the buildings in sight. "They said people heard kids crying and yelling 'I have no teeth!!' from an empty bathroom. I think it was in the Devon building. Also reported that security went into the Mayflower Building and heard pianos playing, doors banging and things moving around- but the place was completely deserted. One guy saw a ghost of a woman in a white dress floating through the hallways. The Quaker Building apparently had the most volatile patients. The show said that's where the scariest haunt-ings are, too."

"No worry. I don't believe in ghosts. I'll protect you."

"With what- a four inch flashlight?"

"Check it out." He pointed to the cracked, half-broken

sign. 'Quaker'. "We'll have to go around and locate a way inside." Brushing past dense foliage, they maneuvered to the back. "Over there! A side window's open." He took her hand as they reached the edge of the wall, then helped her climb over the windowsill, avoiding the broken glass all around. They rested in the empty hall while Jim panned the flashlight.

"A stairway. Abe said Randolph's room was near the back-on the second floor near a staircase!!" She climbed ahead of him to the second floor, stepping slowly across the rotted beams which had fallen from the side walls. She stopped at a broken, rusted wheelchair, its' leather seat now shredded, drooping to the floor. Water dripped on her forehead as she glanced at the paint peeling away in large slabs from the walls. "That must be his room!!" She entered the doorway and saw an old, moldy mattress on the floor, the cotton stuffing visible, stains spotting the surface.

Jim walked quickly up and kicked it, sending four mice scurrying. "SHIT!" he shouted, leaping out of the way.

"Where's Frankie when you need her? Hey, shine that over here." Hidden behind discoloration from years of weathering, faint markings could be seen, clearly made by a human being. She knelt down within inches of the surface, then started to touch the end of a large section about to detach from the wall. "Looks like writing here." The paint chip fell to the floor, crumbling to dust.

"No, STOP!! You'll ruin whatever is there. Just take a few photos."

"You're right." She stood up and scanned the entire wall, graffiti scrawled everywhere as she clicked. "Reminds me of the New York City subways before Giuliani. Hope no one saw the flash in here through the windows."

"Or the flashlight. Let's get back. I'm feeling like something wants us gone."

"Just a few more shots. You go ahead. I have a small penlight in my purse. I'll find you." She turned to the adjacent wall where several more scribblings were visible.

"Just hurry." He stepped around a mouse nibbling on a fragment of cloth and got to the doorway, peering out to the side hall. "If there *are* any ghosts, I hope they work the day shift." Walking slowly with the flashlight, he got to the far end where they first entered and searched into the darkness rimming the beam of light, then felt his shoulders pushed forward sharply. "Oww! Stop it, Natalie!" He spun around… finding no one. "What the…?" Moving ahead, a haze surrounded him and he heard low, muffled laughter… then his right arm was squeezed, pulling the windbreaker off his shoulder. "Let go of me!! Who's there??!!" Stepping back quickly, he flashed the light all around the hallway and saw… eyes… glaring back at him… fading as they withdrew. "It can't be… I… don't believe in… Must have bumped into something. I'm seeing spots… Probably focused on the flashlight too long." Shaking, he went back toward the room. "Natalie!! Let's get outta' here!!"

She came up to his side. "I'm ready."

He was silent as they made their way back through the woods, the door still slightly ajar, a small crack of light penetrating the darkness from the other side.

"So… any success?" Sue inquired, stepping out of the darkened corner.

"Possibly. Got several shots of a room with faded handwriting… and some pretty wild graffiti."

"Jim, are you alright? You look a bit- dazed…"

"I'm fine." He examined the jacket sleeve. Gray markings smudged the white material, the vague impression of a hand imprinted along his arm.

"This place is filthy. Looks like you brushed up against a post or railing."

Jim stared a moment longer, then wiped the spots off.

"Let's go. The exit is up ahead."

Jim moved quickly past her. He trekked at a brisk pace, putting almost 50 yards between them, but slowed as the light from the far exit suddenly dimmed. "What? How could that happen?" He peered ahead and felt his chest pushed back. The grey shroud flew around his face and hovered a few feet in front of him as he froze in disbelief. Misty fog enveloped him, wrapping itself around his chest, a man's grip, blacking out the scene completely. "Oh, my God!! Stop!! Get AWAY FROM ME!!" He threw his arms into the air and tried to step back, falling onto the muddied floor. "Oww!! Ohh… my back!!!" Kneeling to get up, he felt the push again- and a sharp, cool breeze rushing past as he finally got to his feet. "What in the *hell is happening*?" He felt the horror surge through his veins- and saw it. A tall man drifting away wearing a patient's uniform, soiled and ragged… dissolving in front of his eyes.

Jim turned as he heard footsteps, hoping to see Natalie. His heart was pounding ferociously in his chest and he could barely breathe, hyperventilating as he tried to put his hands up to open his collar. He was helpless, as in the dream. "Can't… move!!" He waited to gather the strength for a step backward, but was paralyzed. The EXIT sign at the end of the tunnel became visible again. "I can't *breathe*!! I… I need to sit down." He leaned onto the wall and tried to steady himself as the footsteps became louder. "Natalie??!! Sue?? Are you there?"

"Yes, but we could barely see you!! You got too far ahead" Natalie remarked, emerging in the twilight of the tunnel.

"Hey, your face is totally pale. Milky white. Do you feel OK?" Sue put her hand on his right shoulder.

"Umm… I think so, but something very strange happened. Did you see it?"

"We saw you up ahead, then the lights flickered and you faded out for a moment. That's all." Natalie wrapped her arms around him as he steadied himself.

"It was bizarre. The light from that EXIT sign dimmed… I kept walking… then I felt a push!! I couldn't believe it. I was enveloped in some kind of fog… cold and damp. I could make out the shape of a man floating near me… reaching out."

"No WAY!!" Sue's eyes widened as she leaned closer to him.

"My heart nearly stopped… I was horrified."

Natalie could tell from his expression he wasn't exaggerating. "Are you sure you're all right? Rest a second. It looks like you're about to fall over."

"I'm fine, let's just get the HELL out of here!!" He picked up the pace leading them through the passageway. Then he looked up and saw something dangling over the door.

"AAAAHHHHH!!!! GO!!!" A young woman in shackles leaped at Jim, her hands trying to grab him.

"You're a ghoul I can deal with, but what's that?" He pointed up into the light and saw the bloodstained rope tied into a noose, swinging side to side above them.

The woman glanced up. "What??!! That wasn't there a few

minutes ago." Her eyebrows raised in disbelief.

"That's a hanging noose." Jim focused on its entire length, still swaying back and forth. "From the looks of it, someone just put it up there... and I don't want to find out why." He grabbed Natalie's hand firmly and brushed past the woman into the night. He could see the crowd gathered at the bottom of the exit ramp, floodlights all around. "What in the world's going on down there?"

"Looks like a... TV crew?"

"I think it is. I see a Channel 10 truck. There's the cameraman. They may be interviewing people about the exhibit." Jim walked forward into the spotlights just as the reporter approached. She was an attractive woman in her 30's, chestnut hair, well dressed with a professional demeanor, holding the microphone up to his face.

"Excuse me, sir. What did you think of the event?"

"Well, it was... scary enough for me." He saw the images in front of him again and started to sweat.

"You're aware of the controversies concerning Pennhurst- the abuses, the horrible conditions, unconventional treatments. There was a lot of pressure NOT to allow this exhibit to open tonight."

"There *were* atrocities here. Apparently some of the workers did some harm, which was criminal... but tonight- this wasn't offensive. It's for Halloween."

"How about you, ma'am? Any comments on the controversy?"

Natalie stepped up to the microphone, into the floodlights as the camera crew rotated toward her. "We certainly respect people who were here... the conditions they were under at the time. It's very easy to tell reality from something fake."

"Thank you, folks!! Oh, this is rolling live and will also play later on tonight. What are your names?"

Jim stepped back into the floodlights. "I'm Jim Peterson. That's my partner in crime, Natalie." Jim noticed Natalie smiling as she turned away.

"Thanks so much!!" The reporter turned back toward the camera man. "There you have it. Somewhat of a mixed reaction tonight. Some people here outside the gates, who didn't want to come in, are still angry that a place with the reputation of Pennhurst should ever be opened again- especially with a horror show exhibiting ghoulish patients running around scaring people. Others, like those folks we just saw, were not offended. We'll be interviewing more as they come through over the course of the evening. This is Claudia Ravens, Channel 10 News."

———≫•《❖》•≪———

Across town, Richie Olson was watching TV when he got up from the couch and threw the beer can against the wall. "BASTARDS!! They wanted to stick the knife in one more time!! Now the news people are gonna' start blamin' us again for all that shit… Everybody'll start sayin' I caused it all!! Neighbors talkin' behind my back… He's dead!! Dead meat!! I'll show him something he doesn't want to see…" He grabbed the remote control and clicked the T.V. off. Marching into his bedroom, he sat in front of the computer. "This'll scare the shit out of 'em!!" He crafted the images together, weaving ghouls moaning in agony amidst cracked skulls. The screams got louder… louder… ear splitting… AAHHHH!!!!! OOOOOHHHH!!!!! STAY

AWAY!!! STOP NOW OR I'LL COME AFTER YOU AND RIP YOUR HEAD OFF!!!" The intense shrieking strained the speakers on the desk, causing them to crackle. He hit "SEND." The screen cleared, then he turned and flipped off the computer, smirking. He inspected the business card. "I know where you live too... and I'm gonna' get you, good..."

"Is that you, Richie?"

He heard the tired voice from the other room. "It's O.K., grandpa. Everything's fine. Go back to bed..."

———◦((◦))◦———

Jim pulled the car into the garage and glanced over through the side window to make sure there was no one behind them on the cul-de-sac. "Looks clear" he decided as they entered the house. "Natalie, can you check my e-mail? I was hoping to hear back from the Historical Society on that upcoming lecture. I need to use the restroom."

"Not a problem." She bounded up the stairs and sat down in front of the screen. "Quite a few today. This one seems... odd. Check that first." She clicked on the e-mail and the horrifying scene unfolded, freezing her in the chair. The images gripped her and she couldn't move her arms... the man on the screen screaming in agony... dissolving into a scene of bloody mayhem... crushed skulls, howls and moans of pain from writhing bodies... and then the threats. "Oh, MY GOD!!!" She sat for a minute, stunned in silence. "I have to save this. It's evidence. Whoever sent this is deranged and dangerous. This is *criminal*." She turned off the computer and raced down the stairs.

"Now YOU look like you've seen a ghost. Are you okay?"

"I... don't know. I checked your e-mail. I didn't see one from the Historical Society. I... didn't get far enough... but I did see something... shocking."

"What could be worse than what we just saw at the asylum?" He thought back to the e-mail from weeks earlier.

"Oh, my God!! It was terrible. I've never seen anything like it!! It had screams and people moaning in agony... skulls dripping with blood. Horrible!! Then a voice yelled they were coming to get us. Oh, Jim it was so frightening. I cannot believe someone would send something so demonic."

"I got an e-mail the same day we went out to visit that guy and his less than pleasant grandson. Remember him?"

"Abe. Of course!! What did you get?"

"That same night I sat down to check my e-mails and I saw something I didn't recognize, so I clicked on it first. Turns out, it was this weird, shocking scene... skulls dripping with blood... moans... screams of distress... I deleted it immediately."

"Did you ever empty your 'TRASH'?"

He thought for several seconds. "I never did!! It's got to still be in there..."

"I know someone we can send it to... for analysis."

"Who? Inspector Clouceau?"

"No... somebody who worked on the Cyber Crime unit at the FBI. Jack Clark."

"Not *that* Jack Clark."

"Yes, but please don't worry!! This is serious and it has to be reported. If I forward these e-mails to him, he should be able to run a trace and find their source. The one I just saw was criminal... way over the line, the product of a horribly disturbed mind. Whoever sent it should go to jail for virtual assault."

"Let me see the one you just received and we'll decide how to proceed. Anyway, if the FBI is contacted, it will be Rawlins, not Clark..."

———— ⟨⟨◉⟩⟩ ————

Dexter set the empty mug on the bar and nodded to the bartender for a refill. Floyd flubbed another shot at the pool table, the stick missing the cue ball, leaving a blue streak across the felt. He stomped away, tossing the pool cue against the wall where it slid down, bouncing off the floor.

"Geez, Floyd- what gives? You've been actin' squirrely all night." He peered over as the bartender pulled back the tap and filled the mug.

"It's nothin' man. Just a little bad luck." Floyd grabbed his beer and dropped in the shot glass filled with whiskey, then guzzled it down in a few seconds. Wiping his mouth on his sleeve, he pounded the glass down on the bar. "One more, will ya' Leon?"

"You're hittin' the booze a bit hard tonight. What's buggin' you?" Dexter asked, straightening up on his stool.

"Cindy's not gettin' a paycheck... bills are comin' in. I'm late on the mortgage already." He pounded the empty glass on the table two times. "Come on Leon, fill 'er up. Don't have all night, ya' know!"

"Couldn't you take another part-time job until she gets some work?"

"Bullshit, Dexter... get real! You know I'm already workin' 12 hour days and a second job fixin' rigs on the weekend!

Whudd'ya want me to do, work my ass off 18 hours a day so I can drop dead?" He tossed the shot in the glass and chugged the beer again, only a little slower, taking two passes to finish.

"OK... Bad idea." Dexter slid off the stool, racked up the next game and cleared the first three in a row off the table before missing a tough bank shot. "Your shot, Floyd."

"Forget it... I can't hit a friggin' thing tonight. I say we get drunk."

"Gets my vote." They sat quietly, each downing two more beers when Dexter finally sat up on the stool and started grinning.

"What the hell's got you so happy? Dreamin' about Mary Lou in that low-cut tank top again?"

"Nope... but I think I have somethin' that'll solve your problems. Remember that rich couple from Frick's Lock?"

"Not the stupid box again! Look, there was nuthin' but dusty old junk in it. Move on."

"I know... but I got a better idea. You know they didn't tell the cops about that box. Lyin' about stolen goods is a felony... I think. I'll bet if we go up to that guy and tell him we know about the box, he'd be willin' to pay us somethin' to keep quiet. Remind him about the cameras- the ones in the back you can't see. PECO's probably got it all on tape, somewhere... Wouldn't want that pretty wife of his *in jail*. Bet we could get five hundred... maybe a thousand bucks, easy!! He's got a fancy house, so we know he's got money. He could probably write us a check on the spot."

"You're kiddin' me, right? What are we supposed to do, ride up on a horse with a sword, like Zorro?'""

"No! We surround him somewhere and rough him up...

just a little bit. What do we have to lose? Worst case, he empties out his wallet and we at least get somethin'!! I say we head over after work, follow him around some night. Come on Floyd... cheer up. I'll even drive..."

"You're crocked... but a riot when you're drunk!!..."

"Who gets to be Zorro?"

Pennhurst State School and Hospital circa 1930's

Pennhurst compost piles

Chapter 12

"A creative man is motivated by the desire to achieve,
not by the desire to beat others."

--Ayn Rand

The digital clock's dial highlighted '4:30 a.m.' as she pulled the light yellow blanket from her face. Looking over to her right she heard Jim snoring, his arms wrapped around the pillow. "I can't sleep after that message. I've got to send it to Jack. He can help. No need for Jim to bother Frank Rawlins." She got up, wrapping the pink bathrobe around her as she stepped into the floppy-eared slippers. Glancing back, she noted Jim's eyelids fluttering, a sign of him soon awakening. "I can get it done before he's up." She tiptoed down the stairs, entering her office and turned on the computer.

After typing the same sentence three times- she stopped. "How can I do this without him thinking I'm coming on to him? I can't let that happen" she deliberated as she put her hands back on the keys. 'Dear Jack, I trust you're doing well. This note is written both in thanks and in hope. First, I need to tell you that your kindness was exceptional. I've rarely met a human being who went out of their way to help me so much. You've earned a special place in Heaven for that…' Her finger hovered over the 'DELETE' key for thirty seconds before starting to type. 'I do need your help again. Jim and I received two very threatening e-mails recently. They were… morbid, horribly frightening. We didn't recognize the address and have no idea who the sender was. I think they were sent by someone who's insane and could possibly hurt us. I recall that you'd worked in the Cyber Crime unit of the FBI and thought you might know what to do. I'm forwarding them here and hope you can determine the origin. My deepest thanks for your efforts and your good heart. Fondly, Natalie Peterson.'

The glass-walled sides of the high rise apartment building just off of 16th and Market in downtown Philadelphia showed the first rays of the sun streaming across its upper levels. On the 18th floor, Jack sat at the computer, sorting through the dozens of e-mails he received each day from associates, family, friends, a few old girlfriends and advertisements he didn't want. He peered at one with a headline that lifted his spirits as he tried to shake off the lingering dull headache from the four Belvedere martinis he'd had at McGillin's Olde Ale House. 'To a Friend…' He opened it and sat up close to the screen in the morning twilight. Sirens and horns honking below distracted him as he tried to concentrate on the words which appeared, reading to the end quickly. 'Fondly, Natalie Peterson.' "She likes you, Jack. You know it. Now she wants you in her life again. Sounds like an open invitation to me." He smiled as he clicked 'REPLY' and started typing.

'Dear Natalie, it's so good to hear from you. I'm doing well, busier than ever. Banking regulators and the SEC are pursuing

dozens of cases related to the mortgage meltdown and trans-
actions involving securities fraud- and we get to help. A lot
of work to do- good thing these days with layoffs all around.
I'm so sorry to hear about the threatening e-mails. Many cases
are being viewed as cyber-assault by judges these days- pun-
ishable offenses. We did have one case about two years ago- a
twisted guy who ended up participating in a long series of these
things- harassing someone to the point where they committed
suicide! It's a sad commentary on what we call 'progress' that
technology so promising can be used for such evil... I'll check
on the e-mails you forwarded. We have ways of finding out the
senders even if they utilized proxies and 'secured' addresses. I'll
get back to you as soon as I find out something useful. Please
call me anytime. I'm still open for that rain check on lunch...
Jack.'

She saw the pop-up in the lower corner of the screen as she
scanned the headlines on Yahoo News. "Yes!! I knew he'd help
me!!" She pondered the best way to respond as she heard the
parakeets chirp their first morning songs. 'Dear Jack, Thank
you so much for your help!! You have a gentle soul- one which
is dedicated in kindness to others. I'll always appreciate that.
–Natalie'

He leaned within five inches of the screen as the reply
came back. "Nothing about lunch, buddy boy. Cool down. No
'fondly' either. OK- time to decide. Is she keeping a line out for
you- or does she just want help?" He stared at each sentence,
reading them three times as he noticed the brightening sky.
"Who says she doesn't want *both*? Don't be such a pessimist!!
Look, she likes you! You can see it in her smile. Never let a
smile go to waste..." He saved the e-mails and strutted over to

the Cuisinart for the first cup of the day. "I think this is going to be an interesting relationship." He stretched his arms up before the 10-foot high plate glass showing the full skyline of Philadelphia around him... William Penn standing with his hat on, the PSFS electronic ticker-tape scrolling the headlines around the top of the 1960's era building several blocks in the distance. "You always liked the smart ones. The sly ones with a great personality. Forget all the others with the great curves, but 'lights on, nobody home'. This is a challenge- like your cases. She's going to be my next one, no matter what Frank says..." He took a long sip of coffee as he heard the taxis honking below...

——«()»——

Jim ambled slowly down the steps and walked up to the back of her desk chair. "Cleaning out your In-Box?"

"I couldn't sleep, thinking about those e-mails we got. I had to send them to Jack." She watched his expression as he stepped back from the chair. "Please, don't think anything more than this being a request for help. That's all it is!! He has experience in this. I think he'll be able to find the source and get them to stop. That's all I want." She stood up and wrapped her arms around his waist, but felt him pulling back.

"I thought you were going to let me think about it first! I know how guys are. I've got 54 years of experience in the area. He probably gets a lift every time he hears from you. You're a very attractive woman and men love the chase. Even though you're not putting out any bait, he smells the scent. I don't like it. Plus, we should have contacted Rawlins... not Jack."

"Jim, please don't!! You're working yourself up over nothing." She tried to pull him closer, but felt resistance to her grip. "I promise you, I won't give him any reason to think otherwise."

"He doesn't NEED a reason!! He's a guy and he sees you as 'available'- forget about being married!"

"I'll never forget that! I'm with the one and only man I want in my life!!"

He brushed the hair back from his forehead and hesitated before he spoke again. Taking a deep breath, he pulled her closer. "I know. I over-scrutinize things. That's one of my weaknesses. Being an analyst for 15 years- picking apart financial statements, trying to decide which CFO is honest and which one's cooking the books has made me cautious… Maybe a bit cynical, but… I don't want to be that way with you." He pulled her toward him and kissed her firmly, putting his left arm behind her neck to hold her close.

"That's the best kiss I've had since you proposed."

"Thought I'd worked it up a notch or two since then."

"I'll give you plenty of chances to practice. Let's forget all this stuff and have some breakfast. We have eggs, scallions, a nice big block of pepper jack cheese and sweet green chiles. Oh, I forgot- some tortillas which we should probably use before they get stale."

"I agree. Life's too short to eat old tortillas. Let's move on. Did I ever tell you about this place called The Laisy Daisy in Austin, Texas? It was our favorite hangout when I was in grad school. We used to go there late at night when we were hungry. They had these things called Migas. Grilled chorizo, which is Mexican spicy sausage, along with scrambled eggs, cheddar cheese, onions, refried beans and fresh salsa- all wrapped up in a large, warm flour tortilla. They were delicious. The Daisy gets credit for 30% of my Master's Thesis."

"No way, Jose!"

"They were pretty tasty. I think back to all the times I met my buddies there... Steve, Scott... We had a great time even though we didn't have much money. I mean- this was 1978. I think I made maybe $12,000 a year- tops- as a Research Assistant at the Bureau of Economic Geology. We'd also go over to this little place on the corner called The Posse just down the street from the geology building where they had ice cold beer on tap and a toasted sandwich called The Sheriff. It was our hangout on Friday afternoons. A whole bunch of us would sit at the picnic tables out on the patio in the sun- me, McD, Berge, Cumella- all of us downing beers, laughing and enjoying life. Those were days... we accomplished a lot. Sometimes I wonder if I could ever work back up to that level..."

"Of course you can. Control your mind and you determine your destiny."

"I'm making us Migas for breakfast." He strode into the kitchen and opened the refrigerator.

"Sounds good to me." She took out the cutting board as she heard the wind pick up outside. "You know, with all this rain, I think the basin may just fill up this time. The news reports said parts of New Jersey are under four feet of water right now."

"Always wanted a house on the water." He stood at the stove, flipping the ingredients in the large frying pan until they were golden brown. Taking the large spatula, he scooped it up and placed the food gently onto the tortilla, wrapping the steaming ends together to make sure it held tight. "Here we go. Enjoy."

She pulled her chair up to the glass table and took the first bite. "Mmmm… this is wonderful!! You can make these for me any time."

He ate slowly, thinking back to that day… raising his beer mug for a toast with his buddies in the afternoon sun…

"Hey, Berge!! You made it!"

"You doubted me? Where's your faith- and the beer? I thought you'd have a full pitcher waiting."

"Steve, grab another pitcher of Lone Star and a frosted mug."

"Will do, Jim."

Berge straddled the wooden bench and gave him a bear hug, his muscular arms wrapped tightly around Jim's shoulders. "I'm ready for a few… maybe a few more!!" He watched as Jim grabbed the pitcher, filling the mug right to the top, a full inch of foam starting to lap over the edge. Berge took a long gulp, splattering a few drops on his faded jeans and Earth shoes, cars passing by with suited businessmen loosening their ties on their way home from work.

"Someday that'll be us when we get *real* jobs." Jim pointed to the long line of cars weaving in both directions down the four lane road adjacent to The Posse, the whole crew of grad students listening to music blaring from the outdoor speakers. "Welcome to the Rat Race."

"Welcome, yourself. I'm ready for another beer!!" Berge glanced over at a dark blue 1971 convertible Pontiac Catalina cruising past, the drivers' head swaying to the beat of the radio as the wind blew back his hair. He poured another Lone Star and clicked his mug against Jims', giving him a big smile...

———————◄(◊)►———————

Jim sipped the cranberry juice and then took the last bite of chorizo as he glanced at the camera sitting on the counter. "Let's download all those photos from Pennhurst and print them out after we're done breakfast."

"I'm ready. That was delicious."

"When I first moved to Austin, I had no idea how to cook Mexican food. One time I asked a girl in class how to make guacamole. She said 'Just go to the store. You get them right there.' So I went shopping at the supermarket, but I wandered up and down the produce aisle for ten minutes without finding anything. The next week I saw her and said 'I went to the food store and looked all over the place, but I couldn't find any guacamoles.' She shook her head and walked away." Jim chuckled to himself. "Hey, while you're printing those pictures from Randolph's room, I'll do a quick search on American inventors. Back in a flash."

"I'll be in my office. It shouldn't take very long."

He pulled out the walnut chair, the woven seat cushion inviting him and inspected the endless number of listings. "Well, there are 17,453 on American inventors and that's just at the Free Library of Philadelphia. I could spend weeks going through all this." He paged ahead and saw the name alongside that of Henry Ford. "This is interesting. 'Technical personnel at the early utility plants'. A man named R. Larson worked at Edison Electric in the late 1890's! Could this be the same guy? Henry Ford worked there around the same time. If it was Randolph Larson, he must have been… in his 50's? Says he was a unique craftsman and assistant to the engineers- a mechanical wizard who could build or fix almost anything."

He entered Larson's name with 'inventor' and found 23 listings. "He's in several of these stories on early American inventors. Appears to have been a technical genius… helping to solve some complex problems which ultimately led others to several important patents. I gotta' print this." Then he saw it. 'Carolina News-Gazette, December 18, 1903. Two young bicycle mechanics from Dayton, Ohio- Wilbur and Orville Wright- may have just done something man has never done before- fly in an aeroplane. The two men have been doing flight experiments on the beach for months where they say the wind is helpful to their crude flying machine. With them on this day was R. Larson, one of many technical assistants to Wilbur Wright on the beach at Kitty Hawk. Orville Wright claims to have been the first man to fly. This reporter did not witness the supposed historic event.' His jaw dropped as he read the story a second time. "This guy could be for *real!!*" He clicked 'PRINT' and grabbed the sheets as they fell onto the tray.

"Ready to see some interesting photos?" Natalie pulled up the brown metal folding chair and put it next to her.

"Are YOU prepared to hear something *fascinating*?"

"Yes… What?"

"Look at this. A guy by the name of R. Larson was in this newspaper report from December 18, 1903- the day after the Wright Brothers made their maiden flight!! Says he was there as an assistant. This confirms the picture we saw in that book!!

If we were at The Sands in Vegas, I'd bet a thousand bucks it's the same guy."

"Calm down, Dino. It's not 'Ocean's Eleven'." She took the print-out and read the entire story. "That shows a link to what I just printed. Look at these photos from the wall writings. A lot of it's hard to read, the light was terrible, but there it is. 'I flew with the Wright Brothers'!! Check out this photo- even more interesting- says "Showed Edison the light'. Abe Olson was right!! This guy was either a lunatic or maybe... he really did have some connections with inventors."

Jim held the list of early inventors in front of her. "This seems to bear that out. He's mentioned here several times, although I didn't see him credited with any inventions. Abe said he was a very old man- about 93 when he met him in 1938. That would make him about 58 back in 1903 when the Wright Brothers were at Kitty Hawk. It's plausible. Benjamin Franklin was inventing things into his 80's and Edison himself worked until the day he died."

Her mind was processing each bit of information voraciously, as she had in her first computer class at Penn State in the early 1970's. Excitement built as she held up the next few prints. "Look at these photos. The first lines are hard to read, but he's written the same thing over and over so I could pick out the words from the duplicate lines. It appears to say 'Model T's because of me' and another one... 'Listen to MY phonograph, Tom'. Or, this one, it's almost illegible, but I'm guessing it reads 'Stood next to Lincoln'...? Who knows? He could have been *totally crazy*. This might all be nonsense. How can we possibly find out?"

He examined the photos and felt his pulse racing. "Well,

that exact name *is* mentioned in the story with the Wright Brothers... and all that stuff in the box seems to fit, at least tangentially. This guy was either a total fruitcake- or he knew some of the most famous inventors in the world."

"I actually *like* fruitcake. My mother said nobody really eats it. People just keep passing it on to their friends as gifts every year for the holidays because they hate it. Told me she got one recently dated 1978, but it was well wrapped- and still fresh."

"I have an idea. Didn't you say an old classmate of yours from Unionville high school was a sound expert?"

"Yes, that's Brent... Brent Ellsworth. We saw his brother Rod last year at the reunion party. I know Rod, but I barely knew Brent. He was in an earlier class. Why?"

"I thought you said he was a technical wizard and knew a lot about the history of sound recordings and different types of inventions."

"He is supposed to be an expert on early recordings. You'd like him- his brother said he's a big jazz fan. I remember Rod saying he lived somewhere in northern New Jersey, near Orange."

He held each photo in his hands, staring at the last one intensely. 'Stood next to Lincoln'. "We need to pay him a visit... but first I want to go over to the Hagley Library near Wilmington. They have a large collection of documents and photographs on the industrial history of America, along with an enormous library of books from the last 150 years. I already saw a few items in my web search and have a list. It won't take me long."

"I really enjoyed our visit to the Hagley Museum last Christmas... the freshly fallen snow blanketing the valley around the Brandywine. It was lovely viewing the scene from the upper deck there at the du Pont home."

"The owner wanted to have a good place to view the mills along the river- and he chose a great spot. E.I. du Pont's own history is fascinating. He studied under the famous French chemist Antoine Lavoisier- the discoverer of oxygen and nitrogen. During the French Revolution, his father's shop was ransacked by extremists, so the family fled to America in 1799. In 1802, he paid $6,740 for land along the Brandywine to build his first powder works. The company started making explosives and eventually expanded into different lines, after the First World War becoming a major investor in General Motors. In fact, they had such a close relationship and large investment in the firm, by 1929 GM accounted for roughly half of their earnings."

"Why did they want to get involved with the car industry?"

"The managers at Du Pont saw it as a rising star... and knew it would become a major force in our culture. Thank God they did. The famous industrialist Alfred P. Sloan at GM helped Du Pont restructure their businesses to run more efficiently. Du Pont eventually had to divest their ownership in GM, but the association allowed them to expand into numerous areas, including synthetic materials, paints and derivatives. That laid the groundwork for the firm to develop products for thousands of different applications. You probably didn't know that their digital displays are in many cell phones, PDA's and Blackberry's. The Du Pont logo is really an emblem of the success of the Industrial Revolution in America..."

"From a humble start- a giant enterprise."

"Not a bad investment, either. That initial $6,740 turned

into a company which today has revenues of $31.5 billion. Who would ever guess that an unknown chemist would eventually build a close connection with the automobile industry? Their titanium dioxide plant right outside of Wilmington produces the feedstuff for coatings of all kinds. Du Pont is now the leading provider of automotive paints to Ford. Henry's still smiling."

"Persistence pays... I know you and books. Just don't get carried away there. They may have to pry you from the armchair in the corner."

"Only if they serve me grapes and Opus One in cut crystal glasses... then I might be a bit late. See you soon." Heading south on Route 52 into the small village, the sign for the Fairville Inn flapped in the breeze as the wind picked up, the sky turning overcast... 'Travelers Welcome'... So who else would stay there- the guy next door? Always liked the Mendenhall Inn for Sunday brunch. Some people say that Krazy Kats in Montchanin is superb... have to indulge there at least once."

The drive toward downtown Wilmington brings one vision- the towering presence of the elegant Hotel du Pont, the center of life in the city at Tenth and Market, surrounded by its long standing neighbors. Stately Wilmington Trust which was founded by the du Ponts, the former U.S. Courthouse and the Wilmington Public Library complete the scene. All of them wrap around Caesar Rodney Square, the inviting greenspace where they hold the Jazz Festival every year... flanked by the statue of the patriot on his horse in front of the hotel, a reminder of the dedication of one man, riding all night in a driving rainstorm from Wilmington to Philadelphia to allow the deciding vote on the Declaration of Independence.

It's the Hotel du Pont where thousands of business deals have been discussed over the decades in the opulent Green Room, the food sumptuous and the service five-stars... gorgeous full-length draperies jacketing the guests in a cozy atmosphere of brocaded fabrics rimmed by hand-carved panels and plush carpeting. Even the glass-enclosed display cases along the hallways lined with marble remind you of yesteryear, when J.P. Morgan, Andrew Carnegie, Vanderbilt and Rockefeller built and expanded their empires. It all welcomes each visitor as if to say "A pleasure to have you... May I take your coat?" as you sit in one of the high-backed chairs, prepared to feast on a delicious breakfast or lunch. The walls whispering who sat there before you... and what dignitary is about to arrive.

He pulled the car up to the turn off from Route 141 North and headed down the back way, rolling hills and palatial estates surrounding the road. "Gorgeous homes. Definitely du Pont country." The driveway arced around, exposing a large 'Visitor Parking' area along with an overflow lot next to the two-story stone structure, its white columns announcing an impressive collection behind them. "Hard to believe he finally succeeded after seven devastating failures. Glad he didn't give up. A company more than two centuries old is still producing vital products today. That defines persistence. Now it's solar panels, bioengineered materials and membranes for high-tech batteries- and it all helped build this great library." As he approached the front heavy glass doors, three other cars pulled up, the lot filling completely.

"Hi. I'm here to do some research."

"Hello and thank you for coming to Hagley. Please sign in

here, then step over to your left where that woman can assist you."

He walked over past the two-foot high bronze bust of E.I. du Pont as a woman in her early 30's with dark brown hair to her shoulders stood behind the counter.

"Hi. I'm Linda. Are you here to view the archives?"

"Yes, a quick search. I've already printed out the list and checked the specific items I'd like to see."

"Fine. You can sign in right there. Do you have a Library Card for Hagley?"

"No, but I'd like to get one."

Autographing the line while Eleuthere's eyes watched from above, he saw five other people sitting in the adjacent room as Linda took the list to the back.

"Here you are. This is your Research Card. I've separated the books from the pamphlets. Please take a seat over there in the adjoining room and feel free to ask for anything you need."

As he sat down at the buff-colored table, three leaves swirled around the flagstone terrace in front of the glass-enclosed sitting room, a howling, rainy grey day bowing the branches of the trees. "Yes!! 'Edison- The Beginning of the Incandescent Lamp and Lighting System'... Tom- did you always insist on wearing only *black*? Same range of colors as in the Model A. 'Henry Ford- My Life and Work'... Your life *got me* to work... that Lincoln Town Car was one of my all-time favorite vehicles. By 1913, your Highland Park assembly plant revolutionized the industry and accounted for half of the cars built in America. Henry, you grasped the essence of a new mass culture emerging... and gave us the wheels to explore. 'Jack L. Shagena- How the Wright Brothers Got It Right'. Never seen that photo of *Wilbur* flying!! I always thought it was his kid brother who had all the guts. A lot to read through, but I already know what I want." Seeing Linda peering over at him through the window, he approached with four volumes in hand. "Is it possible to make copies?"

"Yes, right back there... 25 cents each. You can pay me directly. We don't have a debit card hook-up for the copier. It's a bit out of date."

"Is it just me, or are these old machines multiplying?"

"What was that?"

"Oh, nothing. I have cash. You really have a superb collection. I did a long search on-line and it's a wonderful resource."

"Thank you! We're proud of it. A lot of people come by to work."

He walked around the counter and flipped eagerly through each volume as they lay ready on the copier. Edison's daily diary... Orville's photo flanking his own handwritten comments on that fateful day. "Hmmm... That was actually fairly quick. I'm done. I had 20 copies."

"It'll be five dollars, even."

"Nice. No sales tax in Delaware. That- and a business friendly climate is why so many companies incorporate here. Should I put these back in order?"

"Not a problem. I can set them aside if you'll be doing a follow-up."

"That's extremely kind of you. Thanks so much."

"You're quite welcome." She gave him a smile as he walked past the bust and headed toward the entrance, winking at Eleuthere, the bust's gaze following him out the door. Then he stopped. "Hey, what's with all the cars outside?"

"It's Gunpowder Days. We do demonstrations of the use of gunpowder that du Pont made back over two centuries ago. It's also Antique Cars days all this week. We get dozens of vehicles from the 1920's through the 1950's. It's right over there next to the parking lot. Feel free to take a look."

"Thanks." He heard the door swoosh closed and crossed the lot toward a grouping of over 20 vintage vehicles. "Now *that* is a classic car. Could it be... a Model A?" He walked slowly toward the edge of the greenspace where the aging, yet dignified octogenarians were parked, all beaming despite the blustery weather around them. "It is. I'm sure of it." He looked up and saw the sign hanging on the edge of the heavy wire railing. 'AUTHORIZED PERSONNEL ONLY'. Glancing back towards the entrance, he noticed the hill and adjacent fields were vacant. "Nobody around. Everyone must be at that Gunpowder show..." He stepped over the heavy wire rimming the site and walked slowly toward the shiny black vehicle, leaning close enough to see inside. "What a beauty. Mint condition. The real thing... a Model A!!" Checking back around the rear bumper, the plate flashed proudly, emblazoned in gold, dust blue and white. 'Classic Car 1923 Ford'. Pulling the handle down slowly as he watched the entrance to the parking area, he took a deep breath as he climbed in. "I'll just stay for a minute..."

The seat was firm under him, the abbreviated windshield allowing a 1920's view of the world. "Sure made them different back then, but this is a treat. I can't believe it!! There's the keys!!" He turned all the way around. "No one anywhere in sight. What the hell." He gripped the key and the ignition turned over, a pup-pup-pup start unlike anything he'd heard since his buddy Dave started one of the antique jalopies he'd rescued from an auto graveyard. The pops turned to a growling hum, the vibrating seat giving him a free massage. "I could use this every time I do yard work." Then he heard the siren…

"Get *out of the car*!! NOW!!" Two green uniformed security guards ran up to the bumper, one pulling the driver's door open.

"Oh, I'm so sorry… I was just…" He quickly turned off the ignition and stepped out.

"This area is clearly marked NO ADMITTANCE!! You are trespassing on private property. I can have you arrested. What is your name?"

"Jim Peterson. I was just doing some research at the Hagley Library. Call Linda in there- she saw me. I didn't mean any harm."

The taller guard, a man in his early thirties, 6 foot 2, muscular, with thick blonde sideburns below his thinning pate grabbed his mobile phone and pressed the top button. "This is Johnson out at the antique vehicle site. We have a guy here- a Mr. Peterson- who claims he was doing research there at the library. Is this Linda?"

"Yes, Ben. I did have a Jim Peterson here just a few minutes ago. He was a complete gentleman. Why? Did he cause some trouble?"

"Almost. Could have driven off with a car worth well over $100,000. We caught him first."

"Hey! I had no intention of stealing this vehicle!! I just wanted to see… how it felt inside… that's all. Who are *you*? You didn't show *me* any identification."

"QUIET!! I'll handle this." The guard glared at him before speaking back into the mobile phone. "So, what should do with this guy?"

"Oh, he was nice enough to me and the staff here. Just get him away from the car and send him home."

He clicked off the phone and zeroed in on Jim's eyes as he walked within a few inches of him. "I'm Ben Johnson. We both work for High Point Security and we're contracted to guard these antique vehicles. You're lucky. You could have gotten into a lot of trouble here, mister. What the hell are those things you've got in your hands? Let me see them." He grabbed the papers from Jim as he spat toward his feet.

"Those are just copies of materials I reviewed inside the Library. Linda will vouch for that."

"Look- at this point, buddy- you're lucky you're not calling your attorney to vouch for you." He flipped through the pages, then held them back out toward Jim's hand, intentionally dropping them to the ground as he reached forward.

"I didn't think donkeys could reproduce…"

"What was *that*??!!"

"Nothing. Just talking to myself" he said as he picked the last sheet up from the grass.

"You get yourself outta' here- NOW!! If you're not gone in two minutes, I *am* calling the Wilmington Police… and I know the Captain personally."

"I'm on my way." Papers under his left arm, he marched quickly to the parking lot, turning around once to make sure the guard wasn't on top of him. "Close call." The car rounded the gate out onto the entrance road. "Can't tell Natalie. I'll never hear the end of it… but it was, shall we say, an interesting end to a day of research." The trees lining the road were showing their mottled late season garb as the car sped back toward Greenville, his mind wandering through all the files he'd merely glanced at while sitting in the Library. "That place is outstanding and it's right down the road. If Natalie has a cold drink waiting, I may just treat her to a surprise dinner at the Hotel du Pont. Their New Zealand rack of lamb is superb…"

Chapter 13

"If someday they say of me that in my work I have contributed something to the welfare and happiness of my fellow man, I shall be satisfied..."
--George Westinghouse

Jack noted his watch- 11:48. "Not really that hungry, but they have enchiladas in the food court today. Might be worth a try." He grabbed his jacket from the back of the door and strolled into the elevator. "Second thought, maybe just some fresh air." The doors opened and he advanced to the entrance, moving through the revolving exit. The October breeze blew open his suit coat and he tried to button it quickly. "Cooler than I thought." He meandered around the walking path rimming the complex, the small garden area fringed with a grove of poplar and sugar maple trees whose leaves were already near their peak. The rustling *whooossh* give him a peaceful feeling as he went under their shade.

The two threatening e-mails disturbed him as he remembered her words. 'I think they were sent by someone who's dangerous and could possibly hurt us...' "I can't let that happen. Glad I got the trace on them both. I know where Richard Olson lives, where he works, the car he drives- and I can track his car through On Star. I couldn't forgive myself if this nut harmed her- and I could have prevented it!!" Then he reviewed the words from her second note, playing them over and over in his mind. No 'fondly'... no lunch date.

"Sometimes you have to call it a day. Gotta' throw the little ones back in the stream. There's a size limit." He recalled all the times he knew he could have had them. Each time there was a reason. "There's always a reason. Just look hard enough, past the curves and the smile." He struggled over the sharp difference between consummating a desire and earning respect- and wondered which one was more tempting. "No matter how irresistible they are, it's never worth your reputation. What else is there? Without it, we're just animals, satiating our desires. All you have is your work. What you accomplish."

He glanced up the path and saw the sexy trainee he'd had the close call with, strutting in her 3-inch pink high heels and a tight-fitting skirt. He quickly shifted his gaze up to the white cirrus clouds drifting slowly past in the azure sky. "When people look back after you're gone and think about you- what do you want them to say? Not 'He was a real ladies man'." The sun poked through the gaps in the trees, rays warming his face as the breeze died down. "No. It has to be 'I respected him. He accomplished great things'." Jack opened the pocket Day Planner and saw his notes on the sheet he'd written the day before. "Lunch w/Natalie- maybe? Call her again." He tore out the page and threw it into the trash can at the edge of the path as he walked inside.

Sitting back at the desk, he read both threatening e-mails

again and felt a tinge of pain thinking how she could be harmed. "I'm not going to let this jerk hurt her- or anyone else. I'm tailing him again. Leave a bit early today."

———————

"Hey, Floyd- wuddya' say we cut outta' here around 4? Smitty's has Yuenglings for a buck up 'til 6."

Floyd grinned and put the wrench down. "Best idea you've had all week." He thought about the cool atmosphere at home, the big argument with Cindy over credit card bills. "I say we go, then make that side trip."

"Where? For what?"

"I've been thinkin' on this for a while… we *should* pay those rich folks from Frick's Lock a visit. We'll follow 'em around and hit 'em up for some cash. He's good for a chunk of change."

"That was *my idea.*"

"Congratulations. You're an inventor."

"So, how're you gonna' do it?"

"I got a little friend here who's good at persuadin' people." He put his hand on the side of his belt to a small, light brown leather clipped-on pouch.

"You're carryin' heat?"

"When I need it. It's small, but it does the job. Let's finish up here soon and head over to Smitty's for that beer."

———————

Natalie saw the tiny drawings of birds at each number on the clock. "God, I can't believe the day is over! It's already 7." As the hands struck, the soft voice of a whip-poor-will came from the clock, the gentle tones soaring through the kitchen. "Love that sound." She noticed Jim reading a magazine at the table. "Sue's going to be here any minute. She wanted to stop by and see us, then pop over to mom's later. We need to run to Wal-Mart. I have to get some cleaning supplies, a few gardening tools and a couple of items for my mother. Jim, were you listening?"

"Always... every word. You've become quite a Wal-Mart fan. Used to be I couldn't bribe you to go into the place. Now it's your first choice."

"Well, it's not bad for certain things. I mean toiletries, household supplies. Their prices are great and you don't have to worry about expiration dates on those. I wouldn't buy my food there."

"Why not? Wal-Mart has a higher turnover than SuperFresh or Genuardi's. Things don't go bad sitting on their shelves. Even the regular Wal-Marts are stocking fresh fruits and vegetables. I'd buy food there. It's the same brands they have at the other stores."

"I don't know... don't trust it. Their food might not *start out* as fresh as in the regular stores. Oh, that's Sue at the door."

"We can stick with the non-perishables for now, but you'll be buying bananas there soon."

She laughed as she wiped the table clean and tossed the sponge into the sink as she moved to open the side door. "Hi!! Glad you came. I'm having a discussion with Jim about Wal-Mart."

"I'm a Target girl myself." She kept her jacket zipped up as she walked into the kitchen.

"Jim really likes Wal-Mart. Do you have a large hidden stock holding in the company?" Natalie remarked kiddingly.

"I don't, but 25 years ago I wish I'd bought some. Remember back in the 1980's everybody was talking about how Japan was going to conquer the world? They were the masters of technology, experts at efficiency- and the best managers around? Most people don't know that their economic system is built with layer upon layer of distribution channels- set in stone within their hierarchy. I remember saying in my MBA class that a system like that was bound to be inherently *inefficient*. Wal-Mart beat them at their own game. They *became* the distributor- for thousands of different products people buy every day. Sam Walton recognized that bringing goods directly to people, without several layers of middlemen was the way to do business. He structured the company to utilize a network of warehouses all around the country linked with the latest technology to do just that. Did you know that thousands of long term Wal-Mart employees have become millionaires by owning that stock?"

"I'd read that somewhere. Not bad for somebody starting as a clerk, stocking shelves."

"You don't need a Harvard MBA to know that people want quality products at a good price. Do you know how many MBA's it takes to change a light bulb?"

"No. How many?"

"A hundred. One to hold the light bulb and 99 to turn the house."

"Hah!!" Sue flipped through the 'Oriental Trading' magazine looking for gifts as she waited to hear Natalie's reaction.

"Cute. We'll go to your favorite store. It's almost 7:15 and getting dark outside."

———❈———

Jack looked at the specially adapted GPS on the dashboard and noted the car he was trailing was less than 100 yards ahead. "Always wondered if these dudes have a clue when they're being tailed. Hope not. At least... not tonight. This guy's a psycho. Probably doesn't know his ass from his elbow." Natalie's smile at lunch came to him, her hand across the table, the gentle touch... "What a lovely woman. Too bad she's married. Makes for a mess of a relationship, but- you haven't had what most people call 'relationships', dude. Three months here... six months there... what's that? Extended one-night stands? It's gettin' pretty old. Want to be doing that when you're fifty? I don't think so. Time to explore some new territory..."

———❈———

The drive down Rosedale was always quicker. Turning at the corner past the new medical building, Jim veered to the left as the lanes merged along the diamond-shaped greenspace, wilting irises and fountain grasses past their peak bowing in the cool, early Fall breeze. "It all goes by so fast. Wasn't it just Summer?"

"Yes- and Fall is slipping by, too. I'm not sure if I'm ready for snow in the next month. In fact, I'm never ready for snow. Couldn't we just have Spring and Summer?"

"We'd leave out Thanksgiving, Christmas and New Year's,

not to mention Halloween. Can't miss that. It's our favorite day of the year."

"I remember we used to walk all around our neighborhood in Lenape on Lafayette Drive and fill up big brown Acme bags with treats."

"One year I went out with my sister Marcy and we joined up with Adam- one of the wild kids in the neighborhood, who lived just off of Overbrook Parkway in Penn Wynne. Somehow he persuaded us to start eating the candy before we even got to the next house!! I think he was on a sugar high. He was also drinking a milk shake he'd bought earlier- and then chucked it half-full into the nearest mailbox. I thought we were going to be arrested."

"I love Halloween. Boomers have made it into the second biggest holiday after Christmas."

"I thought the holiday after Christmas was New Year's." He tried to keep a straight face, then burst out laughing, almost falling over.

"I think your brain is on a permanent holiday."

"What was that song from the 1950's? 'Your Mind's On Vacation, but Your Mouth's Working Overtime'." He was still grinning, unable to contain his smile.

"Are you mixing medications?"

"It *is* a big thing. How often do you get a chance as an adult to put on a spooky mask, play some scary music and be a kid again? Its pure fun… and I enjoy it every year. Let's keep the 'kids' in us all our lives." He pulled into the lot, noticing the truck that had been following them for the last few blocks.

"Sounds fine with me. Park over there, but I'm not buying any bananas."

"Relax. Look, do you want to get back at the Chinese who now make *everything* in the world, like the Japanese did in the 1980's? If you do, buy it all much cheaper- at Wal-Mart."

"Their stuff comes from China, too. Look, I don't mind paying high prices as long as it's good quality. There's a reason why some places charge more for their items."

"You mean like the top-of-the-line $1,400 refrigerator you bought whose ice maker has never worked?"

"That's an exception. We got a lemon."

"Maybe someday it'll come full circle and we'll actually make things *in this country* again that the Chinese will want to buy from *us*." He noticed the truck coming to a stop in a parking space about 50 feet away across the lot.

Richie's hands were clammy around the steering wheel of the 1999 dust blue GMC truck, its hood streaked and weather-worn and front bumper dented as he pulled toward the entrance off of Route 1, his grip so tight, his hands were slightly numb, the axle vibrating as he veered into the lot. "Piece a shit car!! Next one's gonna be a Navigator… like the rich folks got." He noticed three cars exiting as he turned left toward the edge of the 200-yard wide parking area, looking down at the dashboard to conceal his face each time a car came within 20 feet of his lights. "I'll teach those bastards a lesson… no more lyin' about the people who worked there."

She shook her head as she opened the door and struggled to take off her seat belt. "Isn't there a way to have these silly things automatically disengage as soon as we stop so we wouldn't have to go into contortions and wrestle them off every time?" Natalie pulled it away, getting out of the car.

"Didn't you wrestle the 140-pound weight class in high school?"

Natalie gave him 'the look'. Silence. "I was *only* 105 pounds in high school!"

"You may be onto the next great idea in automotive technology. My idea is having the sun visors able to be split into two separate ones, wrapping around with a link in the corner for the front and side window to block out *ALL* the rays coming at you in the early morning *and* late afternoon. The guy who invents that one will be a millionaire."

"Why not you? It seems so simple" Sue said as she closed the rear passenger door.

"The best accomplishments *are* the simplest ones. They're right in front of our faces every day. We just never take the time to think about them. Unfortunately, it takes marketing and millions of dollars to make them successful."

"OK, Mr. Edison. Let's get some shopping done." Natalie strolled in front of him toward the long row of stacked carts and the double doors opened automatically. "I'll grab a cart." Passing the jewelry counter with Helzberg 'diamonds', she inspected the long row of canned and bottled goods 30 feet ahead of her. "I'll just take a quick look." She stopped in front of the shelf stocked with dozens of cans of soup. "I like Progresso. They have great soups. These are only $1.29!! They're $2.29 at all the other stores. Hmmm…" She turned the can to read the back label. "Doesn't expire until June 2012. Seems good." She put two cans each of the lentil and Italian Wedding soup in the cart, glancing back to see if Jim noticed.

"I think we have a convert!! How about a few zucchini?" He grinned as she kept walking ahead.

"Now where are they?" Sue asked, examining each customer who walked in.

"Who?"

"The 'Wal-Mart People'… You know, the ones who dress so bizarrely. You see their pictures on YouTube all the time." She continued her search, glancing down the aisles. "Natalie, why are you staring at *me*?"

"I think I found one." She laughed, pointing the cart straight at her.

"Very funny…" Sue punched Natalie in the arm and walked away.

"I'm heading over to the household items." She proceeded to the row stacked with brooms, brushes and cleaning agents. "These are all cheaper than what I normally buy and they're all brand names. I may be… starting to like this place. Can't tell Jim." She pushed the half-full cart to the register and saw the self-check lanes empty. "Hope these don't malfunction like some of the other stores. Last time I had an argument about a tomato. Or was it *with* a tomato?" Natalie stopped the cart and touched the screen, scanning each item. 'Please place the item into the bag.' "I didn't know that. Where else would I put it- in my skirt?" Scanning the last one, she pushed the debit card through and got the receipt. 'Thank you for shopping at Wal-Mart!!' came the pleasant voice of a 20-year old girl through the speaker. "That was enjoyable. Now if we could get the staff at all the stores to be that polite…" She maneuvered toward the exit and let Jim take the handle as Sue walked behind, looking out to the broad expanse of the lot.

"Hey Floyd- who's gonna' go up to him first- you… or me?"

"Relax. I got it under control. We put on the masks- and I hit 'em up for cash. It'll be easy."

"OK… but what if he throws a punch or somethin'?"

"You're way too nervous, Dex. Leave it up to me. I know how to handle rich folks who have money. Piece of cake. Just make sure you get him in a headlock from behind. We'll be in and out in a flash.'

Jim pushed the cart out the double doors toward their car and watched as two men in an older F-150 pick-up truck got out slowly, then seemed to follow him past the rows of cars and SUV's. "They look… familiar." Another truck pulled up, stopped and parked within a few spaces of theirs. Jim kept walking, but turned slightly as the man opened his door and got out, moving at a brisk pace toward him. "Now that guy I *have* seen before." Natalie clicked on the remote and their trunk opened as she approached the car.

Dexter nudged Floyd as they headed toward Jim and Natalie. "Hey, Floyd!! Check out the guy over there. Isn't he the one they interviewed way back when about Pennhurst? I swear- it's the *same dude*!! I'll never forget that face!! Kinda' weird lookin'."

Floyd peered over, the arc of the floodlight illuminating the area and recognized the face etched in his mind from the news reports. "Yeah!! That IS the same dude!! The guy who tortured all those people!! He's slime. Let's get him!!" Floyd felt the gun underneath his heavy leather belt as they each put on their ski masks and darted toward the other man.

Richie focused on Jim's back as he approached. "Your number's up, man!!" He walked faster as he felt the gun in his jacket. "I'm gonna' nail you!! No more shit about Pennhurst from you- or anybody else!!" The early evening darkness enveloped him as he started running toward Jim.

"Hey!! You jerk!! You're the ass who hurt all those people at Pennhurst!!" Floyd pulled the gun out from the sheath on his belt, holding it down as he got closer, signaling to Dexter to circle and grab him from the back.

Richie heard the voice, spun around and flew into a rage. "Who the hell are *you*?!! That was somebody else you're thinkin' of!! Better get outta' here unless you wanna' get your ass kicked!!" He grabbed the pistol, but fell hard onto the blacktop as they both jumped him, tumbling against a car bumper, the white cement strip nearby breaking the fall. "Son of a BITCH!!!!" Richie sprung up, his full 6-foot 2 inch, 240 pound frame poised to attack as he touched the back of his head to check for bleeding. "You're DEAD!!" He leaped onto Floyd and smashed his head down onto the blacktop as Dexter tried to grab his neck from behind. Richie aimed the pistol toward Floyd's face, then glanced quickly over, shifting his attention toward Jim and Natalie. The pistol barrel pointed directly toward Jim's head as the shot rang out. Natalie and Sue fell to the ground as Jim dragged them both behind the edge of the car, the bullet ricocheting off the door.

"My God!!"

"QUIET!!... Stay down!!"

Jack saw it all unfolding as he watched from a position parked 50 feet away. Turning off the engine, he grabbed the

45-calibre weapon from his holster and jumped out the door, sprinting over with his gun drawn. "STOP!! FBI!! Drop your weapons- NOW!!"

Richie elbowed Dexter in the face and kicked him over onto his back, jumping over to hit Floyd as he rose, his bloodied face imprinted with gravel. Richie pummeled his head, seeing him go down again, then stared at Jack and fired. The shot missed Clark, just grazing his blazer as he ducked around the oversized bumper of a black Toyota Land Cruiser.

Jack fired intentionally low, hitting Richie in the upper left thigh, dropping him to the asphalt, writhing in pain.

"Uhhhh!!! My leg!!!"

"Don't shoot!!" Floyd and Dexter yelled out simultaneously.

Jack stood in front of them, magnum pointed at Floyd's head as he saw the small gun in his right hand. "Take off those masks and put that weapon on the ground in front of you!! NOW!!" He kicked it away and watched as they both slowly stood up. "Hands out front where I can see them!" Jack leaned down to pick up the derringer and put it under his belt.

Floyd glanced at Dexter, his face white, in shock as he stood next to him.

Jim's jaw dropped as he observed the scene from behind the car. "FUCK!! That guy could've killed us!" He grabbed Natalie's hand and pulled her closer toward him.

"*Both of them* could have killed us!! They each have a gun!!" She shook as she watched Richie get up, leaning heavily on his right leg, the calf wound bleeding into his jeans. "Good Lord!!"

"He jumped *me*!!" Richie yelled out as he wrapped both hands around his leg.

Jim watched as Agent Clark leaned toward Richie, grabbing both his arms and putting them quickly in handcuffs. Jack focused on Richie's face, now convulsing in agony, then saw rivulets of blood dripping through his pants all the way down to his shoe. "You're under arrest for attempted murder of a Federal agent." He turned toward Floyd, whose knees were shaking. "You're both under arrest for assault, you for assault with a deadly weapon." He picked up Richie's pistol and jammed it under his belt, watching his bloodied hands as the wound oozed, his leg a reddened mass dripping onto the blacktop.

"I didn't shoot anybody!!" Floyd thought about taking a swing at the agent, but saw the gun pointing directly at him and stopped.

"Shut up and put your hands behind your backs." He cuffed them both and turned toward Natalie. "Are you all right?"

"Yes, I'm fine."

"You OK, Mr. Peterson?"

"Thanks to you." Jim reached out, giving him a firm hand shake, holding it for several seconds, his left hand on Jack's shoulder. "You kept us alive. We owe you one."

"I owe you two!!" Natalie yelled out, attracting the attention of several people nearby staring in disbelief, about to load shopping bags into their cars.

"Not at all. It's my job. I'm just glad none of you were hurt." He saw Natalie smiling, then peered at Jim in the aura of the floodlights and could see him nodding.

"This one's worth cocktails and dinner- on me. Sometimes it takes a strange twist of events to let you know how to feel about someone- and which way to go." Jim had managed a smile.

"My grandfather used to tell me 'It doesn't matter where you are in life. What matters is the direction you're heading'." He watched in anticipation as Natalie came up and gave him a long hug, more intense than any romantic kiss he'd gotten in years.

"Thank you so much!! We all have to get together sometime. We'll invite Frank and his wife, too."

"I'll be there. Need to bring these guys to the Kennett Police Station. You'll probably get a call for a statement." Jack felt a warmth deep inside, something he'd been searching years for. He looked over at Jim, giving him a wink. "You folks be safe."

"We will."

Sue watched Jack as he led the men away in handcuffs, Richie hobbling, barely able to walk. "*Now* you know why I shop at Target."

Chapter 14

"Power and machinery, money and goods,
are useful only as they set us free to live…"
--Henry Ford, 1926

"You ready? I have the MapQuest directions to Brent Ellsworth's house in Jersey. It's going to involve a trip on I-95 and the Garden State Parkway- not fun." She studied the page with the map and written directions. "How did we ever find anything before the Internet?"

"We used our heads. People don't do that anymore."

"I want to call him first to let him know we're on our way. It'll probably take us over 2 ½ hours to get there." She picked up the phone and dialed as she patted Francis, his whiskers rubbing up against the side of her leg.

"Hello?"

"Hi Brent, Natalie Peterson. How are you? I called you just recently about stopping over."

"Good. You folks coming on by today?"

"Sure are. It's just before Noon. Depending on traffic, we'll probably be there by around 2:30. Is that all right?"

"Sounds good to me. When we spoke, you mentioned Jim's a history and jazz fan, so I took out a lot of stuff on the origins of the recording industry. I think you'll enjoy it."

"Great. We're on our way. See you soon." She gave a 'thumbs up' as Jim stood with the car keys in his hands.

"Ready to roll? Hope traffic isn't too bad. I-95 can be a nightmare on good days."

"I remember when you were working in Baltimore, driving almost two hours to get to the office every day. Always made me so nervous when I didn't hear from you by 5 o'clock."

Pulling onto Route 1 North, they passed the CVS Pharmacy with its glowing 'OPEN 24 HOURS' neon banner. "I forgot my cell phone on occasion. We've become chained to technology. Sometimes we forget- we actually lived normal lives before those things came along."

"It still scared me." She gazed out the window at the sign for Longwood Gardens. 'Flower and Fountain Show at 8 p.m. tonight'.

"Can't believe I got up at 4 in the morning just to beat rush hour traffic. I loved the job- hated the commute. One time on the way to work, I was driving into the Fort McHenry Tunnel during a massive rainstorm. The highway was so slick, I was expecting spin-outs everywhere. Some guy slammed on his brakes, causing a line of cars to come screeching to a halt. I imagined my car getting crunched into an accordion as I stopped about three inches from the guy in front of me. Thought I was gonna' have a heart attack! Glad I don't have to do that anymore." Signs for The Gables and Brandywine View Antiques poked out toward him, their 200-year old buildings reminders of a simpler era.

He watched the traffic ahead. "Ever wonder if we're missing something by becoming addicted to these gadgets? When Edison and Henry Ford were around, most of the country was living on the farm, waking up with a rooster, sunshine and fresh air and going to bed after a hard day's work in the fields. Now we can't get up without our radio alarms, talk to robots on the phone and can't get to sleep without watching the latest DVD. Technology used wisely can enrich your life… carelessly, it'll destroy you. All these contraptions have taken away something precious."

"What's that?"

"Silence. Have you noticed there's never a time when there *isn't* any noise? Even in the middle of the night, you still hear a plane roaring overhead, a car horn or a train rushing by. We've lost the serenity that peace and quiet bring us."

"Pretty tough these days. With 310 million people in the U.S. and over 6 billion on the planet, it's almost impossible. Only way to get that is to move to a remote area- a mountaintop or out in the desert."

"Now we have to escape from *ourselves*. It's been over a hundred years since we had the pleasure of pure silence… around the time of Ford and the Wright Brothers. Wonder if Wilbur and Orville… or even Henry thought about the far ranging implications of their work, creating a world that would never again know what it's like to hear the wind rushing through the trees *without* the noise of a machine interrupting nearby…"

"They have noise-cancelling headphones for that now" she said.

"Yeah, but don't they have a slight 'hum' to them?"

"Shush!! We have lost something. It's not healthy to stay

inside, glued to the T.V. or our computers. Kids today rarely even use calculators anymore. They do *everything* on the computer. Look around our complex- you never see them playing in the streets like we did when we were younger.

"Exactly. At least if we got into trouble, it was healthy."

"They're all inside now, hooked up to the latest X-Box video game."

"I remember seeing a comic strip a while back. It showed a father and his young son sitting at a desk in front of a computer, the father holding something in his hand right in front of the kid's face, as he stared, bewildered. The father said 'It's something we used way back when I was a kid. It's called a pencil…'"

The line of cars snaked ahead on Route 322 East. "We should be on I-95 in about ten minutes. That'll eventually get us onto the Garden State Parkway."

"Technology can be a great tool, but it's getting so sophisticated. With debit cards, some machines at gas stations don't even ask for your PIN number any more. They assume it's been stolen- so they just ask for your ZIP Code."

"Mixed blessing, isn't it?" He pulled into the line of traffic on I-95, swerving suddenly to avoid a car streaking up the interstate. "My God!! That guy almost RAN US OFF THE ROAD!!"

"What an idiot!" she said, shaking her head as the other vehicle proceeded at around 80 miles an hour, weaving in and out of the lanes ahead. "Didn't you say you read a report about the new Chevy Volt, the electric car? Does it sound promising?" She gawked at the bumper-to-bumper traffic forming all around them.

"Good first step for GM, but it has some drawbacks. First is their very limited range. You have to re-charge the vehicle too often, unless your round-trip is less than 50 miles. Another one, not GM's fault, is the fact that there's no broad-based network of re-charging stations around. It'd be nice if you could stop at the grocery store or the dry cleaners and charge up while doing your errands. If America goes to an electric car in a big way, we'll have to develop a countrywide network of those. Hey, that's the next technology application!! An electric re-charging grid throughout the entire United States. What an infrastructure project that would be."

She saw the sign for Philadelphia International Airport, two planes circling hundreds of feet above for a landing, the roar deafening. "Do you think we'll ever get rid of our dependence on oil? Seems like it's a national security issue."

"It is. We import 60% of the oil we consume every year. Hydrocarbons are the base level ingredients for thousands of things we use every day from clothing to pharmaceuticals, furniture, even plastics- all derived from oil. They're even making wine corks out of plastic now. Horrors!! What's the world coming to?" he exclaimed.

"Have they lost their minds? The French would be in tears if they found out."

"Let's not tell the French. A better question is whether we'll ever allow our *transportation system* to become free from oil. Hell, things would be improved if we just used more natural gas, the cleanest burning fossil fuel, which is extremely abundant right here in the U.S." He noticed the traffic diminishing. "There's the sign for the Garden State Parkway. We're on it for a while, then we take Route 280 right into Orange. Even pass by Edison, New Jersey on the way."

"I think Brent has explored quite a lot in several areas of technology. Rod said he was a recording guru."

"It's interesting how we can't imagine living without recorded sound. That didn't exist before Edison invented the phonograph. If a family wanted music, somebody had to go over to the piano and play."

"The way you play piano, I'll take the radio any time."

"Now music's at our fingertips 24 hours a day."

"Often when we don't want it, like the guy who just raced past us with rap music blaring at 110 decibels. That was so loud, his *car* was vibrating." The vehicle ahead of them had a bright bumper sticker. 'Stop the world!! I want to get back on.'

"Can you imagine living the rest of your life without recorded music?"

"No, but I'll make an exception for whatever that jerk was playing. There's the sign for Route 280. Go West, young man." She watched as two tractor-trailers swooshed by them, a roar drowning out the radio.

"I think we'll be there in less than five minutes. What was the address again?"

She pulled the sheet from the side of the car seat. "Says 938 Collegeville Road. Map shows it on the right after we turn off." She sat back and listened as "Fanfare for the Common Man" played on the radio. "WRTI has classical up until 6 o'clock, right?"

"Yes, then jazz." He smiled as they turned onto the side road. "There it is." He heard the familiar notes from one of his favorite composers. "I love Copland. He had a true sense of

America. Whenever I hear the 'Fanfare', I always get a feeling of being in the midst of a great struggle- and then accomplishment by someone who started from humble beginnings. Think he meant to say we're all capable of that. In a way, Gershwin did it, too. 'Rhapsody in Blue' and 'An American in Paris' are masterpieces. He bridged the gap between the more commonly accepted jazz and classical music- and was quite successful at it. My piano teacher once told me a story about Gershwin. Back in the 1930's, Gershwin's music was hot, but he wanted to be considered a serious composer. So he talked with Stravinsky and said "Why don't you teach me how to compose great classical music, like you?' Stravinsky said 'Why don't you teach me how you make so much money?'" He stopped the car in front of the 1960's-era house, a day-glow peace sign and 'Save the Whales' poster pinned onto the side porch awning. "This should be interesting."

"Behave. I don't care if he's wildly liberal, he's willing to spend time with us and share his knowledge. That's a gift we should appreciate."

"I do." He opened his door and went around, closing hers as she walked toward the house. "Look, real sidewalks. We had these in my old neighborhood in Penn Wynne- with long, thin slabs of grey schist rock lining them all along the streets. Don't see *that* much anymore." He strode up to the door and knocked.

Almost a minute later, the door opened quickly. "Hey, guys. Good to see you!!" He looked directly at Jim. "I'm Brent. Natalie, I haven't seen you since... 1971??" He stroked his graying beard, a thick handlebar mustache flowing out an inch on each side.

"That'd be about right. The year I graduated Unionville. How are you?"

"Great. Come on in." Moving past the well worn sofa that stood in front of a wall of 1960's concert posters, he turned back and pointed. "My vintage 60's collection. I think the one over there is worth well over a $1,000. One of these days I'll sell them all on E-Bay for a fortune."

Jim studied the wrinkles and laugh lines revealing Brent's age as he stroked his mustache. "Want to know how to make a small fortune in the stock market?"

"Yes, how?"

"Start with a large fortune."

"I actually cashed in on the tech boom right before it went bust. Had almost all my holdings in the high flyers- and sold just in time. Made a lot of money."

"Before the dot-coms were dot-*gone*?" Natalie thought back to her days in the software industry and realized they both took the same path.

"Exactly. Sold all my stocks right after BMC Software missed their quarter in January 2000 and the whole sector started crashing. Got me enough to live on for the rest of my life, so I can't complain."

"I left Compuware right after that!! Sold a lot of my stock then, too. Thank God I didn't wait. I benefited from technology in a *real* way."

"Jim, I hear you're a history buff. So am I."

He liked him immediately without hearing another word. "I fell in love with history back in grade school. The American Heritage textbooks, depictions of the founding of our country, the epic battles. I was hooked. What's your favorite period?"

"Well, I used to be a huge Civil War fan, but I've been straying back along the old country roads and now find the Revolutionary War period to be much more fascinating. Done a bit of exploring around the area- it's so filled with history."

Jim found his twin. "Agree completely. For decades we've been in a trance with the Civil War- which was a fascinating period- but sometimes we forget our roots. Living just outside Philadelphia, we're surrounded by it all. Drive down any back road and you're bound to see an historical marker or a stone barn built in the late 1700's. We're lucky enough to live near the Brandywine, which runs through Chadds Ford. That area is overflowing with artifacts. Sometimes... the ghosts come out at night." He could tell from her posture that Natalie was perking up. Looking down the hallway, Jim spotted the rifle prominently displayed above several Revolutionary War relics. "Is that... a Brown Bess?"

"Sure is. The real thing. Pretty fragile, though. Cost me a bundle- but it's a beauty. Use it on occasion to keep my neighbor quiet."

"What do you mean?"

"Guy next door is a genuine redneck. He's got a Confederate flag flying and all kinds of rebel memorabilia scattered around his yard. Even plays old fight songs on his 1960's vintage hi-fi for hours every night, which he knows bugs the hell outta' me. It's so loud, I've taken a shot at it a few times, but no luck."

"Why didn't you just call the police? Tell them he's disturbing the peace."

"Police sergeant is from South Carolina- ground zero for the Confederacy. He actually likes this guy!! I've complained several times, but they never come out to do anything... so every once in a while, I pick up 'ol Bessie here and fire off a few rounds."

Jim thought about the day-glo PEACE posters out front and Save the Whales sign and chuckled. "You can't invent this stuff…"

"What?"

"Oh- nothing…"

"It gets so loud out there, I know he's got it turned up full blast just to bother me. So I pop off a round or two. I always miss. Wish I could just blast it to smithereens. These muskets couldn't hit a grizzly bear at fifty yards… but it's fun to actually watch 'ol Bessie work. That hi-fi is one piece of technology I'd like to take out…"

Natalie's eyebrows were raised to their limit. "So, are you going to show us some of your famous collection of sound memorabilia?" Walking closer to Brent, she noticed the hall-way filled with framed posters of the Reconstruction Era.

"Follow me." He led them past dozens of murals, their im-ages piercing, each one holding a moment in time, now almost forgotten.

"Isn't that one by Thomas Lea? I've seen it before. It's breath-taking." The man dressed in weathered shoes and a buckskin jacket was looking out onto a wasteland, a darkening sky hov-ering over a building nearly totally destroyed. Rimming it, a fence shattered near a tree was reduced to charred limbs and a horse stood in front of an empty carriage, its head pointed down.

"Good call. That one used to be in the Post Office at Pleasant Hill, Missouri- where all the 'compromising' was done trying to avoid that horrible conflict. You know, if Jefferson

Davis had just done the math, he would have given up before it was fought. In terms of technology in 1860 before the start of the Civil War, the North had over 84% of the factories and 71% of the railroads- along with 81% of the bank deposits of the country."

"Those aren't odds I'd play poker against."

"He wasn't playin' with a full deck."

"Brick short of a load. Didn't have both oars in the water."

"Lookin' down the wrong end of the telescope…"

Natalie examined the mural, the bleak landscape a chilling reminder of the devastation of war. "So, where do you keep your audio museum? Will we get a tour?"

"Right through here, my fair lady." He filed past three long bookcases into a workshop with 20-foot mahogany tables covered by dozens of crude, antique-looking devices. "First you could probably use a brief introduction." He stood in front of one of the instruments and laid his hand down, touching its base. "The first devices for reproducing sound were mechanical and could not record things like the human voice. The earliest ones have been traced back to the 9th century. By the 14th century, bell ringers controlled by rotating cylinders were developed, which led to the introduction of music boxes by the 18th century. They could play 'stored' music- creating vibrations with friction along an indented surface. These are all music boxes from the period from 1720- 1890."

"Henry Ford had an entire building with mechanical bell-ringing statues transported from Europe to Michigan for the museum he built. Must have cost him a fortune."

"If I were his wife, I would've rung *his bell* for that" Natalie said as she eyed them all.

"Can we hear one?"

"Just one. I try not to play them too often, because they're so delicate- and I can't get parts. They don't have Pep Boys for music boxes."

Jim recalled all the times his father would drive him to 69th Street outside Philadelphia, passing Lit's, J.C. Penny and Woolworths to the Pep Boys store to get parts for their 1963 Buick. He was back there, at the counter… the man with the "Manny, Moe and Jack" hat gave them change and nodded at him as they were about to leave, his father gently grabbing Jim's hand as he led him back to the car. Jim took the metal part out of the bag, touching its brass surface… and smiled up at his dad…

"They're interesting. Play this one."

Brent turned the half-inch wide bronze butterfly tab, rotating it around the shiny exterior three times. The melody from a bygone era flowed out, tinny, but beautiful, each note drifting upward into the room. The sounds of a harpsichord playing a symphony by Handel weaved around them as they savored every note.

"Very nice. Don't see too many of those on the Antique Roadshow."

"Actually, I did see one just like this on there a while back, but not in as good condition." He pointed to the others standing quietly nearby. "These are all rare items. What you're looking at is worth well over $50,000." He moved toward the middle of the table. "This is a very early reproduction of Edison's phonograph, patented by him in 1878."

"We saw one of his originals at Greenfield Village. The demonstration was fascinating, watching the guide play his voice that he just recorded in front of the group." Jim approached the table slowly, his outstretched hand stopping in front of the machine. "May I touch it?"

"Sure, but be gentle. All it takes is an extra jolt and parts start coming off."

Jim lowered his right hand, his index finger extended as if he were encountering the Holy Grail, expecting to see light flashing the moment it contacted the gleaming surface. "The machine that changed what we listen to… and started a new industry."

Natalie moved directly next to him and brought the tips of her fingers around the edges of the horn above the stylus. "Have you actually recorded anything on this?"

"I did once, way back when I first got it. Have the sheet around here somewhere. I purposely don't use it so as to maintain its integrity. Over there are a few of the earliest Gramophone discs from the 1890's. Discs quickly replaced cylinders as far easier to manufacture, transport, store and play. Edison realized that cylinders were on the way out and created the Edison Disc Record Company trying to catch up. The shellac 78's were the most popular format up until the 1950's. They were replaced by vinyl, with the new medium being the 7-inch 45's and the longer-playing 12-inch L.P.'s" He picked one up and held it in front of Jim's face. "This is one of the very first jazz records ever made, recorded in 1917 by the Original Dixieland Jass Band. The Victor Talking Machine Company and the Columbia Phonograph Company are represented over there." He pointed to the very end of the table, where two primitive Victrolas stood, then gave the disc to Jim. "Careful."

"Understood. I remember the old 'RCA Victor' signs with

the little dog, his ear tilted toward the horn. I started listening to jazz back in the mid-1970's. It was like learning a new language. I've actually become a fan of the Big Bands, Sinatra." He turned toward the other side of the room. "Where'd you get all the reel-to-reels?" Jim pointed to a black metal cabinet stacked with several devices, the ¾ inch wide tapes leading from the end of one reel to the next one, waiting decades to be played again.

"I knew they'd be obsolete someday, so I started collecting back in the early 1970's. Been all over the country picking them up. Have 24 now."

Natalie stepped closer. "I remember my dad used to record my mother singing on his reel-to-reel. We liked playing them backwards" she chuckled.

"A while back, my girlfriend told me her brother wanted to sell me three huge boxes of his old 8-tracks. Said they'd be really important someday."

"Did you buy them?"

"Nope. I can live without tapes of 'The Archies' and 'The Banana Splits'. That machine over there is one of the first Ampex units from 1949. Not many people know that the Italian inventor Marconi- the man who invented wireless radio- developed a magnetic sound recording system back in the 1930's using steel tape, the same material used to make razor blades."

"Reminds me of that song 'They All Laughed'. What a great tune! 'They told Marconi, wireless was a phony...'"

"Exactly. They had these big sheets that rotated at high speeds- and sometimes broke, sending jagged strips of metal flying everywhere. The invention went *nowhere*. Engineers decided they didn't want to get shredded while trying to make a recording. The K1 Magnetophone developed in 1935 was the first practical tape recorder. The original silent films were replaced by 'talkies'- enabled by the new technology. You've probably heard of 'The Jazz Singer' with Al Jolson."

"A gem." Jim was mesmerized as Brent pointed to each item. "They have some neat exhibits on sound and electricity at The Franklin Institute in Philadelphia. I remember going there as a kid, walking through a 10-foot tall scale model of the human heart."

"Tape recording here in America was perfected later by John T. Mullin with the help of Crosby Enterprises, based on recorders captured from the Germans during World War II."

"Bing!! Love him!!"

"That's him. Magnetic tape revolutionized the music industry, as you could record and later erase and re-record many times. Les Paul invented the first multi-track tape recorder and the world would never be the same."

"Guitar legend Les Paul?"

"That's the gent. A musician *and* an inventor. Rare combination of creativity and scientific know-how. With the ability to multi-track, popular music entered a new era. Layer upon layer of sounds could be put onto the same recording, giving the listener something they'd never heard before. The effect could be breathtaking. For those interested in pop music, groups like The Beatles brought it to a higher level and by the late 1960's, you were hearing some pretty wild things on records."

"I saved all my Beatle albums, even though I gave the rest of my collection to charity back in the mid-1990's. I figure they'll be worth something someday."

"They're worth something *now*. Have you ever been into a used record store? They charge $30- $50 for some of those things- and if they're in mint condition, more like $100. Save them- they're collectors' items. As Will Rogers said about real estate- 'They're not makin' it any more...'" Brent turned toward Natalie. "You wanted to show me some things."

"Yes. Jim- could you bring the box in from the car? We found some interesting things in an abandoned house, from an old town called Frick's Lock, up near Phoenixville."

"Isn't that near the Limerick nuclear plant?"

"You know your geography. The town was abandoned when PECO bought up all the property - and there are several houses from the 1800's still standing, frozen in time... filled with lots of strange things. Here he comes. Let him show you."

Jim laid the box on the counter and took a long breath. "At least I got *some* exercise today. There's a few items we wanted you to see. First, take a look at this bulb."

"Very crude. Precursor to the incandescent lamp. Seen photos of the early ones, kinda like this. I'm guessing this is circa... late 1800's?"

"Would that pre-date Edison's bulb?"

"Perhaps, but remember- Edison just perfected it. Want to see it go on?"

"Are you serious?!! I thought it was broken. Couldn't see a filament in there..."

"Oh, there is one. Very thin. Watch." Brent connected a clamped set of wires to the base and a faint glow emanated from within.

"It's 130 years old- and it still works!! Natalie laughed.

"That's what I call a long-life bulb."

"Not sure if you ever smoked when you were younger, but here's some antique cans of chewing tobacco. We got three out of the four open- these are what we found inside one." He laid the three rings onto the table.

"Beautiful pieces! This one looks like something Zsa-Zsa would wear."

"I estimate about three carats."

"A woman's best friend. Bottom is dated... 1878." He grabbed a small hand lens and peered inside the ring. "Says 'Thomas'. Hmmm…"

Jim's eyebrows rose. "We never looked inside. Here… take a look at these two."

"Appears to be a ruby. Very nice. Whose collection was this from- Ivana Trump?" He brought the lens up to the edge. "Says 'Henry'. Bottom shows 1908. Let me see that last one. Beautiful… love emeralds!! Dated 1903. Inside says 'Orville'…"

Jim's mind was racing as he turned quickly toward Natalie. "I think I know what those dates are for."

"Wilbur and Orville Wright had the first successful flight in an airplane in 1903. Not sure who the other guys are" Brent said as he admired the green gem.

"Thomas Edison patented the phonograph in 1878… and Henry Ford built his first Model T in 1908!"

Natalie picked up the diamond ring. "My God!! Could these belong to Edison, Ford and Orville Wright?"

"No way to tell- but we have one more tin to open." Jim handed it to Brent. "I couldn't get it to budge. Maybe you can with all the machinery you have in here."

Brent took it over to the next table and picked up a vice-grip.

"These come in handy." He gave it one tug and the lid turned. "Not too hard. Sometimes we need a machine to replace elbow grease." He put the top down on the counter. "Empty."

"Really? It felt pretty light…" The tone of Jim's voice dropped, revealing his disappointment.

"Except for this…" Brent held up a brown, cracked, water-stained strip of paper. "Anyone know French?" He put the strip up toward the light. "I took it in high school, but I've forgotten most of it. Jim, know any French?"

"La fenetre. The window."

"Brilliant. You can be our next Ambassador in Paris." Natalie walked over to Brent and took the piece of paper.

"Learned that in Catholic school. I can count from one to ten, too. Also took four years of German in high school, but I'm not as fluent in that."

"Says 'Pour mes vrais amis, Thomas, Henry et Orville… Vous avez allume une bougie qui a eclaire le monde…'" Natalie squinted as she re-read it slowly. "Think this means… 'To my true friends Thomas, Henry and Orville. You've lit… a candle… that… has brightened the world'!! These rings… must have been meant for Edison, Ford and Orville Wright! Oh, my God!!"

Jim took the paper. "I knew 'le monde' meant 'the world'."

"Randolph Larson *wasn't* crazy!! He knew these guys. He may have been eccentric, but he probably helped them with their inventions. Wonder why he didn't give the rings to them."

"We may never know." Jim walked back over to the box. "We still have these to decipher." He pulled out all four metal sheets. "Found them in the same spot. I think they may be crude recordings from around the turn of the last century, maybe earlier. Who knows? You have Edison's phonograph. Could we play them?"

Brent looked at their grimy surfaces and then up at Jim. "That phonograph is very delicate. I nearly broke it when I tried it last time. That was years ago- and I almost didn't get it back together. Let me look at it later tonight before we do that. I can't replace anything on that machine- and I'm not gonna' break it trying to play those."

Natalie frowned. "I understand. It's getting late, too."

"Look, we can try. I just can't promise anything. It'll have to wait until tomorrow."

"They've sat in this dusty bin for maybe a hundred years- another night won't hurt." Jim put the sheets slowly back into the box, staring at the cracked pine floor. He glanced at his watch. "It's already 5:30. Can we take you out for cocktails, maybe dinner?"

"Well... sure. I'm a bit hungry."

"Any place good close by?"

"Yes, there's a little martini bar where they play great jazz. It's low key piano, bass and drums. They play light stuff- standards, show tunes- perfect for dinner and conversation. Food's excellent."

"What's it called?"

"The Discovery Inn. It's less than a mile from here. Pretty appropriate, since a famous inventor lived in the area. I think you'll like it. By the way, it'll be getting late when we're through and I know you have a long drive back. You're welcome to stay the night. I have two spare bedrooms upstairs. "

"That sounds great. What do you think?" He saw Natalie nodding.

"No objections here. Let's discuss it all over cocktails- and music..."

Jim noticed the young man in his late twenties playing the piano as soon as they opened the door to the Inn. "Nice place- my kind of music.... Love Ellington..."

As they ate, the combo broke into a Cole Porter medley, a few couples taking to the small dance floor. Jim got up and walked over to the piano player, putting a ten dollar bill into his jar- getting a smile and a nod.

"Let me get this." Jim held up the leather folder with the bill as the waiter came back. "My treat- for your hospitality..."

The drive back was filled with blissful silence. "Well, time to call it a day..."

"I'm ready, but what is that I'm hearing?" Natalie said as they entered the kitchen.

"The rebel next door."

"Isn't that..."

"Yep- 'Dixie'. Drives me *NUTS!!*"

"The rebel's war tune. Strangely enough- Lincoln's favorite song. We're heading upstairs. Goodnight." As they walked into the room, Jim echoed the familiar refrain. 'Wish I was in Dixie... hooray!! Hooray!!', the decibel level outside so high, people blocks away were cringing. Then a shot rang out... and the music stopped. The back door slammed shut. He looked over at her. "Peace... at last..."

Chapter 15

"When we got up, a wind of between 20 and 25 miles was blowing from the North. We got the machine out early and put out the signal for the men at the station..."
--Orville Wright, December 17, 1903

The wind picked up, blowing leaves just turning to amber from the trees in the yard. Brent walked onto the back porch and glanced at his watch. "Only 5:00 a.m.. They probably won't be up for at least an hour. Gives me some time out here... in peace and quiet. Never get enough." A mourning dove cooed in the stillness as the breeze died down. He watched as the copper wind chime settled back to vertical, its grey-blue weathered surface a sharp contrast against the burgundy wooden tool shed behind it. He sat down and stretched his legs onto the three steps leading down to the grassy path. "Best time of the day- total silence. Wish most of it could be like this. No traffic, no noise, no rappers with their boom boxes... just quiet. The spirit within..." Taking a sip of the French roast, the horizon brightened slightly in the East, cumulus clouds darting quickly overhead through the still charcoal-blue sky. "I've spent most of my life chasing what you guys invented decades ago, collecting your work, playing your machines, listening to the sounds coming from them. Someday, maybe... I'll hear something new."

He took another sip amidst the serenity of his backyard kingdom, the black 1963 Mercury starting to rust slightly as it perched majestically on blocks at the end of the gravel driveway. "Got you for a steal- and mint condition inside. Need to give you some time. Even have your original radio- and it works!" The dove cooed again and he saw her, nestled in the beige wild grasses lilting at the far end of his paradise. He nodded and heard her voice once more as he sauntered up the steps onto the porch, the door making the slightest clap behind him.

"Good morning." Jim watched as Brent finished the last sip and put the heavy ceramic mug on the counter.

"Mornin' to you. Up early?"

"I love this time of day... before anybody can get to you."

"I need it... re-charges me. When you're ready later, I can fix us up some breakfast."

"Good eats?"

"I make Huevos rancheros- and grits."

"My kind of place. I didn't even know what grits were until I moved out West. Wish more places had them on the menu."

"You'll like it." He moved over to the refrigerator and took out several items before he went to the stove. "Best homemade salsa you've ever eaten."

"I found Paradise, but I never thought it'd be in New Jersey."

"Don't worry if Natalie wants to sleep in."

"She rarely does. I'm surprised she didn't beat me downstairs.

We're both early risers. Feel like half the day's gone if we're not up by 6:30."

"I heard that. Now who's sleeping in?" Natalie stepped into the kitchen, tightening the cords on her bathrobe.

"Just telling Brent about us getting up early."

"Bathrobe fit?"

"Like it was designed for me. I love the furry collar. I heard something about breakfast. Where should we go?"

"Right here- the Cactus Café. My favorite hangout before 7 a.m.. Best food in town. I think you'll like my Migas."

"You make them? There aren't any places that serve them near us. Maybe we should move." She poured the coffee slowly into the mug, smelling the rich aroma as she remembered the sumptuous breakfast Jim had made her. Turning to the window fringed with curtains made of heavy burlap, she studied the pattern. "Your own design?"

"They are. I favor the Southwestern look- but it's hard to fit into the décor of the living room. I figured I could get away with the curtains in here."

"I like them. I'm getting hungry. I'll head up and change so we can eat." Jim started to turn toward the stairs.

"Hey, cowboy. I'm just having my first sip of java around the fireside. Circle the wagons until I'm ready." Natalie took a long gulp as she heard sparrows chirping outside. "Looks like a nice day."

"It should be. About 65 and sunny, with low humidity. My kind of weather. After breakfast, we can take a look at those sheets. The machine is ship-shape and ready."

She took another sip and placed the mug onto the tiled countertop. "I like these desert scenes in the tiles. Goes well with the windows."

"Guy has a shop a few miles down Route 280. Does them all himself by hand- custom made. Designs anything you want- mountains, desert, Victrolas. Cost me a few bucks, but I figure they're collectors' items. They give me the 'feel' of being out in the peacefulness of the high desert around Sedona. Love that place."

"We were there two years ago. Great trip!! Walking around the Honanki and Palatki pueblos. It was wonderful. I'm done my coffee. I'll be ready in five minutes." She stood up from her chair.

"You're optimistic, which I like, but let's be honest and call it fifteen" Jim said as he went up the stairs ahead of her.

Brent strolled to the back door, opening it slowly and waited for the muffled sounds of the mourning dove, but it was gone. The first car horns from taxis on the roadway were piercing the morning solitude. "At least I had a few minutes of Heaven…"

"That was superb!! I like the Ro-Tel tomatoes in your salsa. Brought me back to my grad school days."

"I thought you'd enjoy it. Always puts me in a good mood for the day. Follow me to the workroom."

"We went through almost all the items. There may be a few scraps of paper in there we haven't seen, but these metal sheets are the most interesting. I think they look very similar to the ones they used in the early sound recordings. What do you make of them?" He handed the first two over to Brent and watched his expression as he held them within a few inches of his face.

"Right material. Look old enough. Judging from the indentations, these could be sound recordings. I've seen enough to say they appear to be the real thing." He grabbed a small magnifying glass and examined the surface of each one.

"What do you say we play one on your recording machine?" Jim saw Brent's eyebrows rise as he spoke the last words.

Brent took the second sheet and eyed it slowly with the glass. "Well, they both appear legitimate. There's only one way to find out… Remember, if something breaks, I'll have to stop." He turned to Jim and then saw Natalie's expression sour.

"I understand. Maybe we could just play a small part of it- not all four sheets. I'd like to hear a bit of what's on there."

"Did you know Edison was nearly deaf when he did most of his sound work?" Brent commented.

"Him- and Beethoven. What caused that?"

"Story goes that when he was a young kid, hopping trains and fooling around, he brought some chemicals on board a car of the Grand Trunk Railroad and nearly burned the place to cinders trying to do an experiment. Conductor grabbed him by the ears and tossed him off the train. Edison said his hearing went downhill from there."

"How could he possibly hear enough to make sure his instruments were working?" Natalie leaned onto the table as she watched Brent place the second sheet down.

"Said he could 'hear' better than normal people by *feeling* the vibrations. Seriously. Not sure how he did it, but he was able to conduct hundreds of experiments when he was almost totally deaf." Brent picked up the first sheet again and noticed the markings at the lower corner.

"Perseverance." Jim felt encouraged as Brent looked closely at the metal sheet again.

"Genius- one per cent inspiration and 99 per cent perspiration." Natalie picked up the last two and studied the markings. "You must have done a lot of research over the years."

"I have. Got a library full of books on the early inventors- from the late 1700's to the 1950's- discovery of oxygen to the microchip. I've always been fascinated by them- how they think, what makes them pursue a dream that other people don't see. Most people don't know that Edison wasn't the first person to make a sound recording."

"What do you mean? I thought he was." Jim stepped closer and watched as Brent picked up the third sheet.

"For decades, just about everyone thought he was. A few years ago, scientists at the Lawrence Berkeley National Laboratory in Berkeley, California- 'Berserkely, to some'- got hold of a recording by a Frenchman done around 1860. It was very crude- used to call them phonautograms. They had to hook it up to a computer to play it, but there was a human voice on it."

Jim's eyes widened as he listened. "You mean, they played things like this?"

"Much more crude than these. This was actually recorded on paper and the computer had to 'interpret' the indentations and convert them to sounds- but it was for real."

"What did it say?"

"It was a 10- second recording of a person- probably a man- singing the old folk song called 'Au Clair de la Lune'. Researchers think that person was the inventor Edouard- Leon

Scott de Martinville. He was a Parisian typesetter and a tinkerer. He invented what he called the phonautograph in 1857. It's now considered the precursor to the phonograph of Edison, beating him by 20 years."

Hearing 'tinkerer', Natalie's grip tightened on Jim's shoulder. "Is that for real?"

"Appears so. This guy Scott seemed to be making recordings well before Edison, but they were not what we would consider true recordings. They were made by etching the sound vibrations onto sheets of paper blackened by smoke from an oil lamp. At the time, they weren't even considered for audio playback. Scott apparently just wanted to get a record of human speech that could someday be deciphered."

Jim stood silent for several seconds. "What happened to him? Did he ever get credit for his inventions?"

"Went to his grave thinking he'd been unrecognized as the original inventor of the recording machine- and that they were improperly credited to Edison. Frankly, I think he deserves recognition for the first sound recordings ever."

"Can we at least *try* to play that first sheet?" Jim watched as Brent took it in his hands.

"Well, sure. Never know what you'll find. I noticed they appear to be labeled. This looks like the first of four."

"That's what I think." Natalie gazed back into the box. "Hey, there's a piece of paper in here I didn't look at before. Says 'A mon cher oncle Edouard, le grande inventeur. Felicitations pour votre machine a sons!! Sincerement, Randolph'."

Brent stepped closer to her and held the fragment of paper in front of him. "Looks like... 'To my dear Uncle Edouard, the great... inventor'? Not sure about the rest."

Natalie held it with him. "The rest says… 'Congratulations… on your… *sound machine'??!!'* She turned her head quickly and saw Jim's eyes bulging.

"Could it be?? The guy who owned this box- was the nephew of… the guy who made the first sound recordings?!! Almost seems too hard to believe."

"I've done a lot of reading. There was a Frenchman, last name Larson-Scott, back in the 1860's here in America. Believe he came over to the U.S. around 1862, so he would have been maybe about 17 years old at the time. He claimed to have perfected a crude recording device that had originally been developed by someone else in France, but it was never patented here. As I recall, he traveled around the U.S. trying to record sound, but nothing ever came of it. He dedicated his life to building mechanical apparatus and apparently was quite talented, helping many other inventors. I think he actually did have some interaction with Edison- and even the Wright Brothers. He was never granted a patent, so he died without recognition for any significant contribution to science."

"When did this guy die?" Jim stood directly next to him, listening intently.

"Lived to be a very old man… I believe about 95. Died… maybe around 1940?"

"Could this be the *same guy??!!* The person who owned the house that the box came from- Randolph Larson- by some accounts claimed to know some of the early inventors, but he was kind of a crackpot, or at least that's what people said. I know that a lot of immigrants back then changed their names- shortened them- to sound more 'American'. Larson was admitted to Pennhurst back around 1925 and ranted for years about knowing famous inventors!! He died there in 1940."

"Could be a link. Who knows? We might want to play that first sheet." Brent grabbed it and walked over to the next table, placing it next to the Edison phonograph. Unrolling the strip already on the machine, he placed it aside and carefully reeled the new sheet onto the cylinder.

Jim's mind was racing. The initials 'R.L.' on the brick at Edison's lab at Greenfield Village... the writing all over the walls at Pennhurst... It was coming together... brewing. "We also found a cylinder in the box, similar to the one you have there!! I wonder..."

"We'll soon find out. Could be a little kid screaming for candy- or a dog barking. I've heard a few of those. That's usually what you get on these things." Brent had it loaded.

"In your research, you've probably found that inventions came along that literally changed civilization. After the Civil War, the South was in shambles and our currency was nearly worthless. Many countries around the world thought we were a basket case, doomed. Yet, we excelled far beyond what anyone had expected- partly due to the great inventors and industrialists. The tough conditions today have some people thinking America is finished. I don't buy it." Jim held the fourth sheet in front of him and felt the indentations in his fingertips. "Breakthroughs in technology can change everything..."

"Agree completely. Ready?"

"Go." Jim felt a surge in his veins as he awaited the initial sounds.

Brent rotated the cylinder and at first, all that came out were screeches, piercing to the ear. They stopped... and the sound of hands clapping poured into the tube, flowing out through the room. The crowd clapped much louder for several seconds, followed by a long silence.

Brent took the first sheet from the machine. "That's it. Not much."

"Do you mind if we play *one more?*" Jim stood within inches of his right hand, still on the crank.

"Look, it's just a bunch of people clapping! Nothing special." Brent placed the sheet back on the table with the others.

Natalie picked up the second sheet and held it in front of him. "There's no way we could ever find out what's on here ourselves. How about playing just the beginning of this one?"

"Well... OK, but it's a very delicate machine. Just one more." He took the second sheet and wrapped it carefully on the cylinder, then turned it slowly as Natalie's eyes widened in anticipation. More clapping poured through the tube, then a voice in French sailed through the air.

"C'est Randolph tester le dispositif d'enregistrement..."

Brent stopped the machine. "I'm rough with my French, but I think that means 'This is Randolph... testing the... recording device'??"

"DON'T STOP!!" Jim and Natalie yelled out together, leaning their ears right up to the tube on each side to listen.

"Here goes..."

'... and now our distinguished speaker, the President, will make a few appropriate remarks...' More clapping, growing louder with each second to a thunderous applause, then several moments of total silence.

The voice was high-pitched, with a very subtle drawl, but it broke through the air brimming with energy. 'Four score and seven years ago, our forefathers brought forth upon this continent a new nation, one conceived in liberty and dedicated to the proposition that all men are created equal...'

"MY GOD!!" Brent swung around quickly, still turning the crank. "THAT'S LINCOLN!!"

Jim's mouth hung open as he heard the oration, staring at the sheet as it turned. "THERE ARE NO KNOWN RECORDINGS OF HIS VOICE!! Until now."

"Do you know what this is *WORTH*?!!"

He took two deep breaths. "It's... priceless." Jim pulled Natalie toward him and wrapped his arms around her waist as the voice continued to flow through the cramped room, his presence all around them. The date carved into the stone in Jacalyn's painting flashed before his eyes... '11/19/63'. "Larson was just misunderstood... like most creative geniuses. He *did* help Edison... and he stood next to Lincoln, recording this speech... that helped save our nation." The energy within the words pulsed through him as the stained metal sheet slowly turned... light reflecting from its surface into his eyes...

Chapter 16

"When you do the common things in life in an uncommon way,
you will command the attention of the world..."
--George Washington Carver

"Ladies and gentlemen, we will be landing in Detroit in a few minutes. It's been a pleasure serving you today. Please remember in your future travels... to fly the friendly skies of United..."

"I'm glad you got through to the curator at the Henry Ford Museum. Did they agree to set up a special display case for each one?"

"That was the condition of our gift- the rings are to be placed in the museum for each man in a prominent spot, giving credit to Randolph for his contribution."

"Bet that took some arm twisting."

"Trump. 'The Art of the Deal'. Look- it's a win-win. They get the rings- which are worth a fortune. Randolph gets his place in history. I'd say that's a pretty good trade..."

The silver Lincoln Town Car stopped at the first open space in the Visitor parking lot and they both got out quickly onto

Woodbridge Avenue in the mid-afternoon sun. "We agreed to meet at the Menlo Park lab. You have all three?"

"Right here." She opened the door and Jim went directly up to the guide. "We're looking for Mr. Harold Arlington. We're the Petersons. He's expecting us."

"Of course." The guide put the cell phone next to his chin. "Mr. Arlington's guests are here. I'm bringing them back." He put the phone into his jacket. "Please follow me."

Jim stopped as he saw the gleaming crystal display case. "Nice job. Randolph deserves it."

"Mr. Peterson- thank you for coming… and for your generous gift!!"

"My pleasure. Natalie has the ring." She handed it to him as Jim studied his expression.

"Even more beautiful than in the photos you e-mailed to me. Mr. Edison would have been impressed. It goes right here." He examined the ring closely, then placed it on a brilliant white pedestal within the case, the diamond glistening as he locked the door. "What a testament to the great friendship of these two men. Who knows how many ideas they shared?"

Jim read the sign below. 'Mr. Randolph Larson was an unknown inventor- until now. This ring is a sign of his friendship, assistance and great respect for Thomas Edison. We're sure the feeling was mutual'. He thought back to the writings on the asylum walls… the anecdotes from Abe Olson… and the dusty old box. "With Edison's lights shining on him, he finally has his place in the sun. Let's pay Orville and Henry a visit…"

Jim counted sixteen bullet holes in the red bricks on the side of the Farnsworth House as they walked into the gentle breeze down Baltimore Street in Gettysburg toward Evergreen Cemetery, after passing in front of 'The Little Drummer Boy' packed four-deep with tourists. "You have the sheets?"

"All four- right here." Natalie pointed down into the heavy canvas satchel in her left hand as they crossed the street past the Jennie Wade House. "Good that we got here early. At least we know we'll get a seat on stage."

They headed to the left up the hill to the entryway, avoiding the path to the side where a crowd of over 50 parents stood with their noisy children in front of the bust with the famous words. "I was surprised when the curator from the Smithsonian agreed to lend the machine to the Park Service." Two young boys in Pennsylvania Dutch outfits ran after a squirrel as Jim approached the podium. "Guess it didn't hurt that we promised to donate the sheets to their permanent collection." He noted dozens of people milling around the staging area thirty feet ahead.

"It's nice that we gifted them to the Smithsonian, for the world to see- but what do *we* get out of the deal?"

"What- a lifetime 50% off at all the Smithsonian gifts shops isn't enough?"

"O.K. Whatever…"

"… and I found a private collector who's offered top dollar for the light bulb, the radiator cap and the piece of the wing. Let's just say I paid for our vacations for the rest of our lives…"

"Not bad… as long as it includes unlimited toe rubs…"

"You know, I've been thinking. Bill, the guide at Pennhurst

was right. We have an obligation to help those truly in need. I'm sending a check to the Special Olympics."

"Wonderful idea. People have come a long way in accepting those with disabilities as part of mainstream society. Hopefully it'll bring happiness into their lives."

"You must be Mr. Peterson. I recognize you from the photo you sent." The husky man with white hair in his early 60's took Jim's hand and nodded at Natalie. "Thank you both for coming- and for your generous offer to share this. Do you have the recordings?"

"Governor Corbett- pleasure to meet you. We have them right here." Natalie handed all four to him as she noticed the stage filling with men in dark period suits from the 1860's, rimmed by three men wearing dark sunglasses, tapping their ears and speaking lowly into their collars.

"We've arranged for extra security, as you may have noticed- so everything will be safe. You can both sit right over there. I'll be participating in the dedication ceremony. I'm giving these to our technical man, who will play them through our sound system. James Gettys will as usual be here as the President- but in light of this remarkable find, we'll be using the real thing this time."

"Thank you. We appreciate your having us here. It's an honor to be part of this event. I never thought I'd have the chance to thank Abraham Lincoln personally…but this is pretty close…" He turned to follow Natalie to the row of padded tan metal chairs. Two young men caught his attention as they set up the crude phonograph, laying the first metal sheet carefully along the cylinder as the curator watched. As they finished, Jim saw the Master of Ceremonies tap the microphone.

"Thank you all for coming here today to join us in celebrating the life of Abraham Lincoln- our greatest President- who not only saved the Union, he kept the fire of liberty burning within the citizens of this great nation during its darkest days. Despite a struggle which at times seemed desperate, he persevered- and through his efforts and deep sacrifice, preserved this precious Republic, the fruits of which we all enjoy today. This year we have a special treat for you. This event is being broadcast not only coast to coast throughout America, but also in 17 foreign countries. For today, you are all about to hear- for the very first time- what Abraham Lincoln said back on November 19th, 1863... not from James Gettys, who you all know, but through the work of an unknown inventor- a man unrecognized until now..."

A hum buzzed through the audience as men turned to look at their wives, struggling to hold their kids in their seats. Jim felt Natalie's hand tightly around his, then heard her whisper. "Never thought we'd be able to honor him in this way. Who would ever have guessed we'd be part of a worldwide event?"

"An honor you earned- from your persistence. I almost didn't let you have it..."

The speaker continued despite the yells of small children in the front row. "Randolph Larson was an immigrant to this country back in 1862, in search of what later generations would call the American Dream. He never found it... but now we have... and proof of that can be heard in the very words Lincoln said on that day, recorded at this very spot." A hush came over the crowd as he nodded to the sound engineer, dozens of cameras clicking while Jim watched him rotate the cylinder, a white dove flying gracefully overhead...

Savoring the momentary silence, the light rustling of sycamores soothed him as a cool breeze brushed past his face, the scent of mint in the air. Then the voice never heard by anyone now living drifted toward them and he felt warm, despite the chilling wind. Jim smiled as he heard the final words. *"Of the people, by the people, for the people..."*, a deafening applause lifting him upward as those around him rose from their chairs. Standing proudly erect, the enlarged photograph came into view on the platform high above them all, the face haggard from four bloody, tumultuous years of war... and he read the inscription below the frame:

"America will never be destroyed from the outside. If we falter and lose our freedoms, it will be because we destroyed ourselves... My dream is of a place and a time where America will once again be seen as the last best hope on Earth..."

--Abraham Lincoln

Gene Pisasale

About the Author

Gene grew up in Wynnewood, PA on the Main Line outside Philadelphia. By the age of 30, he had visited most of the 50 states and several foreign countries, trips which fueled his desire to share descriptions of those places through his websites. Gene worked as a petroleum geologist for six years, then in the investment industry for 24 years as an analyst and portfolio manager. His lifelong fascination with history- mankind's many triumphs, tragedies, sorrows and accomplishments- propelled him to start his writing career. Gene enjoys photography, visiting historic sites, cooking and fine wines. He lives in Kennett Square, PA with his wife Phyllis, their three cats Frankie, Francis and Mom, Linus and Lucy their pet parakeets and occasional feline freeloaders Bear and Dadcat.

Gene's first novel "Vineyard Days" is a 'hybrid'- a travelogue wrapped around a murder mystery describing the sights, sounds and tastes of Martha's Vineyard. The sequel "Lafayette's Gold – The Lost Brandywine Treasure" is an historical novel about the Battle of the Brandywine. "Abandoned Address- The Secret of Frick's Lock" is an historical novel of the Industrial Revolution.

Visit his websites at:
www.GenePisasale.com
www.FoodWineTravelHistory.com

CPSIA information can be obtained at www.ICGtesting.com
Printed in the USA
BVOW031249260911

272064BV00001B/3/P